DEVIK

SVESTI FATED MATES   BOOK 2

WAVY MARTIN

OTHER BOOKS BY
Wavy Martin

SVESTI FATED MATES SERIES
Vared

Table of Contents

Prologue

NO, NOT REALLY. I know some people bypass author's notes early in a book, but I wanted to add the following:

For those readers who have read *Vared*, the first book in the series, you may experience a bit of déjà vu as you read *Devik* and *Ash'n*. No matter what I suggested, the characters were insistent they were going to fall in love when, where, and how they wanted. I offered ways to strand them on a tropical beach or trapped in a mountain chalet during a blizzard on some unknown planet, but they were adamant. Honestly, they didn't have to be so rude about it. *Goddamn characters being difficult. I thought I was the writer in charge. A third of my outline tossed in the trash, but do they care? Noooo. Oh, did I type that out loud?*

Since three couples became fated mates in the same timeframe, I did my best to condense where I could and still keep each love story unique to the main characters. Hopefully, I succeeded.

- Wavy

Chapter 1

Four months earlier
December 4, 2036 *(Earth calendar)*
Trezoura *(capital city of the planet Costonia)*

NOTING THE TIME, King Traxen Sovex of House Davelk sighed heavily and rose from his desk. Picking up his tablet, he opened the door to the outer office housing his admin, Ril'n Xeliv.

Ril'n said, "The flitter is ready, Sire. Would you like your robe?" He stood and gathered his own tablet and comm.

Traxen's long braids brushed his shoulders when he shook his head. He gestured to his amethyst shirt with thin white pinstripes. "I'm wearing the royal colors already. There's no need for extraneous pomp."

"Given the topic of today's meeting, perhaps it would be wise to visually remind the Council members who is king," Ril'n said with a small smirk. "Your crown would suffice as well."

Traxen narrowed his eyes at the older male. "If they haven't figured out who is in charge in the past three solars, there isn't much hope for them." Scowling, he bared his fangs and extended his claws. "If they require additional education, you can schedule them some sparring time with me."

His blue eyes annoyed, Ril'n huffed, "You sound like your father, Goddess rest his soul. He disregarded tradition as well."

"You know I consider your words a compliment, don't you?" Traxen retracted his claws with a smile. "I wish he were here to tell the Council himself. He was king when the Zuvgran released the virus on Costonia thirty solars ago and we suffered so much pain and death. He should have been the one to tell them we now have hope for our species."

His expression solemn, Ril'n said, "I agree. He worked tirelessly to keep us from fracturing at the horrible loss of our females. His unexpected death was another blow to the Svesti. No offense to you, but I had hoped to be working for him another fifty solars."

"No offense taken. I would have preferred never ruling at all if it meant he was still with us." Traxen sighed. "I miss him, too." *I hope Ril'n will be around for those fifty solars, and not just as my admin. His knowledge and guidance has been needed.*

"He would be proud of you, Sire. You inherited the throne much earlier than expected and have done a fine job thus far." Ril'n shifted on his feet. "If you tell anyone I said that, I will deny it, of course."

A chuckle escaped Traxen. "Praising me hurts, doesn't it, you irascible male?" *You're like a grumpy uncle.*

Humor lit his admin's eyes. "I certainly wouldn't want your head to become too big for the crown. The paperwork alone to resize it would take days."

Smiling, Traxen walked through the door Ril'n opened and nodded to the two guards. The four Svesti males continued to the upper levels of the palace to the royal hangar. One of the guards held the rear door open of a shiny, black flitter.

Traxen nodded as he entered. "Thank you, Previv." The male nodded. *He's one of the youngest Svesti left. A whole generation lost because of that crekkin' virus.*

When the four were seated and on their way, Traxen said, "I understand your brother is stationed on the *Invictus*. Did you have time to visit with him while he was on leave?"

Madix Previv said, "Yes, it was good to spend time with him. It's been a while since he was on Costonia. He took a shuttle back to the ship in orbit early this morning."

"Good. Family is important." Traxen spoke to the other guard, Bavin Hossix. "How is your brother? Is he due back soon?"

Hossix, a male twice Previv's age, said, "He is doing well. His ship is not scheduled to return to Costonia for another three or four solars."

Traxen nodded at his guard's words, then turned his attention to outside the flitter. It was only a short distance to the Council chambers, but he surveyed the ground below them, nonetheless. He'd been to many planets in his forty-four solars, but none impressed him with its beauty as much as his home world.

Most of Costonia's previous rulers had made integrating newer technologies with the wide variety of plant and wildlife a priority. *We're over the main thoroughfares of the city, but you can barely tell. Our buildings work with nature instead of overpowering it. Even our walkways simulate the abundance of pink stone found here. Although, instead of gravel as might be found in a country setting, the facsimile is permeable, level, and slip-resistant for the comfort and protection of our elderly and infirm citizens. If it weren't for the number of people out and about their business, one would believe they were flying over the countryside.*

Their driver hovered over the primary government building while waiting for the door to the secure hangar to open in the roof so he could land the flitter. Unlike the majority of Council representatives, Traxen parked onsite. *Sometimes it's good to be the king. I don't have to walk or travel underground to get here. Saves me time.*

In the main hallway leading from the hangar to the Council chambers, they met up with Canaan Durek and his son, Vared. Not only was Canaan Traxen's main agricultural advisor and a Council representative from House Ruxila, he was also Traxen's uncle on his mother's side of the family.

"Good day, Uncle. I'm glad to see you ensured Vared made it on time," Traxen said with a grin.

"Traxen, you're looking well." Canaan gave him an affectionate smile.

Vared grumbled, "I don't know why you need me here, cousin. You know I hate Council proceedings." His tail flicked in rapid movements.

"Given the nature of today's business, it will be helpful to have your charming self glaring relentlessly at those who will try to drag it out. You're the Commander of our flagship, *Invictus*, and there can be no doubt as to what orders you received from me regarding this important mission." Traxen turned his head slightly to look into lavender eyes so similar to his own. "Is Tolvex coming?"

Vared shook his head. "Devik said his farewells to his father days ago—there's only so much of the male Devik can handle. He spent the past week with his brothers and is holding a shuttle for me so I can immediately return to the ship after all this."

Ril'n spoke. "As you are exceedingly proficient at avoiding Council meetings, Commander Durek, may I offer you the reminder to please stand a couple paces behind the king and to his right once the Council begins."

Vared grunted. "Xeliv, it always amazes me how you are able to chastise someone while simultaneously appearing to be helpful. It is a rare and irritating ability." His tail swayed slower.

"Thank you, Commander. However, I must respectfully disagree on the rarity of the ability as I do believe you share the same quality." Ril'n wore a self-satisfied smile. *He does like to tease Vared. And Vared has calmed down. I don't need him punching Council members today.*

Canaan laughed. "You forget, Vared, that Ril'n has known you all your life."

Traxen smiled as he remembered some of the pranks he and his younger cousin had played on Ril'n as younglings. *Maybe this is the male's way of getting his revenge.*

The sound of multiple voices grew louder. Traxen noted the increase in Royal Guards the closer they got to their destination. *Hopefully their presence will not be needed for anything but crowd control.*

It took several minutes to traverse to their seats once they entered the Council chambers. *Everyone wants a few moments of my or Canaan's time to talk about issues important to individual Houses. There is a reason Ril'n is my admin. Why wouldn't they want my undivided attention in my office with an appointment rather than my barely polite attention now when dozens of people are vying for it?*

Traxen glanced around before finally taking his seat at the dais, Canaan to his right. Gleaming, burnished, hand-carved *trulet* molding, comfortable seating on tiers at long, curved wooden tables, majestic murals on craftsman-painted walls, and heavy woven tapestries were all designed to give the space a sense of history and dignity, as well as reinforce the gravity of the work conducted in the room. The impressive area was filled with over two hundred representatives of the twelve Houses. *One would think their surroundings would encourage them to act with sobriety, but no. The way most of them act, we could have the Council meetings on one of our long-unused playgrounds and no one would notice the difference.*

Very few Council members were absent, which only emphasized how important today's briefings were to their species. His braids barely moved when he returned Narilla Rivezt of House Yula's nod of greeting as she took her seat on the dais. Like him, Lady Narilla had dressed for comfort rather than public posturing. Her silver hair shone in the sunlight streaming through one of the high windows. As his head medical advisor, she was one of the few Svesti females to survive the Zuvgran virus. *Lady Narilla would've been just under ninety then. She hasn't attended a Council meeting in person for many solars. She looks healthy. Hopefully, she'll live another forty or fifty solars.*

Traxen had the utmost respect for the female healer. While she didn't care to travel to Trezoura very often as she preferred the mountains on the southern continent, she had a great deal of knowledge and wisdom she happily shared with the other Master Healers via comms. *Perhaps her presence today will help keep the Council in check. One can only hope.*

Traxen kept the frown from his face as he counted only eight females present. *I hate that we have so few females left after the Zuvgran treachery.*

It took a little while, but the Council chambers eventually quieted when Traxen called the meeting to order. He covered a number of smaller, less important items before reaching the primary reason for the proceedings. Then he stood.

"Thirty solars ago, the Zuvgran released a virus on our world that killed most of our females. Our scientists have worked since then to find a way for our males to procreate to keep our species from extinction. I won't go into all that has been attempted and unsuccessful." Traxen's impassive face took in the solemn contingent in front of him.

"Today we have new hope. All of you should have received the latest findings from our scientists. They have found a race called humans who are biologically compatible with Svesti and can bear our young." Traxen's face was grave. "Although we have been protecting its region of space from Zuvgran expansion over the past century, Earth is not yet aware of other life in the universe."

"I have asked Commander Vared Durek of our flagship, *Invictus,* to attend these proceedings to publicly receive his orders. Commander?"

Vared stepped forward and Traxen turned to him.

"Commander Durek, you are to travel to Earth and make an assessment of their government and populace. Determine how best to discreetly initiate first contact with humans, then do so. Be honest about our needs and intentions to negotiate a treaty for breeding and troth contracts with their females to save our race. If you are able, negotiate for some females to return with you to Costonia in hopes of Choosings from among the King's Court and Council. May the Goddess guide you and protect those under your command."

Vared thumped his chest with his fist and bowed his head. "As you command, Sire."

Traxen eyed his cousin for a long moment, then said, "Dismissed." Vared left the room.

Chaos erupted in the Council chambers. Traxen sat and listened to the complaints of "You should not have made that decision without the Council's approval," "We should invade Earth and take their females," and "The young from such pairings would no longer be Svesti; there must be other options. Cloning, perhaps," or similar comments. He let the Council members rant and rave for a while, noting which Houses or Council members might be a problem in the future. He was certain Ril'n was doing the same.

Finally, he said, "Enough! As King, opening negotiations with another species is well within my purview of power. I also am the highest-ranking military officer. The decision is made. We may discuss your concerns in an orderly fashion so I can take them into consideration as this situation progresses."

"Are our scientists certain humans are the only compatible species?" asked Marek Tolvex of House Vramel with a grim countenance. "They haven't even achieved space travel outside their own solar system. It would be like mating with *naroons*." Several chuckles escaped some Council members.

Traxen dipped his head at Lady Narilla, who stood and addressed the Council. "Esteemed colleagues. For thirty solars, I have worked with other Healers and our scientists to find ways for our species to procreate without fertile Svesti females. As Council member Tolvex correctly pointed out, humans have not traveled beyond their own solar system and as such, were not considered as a viable option until recently. Our scientists discovered that other races have been kidnapping humans to utilize as slaves and recently had the fortune to meet a human female who was amenable to non-invasive testing." She smiled. "I met with this female a number of times. She was well-spoken, intelligent, and retained her ability to care about others even after the horrific treatment she received in captivity. I would say humans are more than *naroons*." Quiet laughter was heard about the room.

"Is this female here now?" asked a Council member.

"No. She was given escort to a colony after she helped us. Given her circumstances since her kidnapping, she was unwilling to consider a breeding or troth contract with a Svesti male at this time. We honored her wishes," said Lady Narilla.

"Our biggest concerns are the gestation differences between Svesti and humans. Humans gestate for approximately eight to nine lunars, while Svesti gestation is five lunars. We are uncertain what length a Svesti/human pairing will be. Additionally, Svesti young are a little larger than human babies. It is possible this may result in increased surgical intervention during births." Lady Narilla's entire demeanor emanated calm assurance.

"Humans are, on average, one to two heads shorter than Svesti. They are typically smaller than we are."

Pluvi Frulix of House Srotix interrupted Lady Narilla and asked, "Will we able to manipulate the DNA of the hybrid young?"

She frowned. "Why would we?"

"To ensure the young are full Svesti."

Her silver hair swayed as she shook her head. "DNA does not work that way, Frulix. Half of the DNA of any young would be human. Our simulations do show that in the majority of instances, Svesti DNA would likely be dominant."

"What does that mean, Lady Narilla?" asked Canaan Durek.

"It means it is highly likely that the young would have claws, fangs, and a tail—or some combination of those traits. The young may also end up taller than humans as adults."

"But they would no longer be Svesti," said Frulix.

"Of course, they would be Svesti," said Lady Narilla.

Someone shouted out, "Only clones would have pure Svesti DNA."

"During the cloning process, DNA degrades over time. All cloning does is delay our extinction," Lady Narilla said. "You have the previous reports about that."

She answered questions patiently and addressed concerns for another ten minutes. Then it was time for those in favor of invading Earth to state their cases.

Traxen listened, then said, "Starting a war with humans is not in our best interests."

"But they are no match for us," said Frulix. *This male is all over the place. I think he just wants to foster resentment.*

"That may be. However, it is expensive to invade a world and house unwilling captives. Suggesting we just take whatever females we want sounds like you are condoning slavery and rape. Do you want the future of our species to be products of rape?" Traxen growled. "We do not treat females of any species in that fashion. We are not Zuvgran, and we will not act as such." *Do they even hear what they are saying?*

The longer the Council members postured, the more difficult it was for Traxen to stay impassive. *I would rather be on a Jalaxian military ship for a species cultural exchange again, sparring for respect than listen to this drivel. It was less painful to endure.*

Upon return to the palace later that day, Ril'n informed Traxen he had an appointment in a few minutes.

"With whom?" said Traxen. *I am not in the mood for more Council complaints right now.*

"Merix Hunnek."

Traxen's irritation lifted. "Send him right in as soon as he arrives, Ril'n."

Compiling his own personal notes of the Council proceedings, Traxen worked diligently to indicate where follow-up was required. He kept a list of items he wished to discuss with his Spymaster. *He'll be busy.*

The door opened and Ril'n announced Merix's arrival. Traxen stood and greeted the older male with a hug. Silver shone in spots in Merix's dark brown braids.

"How are you Merix? It's been a long time."

Merix's brown eyes glinted with humor. "I am well, Sire. And you?"

"Call me Traxen, for Goddess' sake. You've been a part of this family since before I was born."

"We aren't blood relations, Traxen," Merix grunted.

"Better, we're related by choice, you old male. How have you been?" Traxen looked at Merix fondly as he clapped him on the back before sitting back down. He remembered Merix visiting the palace often with his daughter, Latessa, when he was a youngling as Merix was a good friend of Traxen's father. Despite a grumpy demeanor, Merix always had time for him and taught him many things over the years. *I am a lucky male to have so many good influences in my life.*

"I'm well. We're leaving in the morning, but I wanted to drop this off for you." Merix handed Traxen a data device. "My latest suggestions to upgrade aquiponics areas on space cruisers. Most are fairly simple to incorporate, such as adding fans to simulate breezes, but I'd like aquiponics areas to have their own anti-grav units as backup to the main ship. I think I've come up with a way to do so, but your engineers should look at my designs and test them first."

They chatted about Merix's suggested improvements for a while before Merix said, "Human females?"

Traxen tilted his head. "You heard about that already?"

"Word is spreading quickly."

Nodding, Traxen said, "Not surprising. Yes, human females. You'll be one of the first Svesti to meet them."

Merix's eyes teared up before he glanced away. "I miss having females around. Our youngest Svesti have no idea what they've been denied."

"I miss your mate and Latessa, too."

A small laugh escaped Merix. "You and Latessa used to get into so much trouble. I'm sure some of my silver hair originated with you two."

Traxen pretended to be affronted. "Latessa was the instigator in every instance."

"I doubt that." Merix turned serious. "I'm glad she had friends like you in her life."

"She was like an older sister to me, Merix. Always looking out for me, while encouraging me to live outside the title of prince." Traxen pondered for a bit before asking, "What do you believe she'd think about the humans?"

Merix gave him a small smile. "She would have insisted on traveling on the *Invictus* with me to welcome them."

Traxen grinned. "You're right. She would've been the biggest supporter of a treaty with Earth."

"Your mother tells me you leave tonight for the *Invictus*," the older Svesti male said as he walked with his nephew in the gardens of his sister's home.

"Yes, Uncle," replied the younger male.

"Here." The older male handed his nephew a small comm. "This is untraceable. Use it sparingly. Contact me when the human females are on the *Invictus*."

"As you wish, Uncle."

"I will have orders for you when we know more of the humans. I have plans in place to ensure the Svesti remain pure, but I will need your help."

The younger male nodded. "I understand, Uncle. I am happy to serve."

Smiling, the older male gazed at his sister's child affectionately. "You have always been my favorite. When the Svesti realize the House of Davelk no longer serves our best interests, new leadership will be needed. When that time comes, I would like you to serve as my heir."

The younger male looked at him in shock. "I am honored by your faith and trust in me, Uncle."

The older male grunted and glanced around to verify they were alone. "The Zuvgran are working on a virus tailored to human fertility. It is not yet finished, but the hope is the first females from Earth will be infected and the virus will spread quickly upon their return to Earth."

"You have contact with the Zuvgran?" the younger male asked quietly.

"Our interests are in agreement for now. It is a short-term alliance."

"You know best, Uncle. Always Svesti."

"Always, Svesti." Slapping his nephew on the back, the older male said, "Come. Let's see what your mother has made for evening meal."

Chapter 2

Emmy Norton alternated between terrified and pissed off. She'd come home to her Canberra apartment to find strangers packing her belongings and carrying them out. Ducking her head and pulling her hoodie over her French-braided hair, she walked right past her open door down the hall to the rear building exit. She wasn't sure who'd caught up with her, but she wasn't sticking around to find out.

Sneakers light, she hurried down the stairs. Glancing quickly behind her, she opened the door to the street and bumped right into the two men. Steely eyes in set faces over black suits stared at her. *Crap. I hope Lobo didn't discover he was hacked. I didn't realize when I was tracing those corporate shell companies, I was actually hacking the notorious crime boss until it was too late.* Then she saw the ear buds. *Oh, fuck! Looks like Australian Federal Police or Protection Security Officers.*

"Miss Norton, please come with us," the taller one said.

"Hey, how do you talk without moving your lips?" She looked at the other man. "Are you a ventriloquist, mate?" Trying to edge around them, she stopped when the shorter one grabbed her arm. "Let me go. Haven't you heard of personal space?" She tugged, but he held on. He wasn't hurting her, but his grip was tight enough that she knew she wasn't going anywhere.

The men crowded close and walked her to the front of the building. *Guess I have no choice for now.* She saw people loading her computers into a moving van. Trying to suppress a grin, she bit the inside of her cheek. *Well, good luck trying to get into those, morons. They're set up to erase everything if the correct sequence isn't entered.* Another woman was loading up Emmy's suitcases into the back of a black SUV. She walked up to them and spoke to Tall Guy. "Sir, we're almost done."

Curtly nodding, he said, "You know what to do. We'll take Miss Norton to her meeting."

"What meeting?" Emmy said.

"Into the vehicle, miss," Short Guy said as he opened a rear door of the SUV.

"I asked *what meeting*? Who are you and where are you taking me?" Emmy's voice rose. *You're panicking, Emmy. You know you don't think well when you panic.*

"All will be explained at the meeting, Miss Norton. Now please get in."

Tall Guy got into the driver's seat.

"Don't you guys have to show me some identification or something?" Emmy stalled.

Short Guy sighed. "Miss Norton, you're wasting time. You're going to be late."

Late? How can I be late for an arrest? Curious, she stopped resisting and got in. Hearing the doors lock and realizing there were no door handles made her regret her decision. Short Guy got into the front passenger seat and a blacked-out partition rose between her and the men. The side windows tinted even darker so she couldn't see outside at all.

Emmy tried to visualize where they were headed. She'd grown up in Canberra, but eventually there were too many turns. It was also difficult to judge how fast they were traveling. At the bottom of what felt like a steep hill, the vehicle stopped.

The door opened, and Emmy got out before being asked. They were in a concrete garage. The men escorted her to an elevator. Emmy clenched her hands in the pocket of her hoodie while Tall Guy used a card to open the door. When they were inside and he was required to scan his eye for the elevator to move, her nerves began jangling more. *This is not good. I wonder if they know about...*

Her thoughts cut off as the elevator reached its destination and the doors opened. *Holy crap!* Emmy tried to take in everything. Her eyes skipped past the large conference table in the center of the enormous space but roved over the huge computer screens lining the walls. Her fingers twitched, wanting to play at one of the workstations. No outside light reached the room since there were no windows, but the artificial lighting was good enough to see that the sole exit was the elevator. The only other door seemed to lead to a bathroom.

She sucked in a breath when she realized the Prime Minister and the Governor General were in the room. *Okay, I know who they are from the news. Definitely government, not Lobo. I'm more likely to live if it's government.* Several people she didn't recognize were milling about. *This is big. Keep it together, Emmy.*

"Miss Norton, good. You're here. What you're about to witness is top secret," the Prime Minister said as he shook her hand.

"I'm not sure why I'm here," Emmy said.

"You're here because..." The Prime Minister broke off his words as a whitish-blue light filled a corner of the room. *What the fuck?* When the light faded, there were three very large, lethal-looking, not-human beings standing there. They were all in different shades of bronze—gold, red, and caramel—and looked like they had short fur on their skin. Emmy blinked rapidly in disbelief. *Holy shit. They have tails and fangs. And they have weapons all over them.*

Emmy felt her fight-or-flight response kick in, with flight being her primary choice. Breathing rapidly, she began inching toward the elevator. The beings all turned their heads to her. *Were they sniffing the air?* She froze, darting her eyes between them.

Geez, these guys are over two meters tall and have predator written all over them. Short Hair with those huge biceps looks like he could be a wrestler. Ponytail looks like he belonged on an American football team as a... What do the Yanks call it? Oh, a linebacker. Braid Guy showing off abs for days is a little shorter than the other ones and leaner. That's a cool tattoo, though. Wait. Are his eyes teal? Is he staring at me? Oh, shit. I'm staring back at him.

After some long moments when no one started shooting or fighting, Emmy relaxed slightly. *Okay. Maybe I'm not going to die today.* Curiosity pulsed, pushing down some of the fear, and she took a hesitant step toward them.

The Prime Minister introduced her to the aliens, explaining that they were Svesti, and had been protecting Earth from another race called the Zuvgran for over a century. She kept her hands in her hoodie pocket. *Nuh-uh, not touching aliens today, not even to shake hands.*

Short Hair was Commander Vared Durek. Ponytail was Lieutenant Karid Wurvez and Braid Guy was Lieutenant Devik Tolvex. The Svesti took over and explained that the Zuvgran had released a virus on the Svesti home world thirty years ago that decimated their female population. *Obviously, English is not their first language, but I'll give them points for trying.* Their accent reminded her of the romance languages.

They said their scientists had figured out that human females were compatible and wanted to negotiate a breeding program with Earth. *Nope, not me. Guess life sucks all over the universe, boys, not just here. Move it along.* Emmy felt a twinge of shame at her lack of empathy, but she'd just met them and it was not her problem. She had enough of her own. Like why she was even in a room that was probably an underground bunker.

Surreptitiously, she wiped her sweaty palms on the material in her pocket. The Svesti looked gladiator-like, but the technology they were using made Emmy salivate. When the Prime Minister said the Svesti had hacked into Earth's genealogical databases to find individuals who had a particular DNA strand, Emmy's eyes narrowed. He explained she had the strand and it would allow her to interact with some of the Svesti technology faster and easier.

The Svesti said they had to port out to meet some other people. *That must be the light-thingy.* Emmy's shoulders relaxed a little with the Svesti gone. She felt as if she were on more solid ground when it was only humans.

Emmy rounded on the Prime Minister. "I am NOT doing the dirty with aliens or having alien babies."

She heard a cough behind her as if someone was suppressing a laugh.

"We don't expect you to."

"Then why am I here?" *That's right, Emmy, a good offense is the best defense.*

"The Svesti want us to send an emissary to their home world. We'd like you to go."

Her jaw dropped. "Why the hell would you want me to be an emissary? I'm nobody."

"Because we want you to hack into their technology and give it to us."

"I design websites. Hacking into alien technology is a bit above my pay grade."

The Prime Minister's face hardened. "You are Phoenix. We know this. We've been keeping track of your activities."

Emmy kept her face impassive. "Who or what the hell is Phoenix?"

He leaned forward. "The only reason you haven't been arrested yet is that you haven't crossed the line into using your hacks for money or treason, Miss Norton. It's been our choice to leave you alone because when you come across something truly heinous, somehow law enforcement finds verifiable evidence of those crimes. We would have recruited you, but your history shows you do not work and play well with others." He nodded at someone at a workstation and the computer screens started scrolling a list of Emmy's hacks.

Oh, shit. Emmy focused on keeping her breathing even as she perused the list. *Okay, they've only found about a tenth of them. Now what?*

"So, you are going to be on a Svesti space cruiser in the morning, Miss Norton. You will travel to the Svesti home world and return in a year and a half. You will hack their technology. We want everything you can find—military, science, star charts, engineering schematics. You are smart enough to know what will interest us."

Emmy crossed her arms. "And if I refuse? I'm not this Phoenix."

"Then you will be arrested and charged. Any additional crimes we find on the computers confiscated today will just add to your sentence. Right now, you're already looking at a minimum of fifty years."

"And if I agree, even if I'm not this Phoenix?"

"Then you will be granted immunity for any crimes committed prior to this date. But only if you successfully return with useful intelligence."

Emmy closed her eyes and ran through all the options. She was silent for a long time. Finally, she reopened her eyes and spoke. "I want it in writing—the immunity, with no specific mention of this Phoenix. And I want wine."

"Wine?" He looked surprised at her request.

"If I'm going to be hanging with aliens for eighteen months, I want some wine with me to make it bearable." She only added the request to see his reaction.

"Anything else?"

"I'll have to see what your goons packed for me first."

"Fine." He looked at Tall Man. "Escort Miss Norton to her room. Ensure she's fed and gives you a list of anything else that might be required."

"I wish I could say it was a pleasure doing business with you, but it wasn't." Emmy turned to follow Tall Man.

"I'll have the immunity agreement drawn up, Miss Norton."

She barely refrained from giving him a one-finger salute as she entered the elevator.

Emmy finished packing, leaving out her favorite graphic T-shirt that said "My dream job would be a karma delivery service." She set her green cargo pants and boyfriend blazer next to the shirt. *What else do I need for an alien space cruiser? Underwear, socks, and hiking boots—just in case I need to kick an alien in the balls. That should do it.*

She grinned. She'd taken particular pleasure in telling Tall Man what feminine hygiene products she required to get her through eighteen months. *Of course, he'd sent the female officer to get them. It's 2037 and a normal bodily function still embarrasses men.* She'd added some more underwear to the list, which wasn't really necessary. The female agent even bought some batteries. She must've been the one to pack Emmy's vibrator. *I'll probably need BB—Big Boy—to release tension.*

Emmy was happy to see the laptop they provided. They added some flash drives for her. She had no doubt they'd put some kind of spyware on it all. She'd wipe everything clean once she was on the space cruiser. And they'd brought two cases of wine. Her grin widened. *They needed me to do this. Otherwise, they would've ignored my wine request.*

Lying on her back on the bed in an oversized T-shirt, she reran the day in her head. *Was there something I could have done differently?* She shook her head. *I was screwed from moment one.*

Where did they get my DNA? Oh, crap. That's right. I did that test years ago when I thought I'd try to find out who my father was. Heavily, she sighed. *And the stupid-ass, eighteen year old I was didn't delete it all out of the system. Nice going, Emmy. That mistake is really costing you now.*

Pondering the life choices that led her here, she had to admit, the whole have-to-hack-aliens thing never crossed her mind as a possibility. She was well outside her comfort zone and she knew it. *Just do what you always do, Emmy. Learn everything you can as quickly as you can and keep yourself separate. You'll get through this.*

I'm going to be in space tomorrow. With aliens. Fuck my life.

Chapter 3

Devik looked around the bridge of the space cruiser *Invictus*. Vared asked for their input on how the day had gone. As the ship's security officer, Devik gave his opinion about how he didn't trust most of Earth's leaders or subordinates, but their security personnel was another matter. While they were no match for the Svesti, he still recognized fellow warriors.

Devik also wasn't sure that the weak human females were a good match for Svesti males. The females had no natural defenses. Not a claw, fang, tail, or even horns to protect themselves. *They're so tiny and different. I'm concerned they would split in two trying to deliver Svesti young. It seems risky.*

Devik smiled when Karid asked what use the human mammary glands were with no young to feed. The bridge crew teased his friend who took it all in good humor, as was his wont. Devik wasn't sure they realized Karid was trying to lighten the tension on the bridge. First contact with a new species was always fraught with potential issues.

He shook his head, braids swaying slightly, when their communications officer, Triv'n Brauvix, asked about fated mate bonds. *We haven't seen a fated mate bond in over a century. I'm not sure we'd recognize one if it were to happen*. Brauvix was still young, not as experienced and hardened yet as Devik and his long-time friends—Vared, Karid, and Ash'n.

Tapping his tablet, he entered the list of what Vared wanted done to prepare for the females' arrival. As he went about his duties, his thoughts kept returning to the human females they'd met today. Different colors of hair, eyes and skin, though there was that one whose skin was a paler shade of his own caramel bronze, but with light yellowish-orange undertones. Her intelligent brown eyes looked terrified as she'd attempted to sneak away. Something caught her interest, though, and she cautiously approached them. Underneath her fear scent, she smelled delicious. Like *tempika* berries in a dessert—tart but with a sweet aftertaste. It reminded him of the Hot Season. *Hmm, maybe I'll put her in quarters near mine.*

Hot Season reminded him of his three older brothers—Solen, Pex and Rassix, who had spent so much time raising him after the virus took their mother and sister from them. He frowned. *Father changed so much after we lost our females. So rigid—when he wasn't absent. Even Solen eventually remembered how to laugh and have fun and he also lost his mate to the virus.* He knew he owed much to his siblings.

Shaking off his thoughts, he got back to work. There was much to coordinate for the arrival of the females on the morrow.

After he and Vared sparred with wooden staffs, Devik's ribs and back ached. He and his friend drank from their water pouches in the training area, cooling down from their exertions. They discussed where to place the female quarters, as well as what access they should have to the ship.

Vared said, ""Very well. I'll have Brauvix explain some of the technology they may use regularly. He's competent and eager."

"He's coming along." Devik took a long gulp of water. "Were we ever that young?"

Vared smiled. "Are you saying we're old?"

"I admit with all this talk about the human females, I've begun to wonder," Devik said.

"Wonder what?"

"If there is something more than serving our race. There is hope now that we may be able to have younglings and continue our lines. Female companionship. Families that consist of more than males. I did not think about it when there was no hope, but now the change excites *and* worries me." Devik felt that itch between his shoulders that warned him that there was something he needed to pay attention to.

Vared checked the surrounding space, ensuring no one was close enough to hear his words. "I think the change will come with its own set of problems—larger than the personal considerations. According to the king, there are those who wish to invade Earth and take their females, while others believe the younglings will no longer be Svesti. The Council is divided, which does not bode well."

Devik could not contain the growl rising in his chest. "Do you believe the females may be in danger?"

"Unknown, but we must proceed as if they are," Vared said with a frown that highlighted the scar on his cheek.

Devik pondered his friend's words as he headed to his quarters to shower. *Females are life givers. We're supposed to watch over them as we would the Goddess.* He did not like thinking the females were at risk, especially since they could not protect themselves. He'd have to keep a close eye on them and ensure they remained safe. *The one with the tempika scent and baggy clothes interests me. What is she like when she is confident? I won't mind watching her closely.*

Ash'n Rivezt said, "I don't know the specifics, Devik. I only received the final report from the scientists, not how they came by the information."

Devik narrowed his eyes at the healer. "Then how do they know human females are compatible with Svesti? I understand genetically; DNA is easily obtainable. But how can they be sure the females can physically accommodate a Svesti male? We are so much larger than they are. It concerns me."

"I've only heard rumors, not facts." His friend's blue eyes were uncomfortable.

"What rumors?"

"The scientists visited pleasure planets."

"Do not tell me what I think you're telling me," Devik growled.

Ash'n shook his head, his dark ponytail brushing his shoulders. "No, not that they partook in anything, but they paid to interview pleasure workers of multiple species at various establishments. The rumor is there was a human slave at one, who supposedly 'serviced' clients larger than Svesti."

"And they left her there?" Devik's fists clenched, his claws biting into his palms.

"Again, rumor is that they offered to purchase her in exchange for her allowing them to test her further. Then they were going to free her with transport to wherever she wanted, including the Svesti home world."

"What happened to her?"

"Supposedly, she was on her way to a colony. Her ship was attacked by Zuvgran. No one knows after that."

Devik felt his temper rise higher. "So this human female, who may be the reason our race has hope, was left in the hands of the Zuvgran? That is not right, Ash'n, nor honorable."

"I agree, but we have no proof," Ash'n said, frowning.

"If it is true, and there was no attempt to help her, I'm not sure our race deserves to survive." Devik knew his frown was deep. "I understand we cannot save every slave, but one that helped us in such a manner deserves better. There is right and there is wrong. Not helping her escape the Zuvgran is wrong. Who knows what has been done to her?"

"I wish I had better information for you, my friend, but that is all I have heard."

"I'm starting to think I should not have asked." Devik's tail whipped behind him.

Devik's comm chimed. "Tolvex."

"Get up to the War Room, Tolvex. I need to brief you on something," said Karid.

"On my way." Devik knew his stride was stiff as he left the med bay. He suppressed a growl. *I need to calm down. Hopefully, it was only a rumor.*

Karid locked the door to the War Room as Devik sat down.

"What's going on?" asked Devik.

"This is classified information. Only you, me, and the Commander know," Karid said.

"Go on." Devik was curious about what required such secrecy.

"The king's intelligence suggests locations for four Zuvgran labs." Karid grinned, fangs flashing.

Devik leaned forward. "Where?"

Karid tapped the surface of the table and a hologram appeared above it. "Right now, we're only interested in this one." He pointed. "XB9428B, which is on the outside of our scanning range en route to Costonia."

Devik ran some data on his tablet. "There doesn't appear to be much on the planet."

"Vared suggested the labs may be underground. He wants deep-level scans as we approach Theron for as long as we can. We're looking for anything that might prove there's a lab there."

"If we modify some parameters, we can see if there's any trace of Zuvgran spacecraft in the vicinity," Devik said as he started tapping on his tablet. He looked at Karid. "Will we be sending a team to investigate any anomalies?"

Karid shook his head. "Unfortunately, no. The king was quite adamant that we are only to escort the human females to the home world."

"That's a shame. To be so near and not look closer if we find anything seems a waste." Devik's lips turned down.

"I agree. However, we have our orders," Karid said as he sat back.

"Then that's what we'll do," Devik said with a smile. "What did you really think of the females?"

"I think life is going to be interesting in the near future, my friend. I got the feeling the humans are not similar in temperament to the Svesti females we remember." Karid grinned. "I'll bet you a bottle of Estalan liquor that Vared loses patience with them sometime tomorrow."

"Not taking that bet, my friend. Too vague." Devik smiled. "Specify a reason, and maybe I'll reconsider."

"Hmm, let's see." Tapping his upper lip with a forefinger, Karid said, "The females being too fearful."

"I say Vared will get angry because the females will question his authority or want something he's unwilling to give."

"You have a bet." Karid and Devik each clasped the upper forearm of the other.

The next day, Devik was busy. He had to port each female individually to a med bed, adding a light mist to anesthetize each per Ash'n's specifications. Then he ported their belongings to a cargo bay so some of his team could scan everything for potential danger. Only if all was as it should be would the belongings be delivered to the females' quarters. While he hoped that no one on Earth would send anything harmful, he would not be doing his job if he did not take the proper steps to ensure all was safe. Fortunately, his teams reported there seemed to be nothing to be concerned about.

Devik took care of delivering the belongings himself, using a maglev to transport everything. He used his security override to drop off the suitcases, bags and boxes. Grinning, he noted that Lady Natasha had brought a couple crates of what looked to be clear liquor with her. Lady Rachel had one crate of something called Chardonnay, while Lady Emmy had two crates of what said Pinot Noir on the labels. Sniffing, he thought he smelled fruit. *I would imagine they are alcoholic drinks.* He inhaled deeply at the faint scent of *tempika* berries emanating from the last suitcases. *Yes, I'll enjoy smelling that as I pass by her quarters each day.*

Chapter 4

Emmy woke in what looked like a futuristic med bay with a Svesti next to her. He was a golden bronze with blue eyes and long hair in a ponytail. He introduced himself as Healer Rivezt. For whatever reason, he didn't kick in her fight-or-flight response. *No weapons like his buddies yesterday; that must be it.*

"How are you feeling, Lady Emmy?"

Lady? I'm no lady. She conducted an internal assessment before sitting up on the med bed. "I'm feeling groggy and have a slight headache."

A curvy woman with long blond hair and brown eyes walked up. "I'm Dr. Natasha Petrov."

Emmy realized the doctor was wearing a medical gown. She looked down at herself to see that she was wearing one, too. *Who the hell undressed me?* "Hi, doc. I'm Emmy."

"When you're feeling up to it, the other human women would like to chat," Natasha spoke with a slight Russian accent.

Emmy walked over and met Talia Sullivan, an American woman with reddish-brown hair and brown eyes. She was a little shorter than Emmy, but sturdier. She looked to be several years older than Emmy.

With Talia was a Brit named Rachel Llewellyn—a tall, lanky blond with blue eyes, and a Canadian named Ava Taylor. Ava had red curly hair and green eyes and looked to be a little younger and shorter than Emmy. The last woman to awake was Lin Chang, a petite Chinese woman with short black hair who seemed to be about Emmy's own age of twenty-seven. *I wonder what their stories are? Did they volunteer to come or were they forced like me?*

Natasha said, "The doctor, or healer, as they call him, is Ash'n Rivezt. He implanted translator devices behind our ears which also serve as information conduits. Supposedly we all know each other's languages now, Svesti, Galactic Standard, and a couple other ones. He said that we needed to be anesthetized because uploading more than three languages at a time can cause severe headaches and disorientation. The trackers are in our left arms. Supposedly it is not safe for females on many worlds and it allows them to find us should we be abducted."

All the women reached for their ears and arms trying to feel for the foreign devices.

Emmy nodded curtly. "Get me to a computer and I'll see about disabling the trackers."

Talia, Rachel, and the doc informed them that the Svesti had decontaminated them for viruses, did some medical checks, gave them some vaccines, corrected health deficiencies, removed contraceptive implants, and genetically altered the women to increase their longevity. *My birth control better still work. I don't like being unprotected. And living longer—not sure how I feel about that. Are we going to have to live an extra fifty years in ninety-year-old bodies?*

Talia said she wanted them to save their anger for the Commander who'd ordered it all. The doc said the healer informed her that the trackers were in case they were abducted or met up with space pirates. *Great. Slavery is all over the universe. Just my luck.*

"There are nanosuits for each of you in there." The healer pointed to an adjoining room. "Once you change, the Commander wishes to meet with you all in the War Room and introduce you to some of the bridge crew."

"We'd like our own clothing," said Talia.

"I was instructed to give you the nanosuits. They will help keep you safer as you females are fragile." *Fragile, my ass.*

"Fragile?" Rachel snorted.

"Are you saying we are not safe on this ship?" Talia pursed her lips.

"No, no one on the *Invictus* would dare harm any of you." Rivezt looked affronted, and his blue eyes deepened to cobalt.

"Are we expecting to be in a battle sometime soon? Or boarded by space pirates?" Talia countered.

"No, of course not."

"So these suits are to minimize bruising and the like if we happen to trip over our own feet or walk into a wall?" At Talia's words, Emmy suppressed a laugh. *Damn, she's good. She's got him so twisted he doesn't know up from down.*

"Uhh..."

"I think we can dress in our own clothing for now. You can give us the nanosuits and we'll take them with us," Talia said firmly.

Emmy was happy Talia got her way and she could wear her own clothes. While they were changing, Talia said she was an author and stay-at-home mom now turned Ambassador. *How did that happen?* She asked if any of the women had been given titles or instructions by their respective governments. All of them had been told to learn as much as possible, focusing on their given fields.

Emmy knew her anger had to be showing when she said, "I was told to get into their computer systems and try to get schematics of any and all technology. They also wanted star charts and maps. I was threatened with jail time if I bring nothing back. They didn't seem to care what would happen to me if the Svesti caught me."

Talia asked, "Are you all comfortable with me speaking for our group? If not, then let's hash it out now amongst ourselves so we can show a united front in the meeting."

Emmy looked at the other women, then back at Talia. *I don't want to be in charge, that's for sure.*

"We're good with you as our spokesperson," said Rachel. "You've got an official title to back it up, although I'm not sure how much it really means here." Emmy nodded, as did the others.

"Let's go give them hell," Ava said with a feral grin. "Let's show them they shouldn't screw over human women." *I like her. If I made friends, I think she'd be first on my list.*

Emmy noted the same three Svesti she'd met yesterday standing in a large room that Rivezt said was the War Room. She took a seat at the conference table between Ava and Lin, keeping her distance from the aliens.

She was glad they reintroduced themselves. She'd been too hyped up on adrenaline the previous day to remember who was who. The only one she remembered was Lieutenant Tolvex with his teal eyes, caramel bronze skin, unusual tattoo, and abs-for-days. *Hmm, so he's the head security officer. Good to know.* Commander Durek was Short Hair, the gold one. Lieutenant Wurvez was Ponytail and the tactical officer.

Bored, she listened to the Commander give a fairly standard welcome speech and information about a space station called Theron. The synthesizers and comms he mentioned perked her interest. *Oooh, technology I can play with. I'm liking this.*

Commander Durek said they were traveling to Costonia, the Svesti home world. When he informed them the women would be presented to the King's Court and Council for "their Choosings," the shit hit the fan. *What the fuck is he talking about?*

Talia, their spokesperson, said, "Choosings?"

Durek said, "Yes, you will meet a number of our nobles and select those of which you may wish to have court you for a troth contract, or if you prefer, a breeding contract."

"I didn't agree to that!" Emmy yelled. Her exclamation was joined by the other women protesting. She glanced around and saw Tolvex frowning at her. Wurvez and Rivezt both were watching Talia with thoughtful expressions.

Emmy's knee bounced as she watched Talia straighten before asking "Why would you believe we are interested in either type of contract?"

"I am confused. Did your leaders not inform you of our agreement?" Durek said.

"What agreement?" Talia said.

"You are the first females to volunteer to become Svesti mates or breeders."

"Oh, hell to the no!" Ava shouted.

Emmy resisted the urge to cover her ears. *Damn, that girl has some lungs on her. Maybe I should've sat next to the doc.*

When Talia asked him for proof, the commander turned scary with his facial scar whitening and lavender eyes going dark. *If looks could kill, poor Talia would be dead now. He's pissed she's questioning his honor.* Emmy was impressed Talia remained calm when she explained the women's point of view.

Emmy tried not to jump when Durek crossed his arms and growled. *Shit. I would not want to meet him in a dark alley.* Durek nodded at Tolvex and Tolvex tapped on his tablet. Holographic videos appeared above the conference table, showing each country's leaders agreeing to give them a woman for a breeding or troth contract. *That tech is so cool.*

Her shoulders tensed as she realized the Prime Minister and Governor General did, in fact, agree to the Choosing. Restless, she tapped her fingers on her leg. *I wish I were back on Earth. I'd hack their accounts and bleed them dry. Maybe expose some of their secrets, too.*

"Our own governments pimped us out," Rachel said, her blue eyes glacial.

"I can't believe this." Lin's eyes filled with tears. "I fought my parents for years about an arranged marriage and now this happens?" Emmy couldn't help but reach out and squeeze Lin's hand under the table. *Yeah, I hear you. We've been screwed and we're going to be screwed for real. Geez, Emmy, you have a sick sense of humor.*

Talia lost her grip on her anger. She stood, placed her hands flat on the table with locked elbows and faced off with the commander. She listed every wrong that men perpetrate against women on Earth. *Damn, when I grow up, I want to be her. I think I have a girl crush. She's fierce.*

Durek stood up and began yelling at Talia. *Oh, shit. Maybe I don't want to be her. I don't know if he's going to hit her or kiss her. Wonder if those fangs would get in the way?*

Angrily, the commander ended the meeting. As the women stood up to leave, Emmy glanced at the Svesti. Wurvez looked like he was trying not to grin, while Rivezt seemed thoughtful. Tolvex was staring at her. She glared back at him before turning to follow the other women. *What the hell is his problem?* Before she left the room, she couldn't resist looking back at him.

Chapter 5

During the meeting, Devik found himself distracted by Lady Emmy's scent. The *tempika* berry smell had fluctuated between curiosity, anger, awe, and fear. *I don't like that she was afraid.* He watched the females leave the War Room before turning his attention to the discussion about the females' reactions.

Vared had been quick to anger, but with Ash'n being his usual understanding self and Karid lightening the atmosphere with his humor, Vared quickly calmed and sent them on their way.

Devik elbowed Karid when they left the room. "You owe me that Estalan liquor, my friend."

Karid widened his gray eyes. "Two out of three?"

Devik chuckled. "I think not, you *naroon*. Be sure to pay up."

Karid slapped Devik's back. "I'll get it for you on Theron." He grinned. "And I'll be happy to help you drink it."

Shaking his head, Devik laughed. "You never change, my friend."

Still chuckling, Devik headed to his quarters to dress in his workout clothes. He wanted to spend some time sparring with his security teams. If there was a threat to the females, he wanted to be ready.

As he approached his door, the scent of *tempika* berries was stronger. He turned to see Lady Emmy leaving her quarters with two large glass bottles.

"Lady Emmy," he said.

She froze and stared at him with wide, brown eyes, tightly clutching the green bottles. As he got closer, he could see there were tiny specks of blue and green in her irises. "Yes, Lieutenant Tolvex?"

Ah, she was cautious. I can't blame her with everything that has happened. Trying to put her at ease, he smiled. "I wanted to say that I am sorry your leaders lied to you females. It was dishonorable of them."

She shrugged. "It's not unusual. Men, especially, make a habit of lying to get what they want, whether it's money, power, or women."

Devik's tail flicked rapidly. "That's not right, Lady Emmy."

Tilting her head, she said, "No, it's not, but it happens. A lot." Her fingers relaxed on the bottles. "And call me Emmy. I'm not a lady."

"Protocol states I should call you Lady Emmy," he said, his tail still.

Narrowing her eyes, she said, "And you're a big believer in protocol?"

He nodded. "There is right and there is wrong."

She laughed. "There are many shades of gray, Lieutenant. Not everything is black and white."

"You may call me Devik or Tolvex." Her laugh warmed him. *I like her happy.*

"Only if you call me Emmy."

"As you wish. Emmy." He smiled.

She shook her head. "I have to admit, initially, your fangs scared me. But now I see they suit you."

He wrapped his tail around his ankle so it wouldn't reach for her. "I'm not certain what that means."

She smiled, her blunt teeth white. "It means I'm getting used to them."

"Do the males on Earth really do all the things Lady Talia said in the meeting?"

"Unfortunately, yes. Not all men, but too many," she said hotly. "And to be told we have to choose Svesti to marry or have babies with doesn't help."

"The Choosing is so that you can find a male that suits you." *Why does that make me angry, too?*

"From a limited pool of men already chosen by other men. We don't want to choose anyone." Her brown eyes flashed and her cheeks darkened.

"I did not mean to upset you. I apologize." He bowed his head slightly.

Surprised, she looked at him closer. "I'm not angry with you, Devik." She sighed and looked away. "I'm angry at the situation."

"You have every right to be." *I wish I could fix it for you.* "I did not mean to interrupt you. Were you going somewhere?"

"We're meeting in Talia's room to get to know one another. It looks like we're going to be together for a long time."

His lips tipped up. "That sounds like a good idea. I hope you make new friends."

She mumbled under her breath, "I don't make friends."

His brows drew together. *What does she mean?*

In a normal tone of voice, she said, "Can I ask you a question?" She shifted her weight from side to side, drawing his attention to her legs and hips. *Hmm, lean, but with a softness. Those pants hide most of her curves. Pity.*

"Of course." Smiling, Devik raised his eyes to meet hers.

"Brauvix gave us a quick lesson on the synthesizer, but I was curious about how it works. Where does it get the materials?" *It's like an unexpected spice on the berries when she's inquisitive.*

"It's very complicated. I don't fully understand it. But what I do know is the recyclers break down anything you put in them to its base elements, which the synthesizer uses."

"So like hydrogen, oxygen, sodium and so on?" Emmy's eyes lit up.

"Yes. There's also a small supply in the synthesizer itself. There are no dangerous elements kept in the quarters. If necessary, the synthesizer will also draw from the air if the element is available. There's a significant amount of base coding in the software. So if you tell it you want a plate of a specific food, the coding for a basic plate is there, as well as for the food." He felt a little heat on his cheeks. "But I have no idea how it receives more elements if it runs low. I do know that there are various lights inside that will harden materials, such as a liquid polymer to make the plate."

"So a bit like when the dentist fills a tooth."

Devik felt his brows draw together again.

She saw his confusion. "A dentist is a doctor or healer for teeth. If there is a cavity, they clean out the damaged area and fill it with a liquid, then hold a special light over it to make the liquid as hard as a tooth."

He nodded. "Yes, that sounds like it's the same process."

"So, can we code different things in the synthesizers in our quarters?"

"Small things and nothing dangerous. You can program in shapes, sizes, and materials. If you wanted a triangular plate, but smaller than the standard, then you could modify the standard and save the instructions under a different name. Foods tend to be more complicated. It's best to have our experts do the programming. Then they would update all the synthesizers onboard." He smiled. "But you can modify a food that's already programmed by amount, temperature, and add or subtract spices."

Her eyes shone. "I think I'm going to enjoy the tech onboard."

His grin matched hers. "I hope you do, Emmy." His comm chimed. "I apologize. I'm supposed to meet my security team for some training. I must go."

"I understand. Don't let me keep you. Thanks for explaining the synthesizers to me." She smiled at him.

"I'm happy to answer any questions I can, Emmy. Enjoy your time with the other females."

Devik was going to be a little late, but it was worth it. *I'm glad she's losing some of her fear.*

Back on the bridge after his sparring sessions, Devik answered his console comm. "Yes, Commander?"

Vared said, "Tolvex, I'd like to see you and Wurvez in the on-call room."

Karid stood and nodded at Devik. "Crulex, you have the bridge."

Hozan Crulex, the science officer on duty, said, "Yes, Lieutenant."

Once in the on-call room, Vared said, "I have three requests to transfer to security."

Karid said, "Were we looking to add to the security teams?"

Vared shook his head. "No. Devik?"

"I don't believe I need more people for my teams." Devik tilted his head. "Although, if you believe the females may be at risk, it wouldn't hurt to begin training some males as backup. Who is looking to transfer?"

Vared said, "Klero Rovex, Nerid Mantoor, and Lerix Sproid."

Devik brought up the personnel files on his tablet. "They've been on the *Invictus* for four years, slightly longer than Brauvix."

"Don't they work in supply areas?" Karid's brows drew together. "If I recall correctly, they are all friends."

"According to their files, they went through warrior training together and currently share quarters," Vared said.

Frowning as he looked at the performance evaluations, Devik said, "Rovex has had some issues with his temper and occasionally his attitude, but otherwise has good ratings.

Mantoor's team leader believes a lack of confidence has kept Mantoor from reaching his full potential. Sproid is considered competent, but quiet. His team leader feels Sproid does not take initiative often enough."

Nodding, Vared said, "Not exactly what I would look for to add to your teams."

"Why do they want to transfer?" Devik asked.

Karid grinned and wagged his brows. "If I had to guess, I would say they hope to have more interaction with the females."

Devik's braids brushed his shoulders as he shook his head. "They should realize the females' protection would go to more experienced personnel."

"Are we in agreement, then?" Vared's lavender eyes met Devik's. "Deny their requests?"

"Yes." Devik nodded. "If you want, you can tell them that if we are looking to add to security, we will keep their requests in mind." *I'll have to watch them in the training area and make an assessment of their warrior abilities. Maybe I should start a small program for those who may want to move sections or garner more skills. I could get a better idea of who might fit in with my teams if we need more males. I'll have to come up with a good plan before I present it to Vared for approval.* Jotting notes in his tablet, he left the meeting.

A Svesti strode across the cargo bay, occasionally glancing between his tablet and the containers. When he was sure he was alone, he sequestered himself in the furthest corner, inserted an earpiece and tapped a small comm. He heard, "I was hoping to hear from you."

"The human females are onboard," he said.

"How many?"

"Six."

"Anything else to report?"

"Rumor is the *Invictus* will be stopping at Theron for a resupply. I do not know when. Most likely within the next couple weeks." His eyes scanned the bay for movement.

"Will the humans be going to the station?"

"Unknown."

"Find out. Encourage it if you can. We need to know when they'll be there. This may be our only chance."

"As you will."

"Much depends on this."

"I am aware, sir."

"Also, encourage the females to dislike Svesti."

"How do you mean?"

"Find ways to make them believe their lives are at risk. Be creative, but be untraceable back to you. And of utmost importance, be careful. We don't want them to die since we need them for the plan to be successful. We need them to return to Earth, sooner rather than later."

"I will do what I can and share more when I know more. You are certain they cannot trace this comm?"

"I am certain. I would not put you at unnecessary risk, Nephew."

"I would not expect you to, Uncle. How is Mother?"

"My sister is fine."

"Please give her greetings from me when next you speak."

"Of course. Anything else?"

"No."

"Always Svesti, Nephew."

"Always Svesti, Uncle." The male stuffed the earpiece and comm in a pocket. He smiled as he entered the corridor. *Time for the evening meal and an excellent opportunity to find out when we will reach Theron.*

Chapter 6

Emmy nibbled on a cookie and looked at the other women sitting on the large oversized couches in Talia's living quarters. Everyone was finally relaxed after countless vodka shots and glasses of wine. Talia was the only one wearing a nanosuit. *I'm going to have to check out mine later and try to figure out the auto-fastening and sizing feature. All this new tech is amazing.*

She snagged some chocolate from a plate, as well as another cookie.

"What do we know about the Zuvgran and the virus they unleashed on the Svesti planet?" said Rachel as she tapped on her tablet.

Talia said, "From what I understand, it was about thirty years ago and it killed most of the Svesti females." She frowned as she sipped her wine. "I can't even imagine how awful it had to have been."

Natasha tapped on her tablet. "It says here any females who survived were rendered infertile." She was quiet as she read. She looked up, her eyes narrowed. "From what I can tell, it directly attacked the reproductive system. Unlike humans, Svesti females produce eggs throughout their lifetime on a three to four month cycle. The virus acted on the egg production and caused the eggs to solidify. The female survivors were suffering excruciating pain. If I understand it correctly, it would be like us having multiple cysts in our ovaries and fallopian tubes simultaneously. On female babies, since they had no eggs, the virus somehow solidified the growing ovaries and tubes. None of the babies survived."

Lin's eyes watered. "That's beyond cruel. Those poor women and babies."

"Svesti doctors had to remove female reproductive systems on the adult women to keep them pain-free," said Natasha angrily. She downed a shot of vodka.

"What do these Zuvgran assholes look like?" said Ava. She burped, then drank some wine.

Tapping on her tablet, Emmy found information on the Zuvgran. *Ugh, not something you'd want to meet in a dark alley.* She found a picture and turned the tablet for the other women to see.

"Scary looking," said Ava, shivering.

"Like a gray devil," Lin said, making a face. "I hope I never meet one."

Rachel read from her tablet. "It says the Zuvgran are comparable in height and weight to the Svesti, although the average height of a Zuvgran is a little shorter—but not much. They have gray skin, retractable fangs and claws, and shorter, but thicker tails than the Svesti. They also have two small, straight horns on their upper foreheads."

Emmy's knee bounced. "There's a long list of ships, colonies, and planets they've attacked."

"They're ruled by an Emperor and their government is military-based." Rachel looked up with a frown. "They seem to have a patriarchal society, with females having little to no rights."

Emmy's stomach turned as she said, "When they attack, they kill the majority of males, keeping some as slaves. Children under five and the elderly are executed outright, while most of the females become slaves."

Natasha said through clenched teeth, "Their scientists like to experiment on live subjects." She read some more. "Biologically, they are compatible with a number of races and their DNA tends to produce young with the gray skin prominent, even if the child retains the overall look of the other species." She held up her tablet to show a child who had dull-colored wings and was gray. "This is a Pellotian-Zuvgran hybrid. Pellotians normally have green skin and colorful wings."

Rachel added, "Hybrids are considered slaves and many are killed immediately."

Emmy tossed her tablet on the couch beside her. "I can't read anymore. It's making me sick." Her fingers drummed on her knee.

Ava mumbled around some chocolate, "Definitely ruining the happy vibe we had going."

"Can we talk about something else?" Lin asked softly.

"I think that's a good idea," said Talia. "Ava, can I get a copy of the recipe for these cookies? They are fantastic."

"I'd like a copy, too," said Natasha.

Ava smiled. "Sure."

"I'd get a copy, but every time I bake cookies, they tend to be hard as rocks," said Emmy with a grin. "I hope you plan on making cookies while we're on the ship because these are delicious."

"Mmm," said Ava. "I like making snacks, so once I figure out Svesti ingredients, I'll be experimenting."

"We'll happily be your guinea pigs," said Rachel with a grin.

After the midday meal the next day, Emmy changed into some shorts and her "I get my cardio by running codes" T-shirt. Her headache from yesterday's day-drinking with the other women had finally subsided, so she pulled up her curly hair. *I'm surprised I had fun yesterday. But I don't want to get too close to them. Everyone leaves in the end.*

Although she remembered the way to the training area from their tour earlier this morning, Brauvix had mentioned they could query their comm for directions and the ship would show a path on the walls. In the hallway, she tried it. *Whoa! That is so cool.*

Musing, she followed the yellow line on the wall. She'd been afraid to tell the women about being a hacker, but they'd taken it in stride. They didn't appear to be judgmental or working to one-up each other. *Not like some of my foster homes and schools. It's a nice change.*

Before she turned the corner, she glanced back at Devik's quarters. He wasn't nearby, but she thought about the previous day's conversation. It surprised her how deep his voice was. *Like that old-time American actor. What was his name? Oh, James Earl Jones.* Emmy loved deep bass voices; they caused shivers in all the right parts of her body. *Wasn't expecting an alien's voice to wake up my lady parts.*

At the meeting this morning, the commander apologized for yesterday, but he wasn't pleased the women wanted to learn self-defense from Rachel. He requested that they coordinate with Devik beforehand so someone from their command structure could be present. She grinned. *Must've tweaked his male ego. But he did ask nicely about us getting more uploads. Hopefully, he'll let me learn more about the tech. Maybe even allow Devik to do it, since he was nice enough to explain the synthesizer to me.*

Fortunately, she liked all the Svesti foods so far. The *pertiza* at breakfast was like a creamy yogurt pudding and the *brellia*, some kind of meat pastry, was tasty and filling. She was glad to have more in her stomach after the cookies, chocolate, wine, and vodka from their drinking yesterday. Mentally crossing her fingers, she hoped Rachel didn't toss them around too much during self-defense training.

Rachel was already on a mat with the other women around her. Rachel explained their stances should differ from men because women's centers of gravity were lower on their body.

Peeking through her lashes, Emmy watched Devik and the Commander. All the Svesti seemed to be in exceptionally good shape. She preferred Devik's more compact look. *Holy crap. Devik in shorts with those abs is something to see.* She could see his tail through his legs. *Wonder how shorts work with a tail.*

She clenched her thighs. *Am I seriously getting turned on by an alien? Like I don't have enough problems.*

She stepped back from the mat when a Svesti challenged Rachel and brought two friends with him. *Shit. He's almost as big as Durek. I hope she knows what's she's doing.* Out of the corner of her eye, she saw Devik stop the Commander from interrupting. She couldn't help the wide grin on her face when Rachel beat the Svesti and threw him to the floor. *Yeah, you showed him.*

Devik approached and said to Rachel, "I believe you have taught all of us here a valuable lesson. That was impressive to watch. Rovex, Mantoor, and Sproid, get back to your own training." The Svesti went to another area in the room.

Rachel worked the women hard, having them get into proper stances from a variety of positions. *Good thing I run a couple times a week or I'd be flopping to the mat already.* When Rachel stopped her torture, Emmy headed back to her quarters. *I'm going to check out that huge Svesti-sized bathtub and soak with a glass of wine.*

The next morning Emmy reported to the med bay to watch Talia receive an upload. She was as impressed as Natasha was with the medical monitoring technology. *That hologram above the med bed is truly amazing.*

After Emmy had her upload, it astonished her she now knew more about the Svesti. *Those tattoos are clan markings showing their father's house with their mother's overlaid. And there are twelve houses. Wonder if it's comparable to Lords or Dukes on Earth.* She could feel her brows knit as she tried to figure out how the process worked in her head. It was strange. It was like there was no difference in her brain until someone asked a question or she looked at something. Then the information was just there. *Do Svesti even go to school if they can just upload information?*

Emmy spent the rest of the day wiping the laptop and drives the Australian government sent. The Svesti provided her a tablet, so she searched for more information about their software languages. Then she played with the coding on the synthesizer, trying to come up with something like coffee. She took breaks for meals and another training session with Rachel, and when her head hit the pillow that night, she was exhausted. *At least I'm not freaking out so much about the Svesti anymore. Guess I'm getting used to how they look.*

In the morning, a Svesti male entered the med bay with his nose bleeding. Finding no one in the room, he smiled. He entered the Healer's main office, calling Rivezt's name. When he saw the information uploads on the desk in a container, he leaned back on the desk and switched out one upload for the one he had hidden on him.

Shaking his head in mock disgust, he walked back into the main area, grabbed an absorbent cloth for his nose, and left.

I don't think they monitor med bay, but if they do, it should look like nothing more than me seeking medical attention and finding no one to help. The cloth over his face hid his smile.

The following morning, Emmy reported with the other women to the med bay. Rivezt was there with two other Svesti and the commander. Talia was late, so she missed the introductions to Healers Markham and Sinoaz. Emmy hopped up on a bed for Healer Markham to insert the upload about Svesti court customs and dress. *Like I care about what they wear.*

Talia came in before the first three women finished. Emmy waited for Lin, who was in the second group of three. Lin was going to help her look in the aquiponics bay for a plant that might be similar to coffee beans, since Emmy's attempts with the synthesizer hadn't gone well. She spun when she heard Talia whimper. She ran over to her with everyone else in the med baby.

"It won't slow the data or disengage," Sinoaz said in a panic.

Talia's nose began to bleed. Rivezt engaged the health monitoring system. Talia screamed and started to convulse.

Emmy hugged herself and stared in horror. *Talia looks like she's having a grand mal seizure.*

Rivezt did something on the med bed and wires attached to Talia's body while the sides of the bed rose.

"Tolvex. Med bay. Now." Durek barked into his comm. He glared at the healer. "What are you doing, Rivezt?"

"I'm putting her into a coma. It's the only way to slow the progression of data into her brain without killing her."

No one spoke until Talia's body calmed.

Devik entered the med bay as Sinoaz said, "It's finally disengaging, Healer Rivezt."

"Good. Give it to Tolvex."

"What happened?" Devik's teal eyes were hard.

"There was something wrong with the upload for the Ambassador," Sinoaz said. "It transferred much too much data and the controls wouldn't work." His hand shaking, he handed the device and upload to Devik.

"Use my office," Rivezt said as he gestured his head at Devik.

"I'm coming with you, mate," Emmy said. She followed Devik and watched over his shoulder as he inserted the upload into a separate device and ran a scan. "What are you looking for?"

"The size of the upload or additional programming that interfered with the manual override." Devik's tail swished behind him, hitting Emmy's calf.

"Hey, watch that thing," she said as she grabbed it. Its warmth and smoothness surprised her.

Devik jerked upright, teal eyes meeting hers. "I apologize. Our tails sometimes expose our emotional state."

"So what's yours saying now?"

"I'm angry a female was hurt." He growled and looked back at the screen. "The size of the file is acceptable and should not have caused Lady Talia harm."

"What's the available size on the upload itself? Does it show significantly larger than the file?"

"No. And there's no programming file."

"Do you mind if I try something?" Emmy asked.

He looked at her. "You have an idea?"

"Yes. But first we should copy this one to something larger and not connected to anything else, just in case."

"Very well." Devik disconnected his tablet from the ship's computers and copied the upload.

"Move out of the way, mate." Emmy bumped her hip against his arm. He stood and gestured to the chair. She was typing before she even finished sitting. He rested one hand on the desk and leaned over her, eyes on the screen. *Hmmm, he smells good.* Several minutes later, she said, "Do you see it?"

He growled again. "Yes. We should check to see if any of the other uploads are the same."

Emmy hopped up. "Let me go get them." She hurried out to the med bay. When she returned, Devik had placed another chair next to the one they had been using. "Here. Markham gave me these." She suppressed a shiver as his larger fingers brushed her hand when she dumped the uploads into his palm. "Do you mind if I use the tablet to check the executable file?"

He nodded absently. "Go ahead. I'm going to check these, then find out what's in the large file." His tail wrapped around her ankle as they worked. *His tail is warm. For some reason, I thought it would be cool.*

"There are a couple commands here. If I'm reading them correctly, they disabled the manual controls. That's why Healer Sinoaz couldn't disengage the device." Emmy slid the tablet in front of Devik. After looking at it, he turned to Emmy, their faces close. "It was deliberate."

He smells like a warm campfire with cinnamon and vanilla in the flames. "Well, I think the hidden partition was probably the first clue." She grinned at him.

He smiled, fangs flashing. *They really don't bother me anymore. In fact, I think they're cute.* "All the other uploads had nothing unusual on them. I'm comparing the files, but it looks like they're all the same except the hidden one on Lady Talia's."

"What's the large file?" Emmy tilted her head to see his screen better.

"If I am correct, Svesti law." Devik frowned. "Look at the file size. It's astronomically larger than the one on Svesti customs."

"Well, we found out the cause. Now we just have to figure out who did it, mate." An unusual expression crossed his face when Emmy stood.

She glanced down. "Uh, Devik? Do you think you could let go so we can tell everyone what we found?"

He followed her gaze and realized his tail was keeping her from moving. "My apologies, again." His tail released her leg, and she moved.

When they returned to the med bay, Emmy noted all the women except Natasha had left. Durek was sitting, caressing Talia's hair. Her body was calmer, although the medical hologram showed there was still a lot of brain activity.

Devik questioned Rivezt. He discovered Rivezt had left the uploads unsecured earlier in the day because of a cargo bay accident and had seen no others in the med bay.

Emmy angrily explained Talia's upload had a hidden partition with the enormous upload and hidden programming to counteract manual commands to disengage. When Rivezt said the individual uploads weren't marked for specific women, Emmy clenched her fists. "So it could have been any one of us who received that upload. Talia just happened to be the unlucky one. Someone wants to hurt us."

Rivezt was shocked when Devik said it appeared that all Svesti law and cases throughout the centuries was on Talia's upload.

"That explains her brain lighting up like a supernova," Natasha said.

"We also have to check and make sure the information in the upload was accurate and not altered even more," Emmy said hesitantly.

"I had not considered that," Devik said. Emmy's shoulders relaxed when he looked impressed at her comment.

"Tolvex, find out everything you can and find who did this," Durek said.

"I would like to request Lady Emmy's assistance," Devik said. "I believe her talents would be useful." *Oh, good, he's not just dismissing me because I'm female.*

"Lady Emmy requested earlier to learn more about our technology. If she is willing to help, this would be a good start to meeting her request." Durek looked at Emmy with questioning eyes.

"That works for me, mate."

Devik growled. "Why do you keep calling people mate?"

"I'm from Australia; we call everyone mate. It means buddy or friend. They also use the term where Rachel is from." She frowned at him. *No one tells me what I can and cannot say.*

"You're among Svesti now. Mate has a much more intimate connotation here. You may find yourself with trouble on your hands if you continue to use the word as you do." Devik gave Emmy an angry look.

Emmy crossed her arms and glared back at him. "I'll take it under advisement. Mate." *Since it irritates you so much, I will make sure I keep doing it.*

Devik huffed. "Come along, female. We have an investigation to conduct."

"Anything you say." She paused for a moment. "Mate." Emmy followed Devik out of the med bay.

Chapter 7

In Devik's work area, he gestured to Emmy to take a seat. *I wonder if we should synthesize shorter chairs. Her feet don't touch the floor.*

"Emmy, your intuitive grasp of Svesti computer language impresses me."

Her face beamed. "Thanks, Devik. I spent some time studying yesterday. It's all logic, so I basically have to learn Svesti terms for things I already know and how the language works." She shrugged. "I still have a long way to go to be proficient on my own, though. I'm hoping to learn more."

"I would be happy to teach you what I know. And your idea about checking the data on Lady Talia's upload to ensure it was accurate is excellent. I'm not sure I would have thought to do so."

She leaned forward, her brown eyes serious. "I also considered that it was possible the ship's database was tampered with. If we are going to compare, maybe we should compare against an outside source at the same time. Just to be safe."

Devik stared at her. "You are brilliant."

Her cheeks darkened. "I wouldn't say that."

He frowned. "Why would you dismiss a sincere compliment? You should be proud you have an agile mind."

Her eyes glanced away. "I'm not used to receiving compliments, Devik. They make me uncomfortable."

Devik's chest rumbled. *I don't like that she doesn't see her own worth.* "I'm confused. You didn't seem uncomfortable with my praise of your abilities with our computer language."

Her brows knit and she chewed her lower lip. "I think it's because you were complimenting skills I developed, not who I am."

He bent toward her. "I've known many beings who had brilliant minds but were complete *naroons*. You, however, constantly seem to stretch your mind. It's refreshing."

She scrunched her face. "*Naroons?*"

"A very large bipedal mammal. They are blue and very furry and act like younglings in their family groups. They tussle, wrestle, and don't seem to be very smart or think of consequences." He chuckled. "Svesti consider it an insult to be called a *naroon*."

She grinned. "I like that."

"Do you think you can set up the comparisons if I allow you access to the ship's database and the one on Costonia?"

"I'd like to try. Although you might want to check my code before running the program." Her eyes lit up. *She likes a challenge. So do I.*

Devik worked on his computer, then gave her his tablet. "Here. I've reconfigured the tablet for you. You may use it for anything that pertains to this investigation. Keep the one we already gave you for personal use. Choose a password and you can start. I'll review it when you're done."

"Do you want me to work in here or somewhere else?"

"I would prefer here, if you don't mind. That way, if either of us has questions or ideas, we can save time." *Besides, I like having you near.* "I'm going to check security feeds and devise a plan to keep the uploads safe."

Emmy slid off the chair. "Okay, I'm just going to move over to the couch and get comfortable." Out of the corner of his eye, he watched her tuck a leg under her as she sat in a corner of the couch. She was using the arm of the furniture as a desk. *Clever female.*

Devik was content with Emmy in the same room. Hearing her mumble or seeing her push her curls from her eyes coaxed a small smile from him. He suppressed a grin when he noted that she constantly moved some part of her body—she bobbed a foot or tapped her fingers. *I think the only times I've seen her completely still is when she's afraid.* He enjoyed her scent filling his work area. *It smells like home.*

After some time, he looked up. "Emmy, would you be willing to observe Rivezt as he creates the uploads and verify there is nothing hidden on them before he secures them?"

"Of course." She glanced at him and smiled.

"Then I'll check them immediately before he uses them. I believe that should forestall future problems."

"I'm just about done programming the comparison of databases."

"I'll check it when you're finished, then we'll run it from my computer since it's secure in here."

"Sounds good." Her brow furrowed. "Devik, why would someone tamper with the uploads?"

He frowned. "I was informed recently that not all on the Council are happy with the situation."

"What do you mean?" She tilted her head.

"Some Svesti wish to invade Earth and take whatever females they want, while others believe in racial purity. Most, however, agree with King Sovex that a treaty is the best way to save our race from extinction."

"Which group do you think is responsible for Talia's upload?" She chewed on her lower lip.

"I don't know yet, Emmy. But we will find out." Devik's voice deepened as he growled.

"It really bothers you that this happened, doesn't it?" Emmy stared at him.

"Harming a female is wrong and contrary to how Svesti are raised," he said.

Wistfully, she said, "I wish there were more men like you in the universe, Devik. In my experience, there are too many men who enjoy hurting women."

His tail flicked rapidly. "I dislike that there is a Svesti onboard who thinks he can hurt any of you females with impunity."

Her face hardened. "We'll catch him, mate. Did you find anything on the security feeds?"

"Nothing useful. We don't have feeds in or at the door of the med bay for patient privacy. And a lot of males passed in that hall—some with injuries and some without. It may narrow it down some, but not enough."

"We'll figure it out." She smiled. "I'm hungry. I'm going to meet the other women for lunch." She passed him her tablet. "You can check my programming. If you could let me know where I made errors so I'll be aware next time, I would appreciate it."

Devik nodded. "I'd be happy to. Lady Rachel has requested to use the training area every day in the afternoons. Will you be joining her?"

"Yes." Emmy grimaced. "I have the feeling that she's going to work us very hard. And she isn't even throwing us to the mat yet."

Laughing, Devik said, "Unfortunately, pain comes with training."

"I prefer using my mind to avoid physical conflict."

"If that option is available to you, please use it, Emmy." He frowned. "I hope you're never in a situation where you have to use Lady Rachel's training."

"Me, too."

After she left, he checked her work. *Only two errors. She's very good.* Smiling, he made a note to tell her.

Devik sent a message to Ash'n to inform him about the new procedure for uploads. He frowned when Ash'n told him Lady Talia was still in a coma. Ash'n believed it would be the next day before it would be safe to allow her to awaken. *I still don't understand how a Svesti could intentionally harm a female.*

Devik's routine changed over the next several days. In the mornings, he and Emmy continued their efforts to find the traitor. After the midday meal, he met with Vared and the human females. Sometimes Karid or Ash'n joined them. Then he made certain he was in the training area when the females were working with Lady Rachel.

His comm chimed. "Tolvex."

"Devik," Emmy said. "I'm going to be a little late. Talia wants me to brief her on our efforts. I'll be there when I'm finished."

"Thank you for letting me know." He frowned as he disconnected his comm. *I was hoping to see her.*

Devik continued working until his comm chimed again an hour later. "Tolvex."

"Tolvex. Ladies Talia and Emmy are in the med bay. It appears they may have been poisoned."

Devik growled and his tail flicked wildly as he stood. "I'm on my way."

"Negative. I need you to check the security feeds. Jevax found them in the hall near the dining area. See if you can discover how or where they were poisoned. Lady Natasha thinks it may have been something they ate."

"As you will." Devik disconnected his comm and stalked to his desk. Blood dripped from his palms. He opened his clenched fists and saw his bloody claws. Never before had he felt a burning need to disobey orders. *Crek! I should be with Emmy, not searching feeds.* Breathing deeply, he attempted to calm down. He grabbed supplies from his med kit to seal his wounds.

As he looked at the vids, he leaned forward when he saw the females in the dining area walk towards their usual table. *Wait. Why can't I see the whole table?* He changed the feed to a different camera and there was still a blind spot. *Someone has been changing the angles of the cameras.* He saw Lady Talia slide a bowl from the unseen area and offer its contents to Emmy before taking some herself. Both females added berries to their *pertiza.* When they finished eating, they dropped their items in the recycler and walked out.

Devik changed feeds again. *The crekkin' traitor moved the cameras in the halls, too.* The entrance to the dining area was no longer covered as it should be. And others were pointing too low to identify most males. Devik growled low. Further down the hall, he saw the females stumbling, then Jevax approaching and lifting them both before running towards the med bay. His growl deepened when he saw Emmy's head bouncing against Jevax's shoulder. When the group came across Vared, Lady Talia reached for him and Vared ran with her.

When Vared comm'd again, Devik was already in the dining area asking about any berries left out on the tables.

Talen Previv, the head cook, shook his head. "We had no berries this morning, Lieutenant Tolvex. I saw no one in the dining area, not even the females. I was in the back showing Lady Ava how to make *brellia,* and the other males who are normally working here are in the master food stores area. They are taking inventory so I can make a list for our resupply at Theron."

She's so pale and still. Devik sat next to Emmy, gently holding her small hand in his. His tail wrapped around her ankle.

Emmy stirred. "Oh, my head hurts." Her voice was hoarse.

"Emmy?" Devik squeezed her hand. "Can you hear me?"

"Yes, but do you have to speak so loudly?" She grimaced in pain. "I feel awful."

"What do you remember?"

"A purple monkey?" She scrunched her face.

Ash'n and Lady Natasha approached.

Ash'n said, "Good, you're awake, Lady Emmy."

Emmy squinted. "The light is bright."

Lady Natasha said, "You probably have a sore throat, headache, and upset stomach."

Emmy nodded slowly. "That sounds about right. Actually, every muscle in my body aches."

"That's to be expected." Lady Natasha clasped Emmy's other hand. "You were poisoned with something similar to Earth's nightshade."

Emmy froze. Devik's tail gently rubbed her calf. "How is Talia?"

"She's recovering, just as you are," Ash'n said. "We emptied your stomach contents and gave you some medication to counteract the poison."

Emmy looked at Devik. "Anything on the security feeds?"

"Rest, *milara.* I'll explain everything after I brief Durek and Lady Talia." He glanced across the med bay. "It looks like she's wakening again." He squeezed her hand and removed his tail. "I'll be right back."

Chapter 8

As Natasha and Rivezt prodded her, Emmy watched Devik speaking with Durek and Talia. *I'm pretty sure Talia and the Commander are going to sleep together. Sooner rather than later would be my guess. He stayed with her while she was in her induced coma, and he's by her side now.* Devik left the couple while all three of them were laughing and walked toward Emmy.

Emmy lowered her eyes and watched Devik through her lashes. *If you'd asked me a week and a half ago, I wouldn't have understood a human and a Svesti together. But considering how hot I find Devik, I'm starting to get it.*

"What was so funny?" she asked.

Devik smirked. "I told them my suspicions that the traitor isn't trying to kill you females but is trying to make you very afraid."

She frowned at him. "I don't find that amusing."

"I suggested that timid, fearful human females at the Choosing might cause some of the Svesti nobles to reconsider their support of an alliance. They might think those traits would be inherited if they bred humans. Lady Talia joked that perhaps that is what you females should do. Vared said it would not work in her case. All someone would have to do is make her angry and her true nature would show."

Emmy grinned. "Okay, now that's funny. She'd probably rip someone a new one."

Devik gave her a confused look. "Rip someone a new one?"

Emmy giggled. "It means she would eviscerate the offender with words." *I'll just keep the rest of the meaning to myself for now.*

He smiled. "Okay. How are you feeling?" He took her hand in his and rubbed his thumb over her wrist. "I was very worried about you."

"I think I've been worse. But I can't remember when. I am thirsty, though." She smiled as he got her some water. "Thanks."

Devik looked around the med bay, then leaned closer. "I discovered the traitor has been moving the security cameras, creating blind spots all over the ship."

She frowned. "We'll have to fix that."

"I'll start on it while you recuperate."

Emmy crossed her arms and narrowed her eyes. "I want to help. I have a stake in catching this asshole."

"You will continue to help, but you need to rest first, *milara*, and regain your strength." A stern look crossed his face. "I must insist."

Aww, he's so cute when he believes he's in charge. She suppressed a giggle. "Whatever you say, mate." Emmy laughed at his grumble. *He's so easy to tease.*

"I think we can let you leave med bay, Emmy. Just take it easy for a couple days. Your body has been through a lot," Natasha said.

Emmy smiled. "No offense, but I'm glad to be getting out of here."

Natasha softly laughed. "I get that a lot."

"I'll bet." Emmy's fingers tapped on her thigh. "I hadn't thought to ask before, but being here brings back memories. Did you ever have a chance to determine whether or not the changes the Svesti made to our bodies affected birth control like shots or pills? I had a shot about a month ago. I was curious if it's still in effect or if its effects are reduced or eliminated now."

"Actually, I did do some research," Natasha said. "Like you, I had a shot, so I ran tests on myself. It looks like it's still doing what it's supposed to do. However, I don't know whether or not it will last as long as it normally would. I'd have to see if one of the other women is on pills and test them to see if those still work."

"Okay. Should I have you test me regularly, just in case?"

"That's a good idea. I'll draw some blood now. When it's time to test myself again, I'll do yours at the same time."

Emmy grinned. "Thanks, doc." *Whew, I'm glad it's still working. It's still my choice.*

Emmy was frustrated and horny. Devik had been keeping close tabs on her ever since she'd been poisoned. Five days of him watching her with those teal eyes that sometimes turned a dark emerald. Five days of his warm tail at her back while they walked and installed hidden cameras in various places. *At least I was able to convince him to leave the other ones alone so the traitor would be unaware of our efforts.*

A few times, she absentmindedly caressed his tail while working next to each other. As soon as she realized what she was doing, she always stopped. He never mentioned it.

Devik's scent of campfire combined with cinnamon and vanilla calmed and excited her. She still wasn't sure how that was possible. He was always in the training area in those shorts that hugged his firm buttocks when Rachel was teaching the women. She wanted to trace the lean lines of his muscles with her fingertips and tongue. She was seriously considering wearing a double layer of underwear when training because she was always wet.

Every morning, Emmy awoke with the remnants of a sexy dream in her head and her hand between her thighs. Despite masturbating, she couldn't take the edge off.

Stomping into her quarters, Emmy stripped down and headed for her nightly bath. As she sipped her wine, she wished she was back on Earth. There, if she was feeling this way, she could find someone to fuck then disappear from their lives. No attachments—that's how she liked it. She didn't have that ability on the *Invictus*. She was stuck on the ship for another six weeks and doubted she could disappear as easily on Costonia either.

Emmy stepped out of the bath, water dripping down her flushed body. Forgoing the drying tube, she grabbed a towel and briskly rubbed herself. She looked in the mirror and nodded. *Big Boy it is tonight. Maybe BB will do it for me.*

Walking naked into her bedroom, she found her favorite sex toy and moved the top sheet over before she laid down. Wetting a finger, she traced her stiff nipples, then pulled and tugged on them. She turned on her vibrator, with its veiny lines and large balls, and rubbed it on her clit.

Closing her eyes and letting her imagination take over, she thought of Devik. *How would those fangs feel?* Breathing heavily at the thought of him nipping at her breasts, she arched her back. *Would he pinch with his claws?* Gasping, she slid BB into her pussy slowly until the latex-covered balls rested against her ass.

Leisurely pumping her vibrator in and out, she turned the speed control higher. *What can he do with his tail?* The idea of his tail playing with her nipples or her clit made her pussy clench around BB. She moaned louder and in a higher pitch as her excitement grew.

Emmy heard a sound and opened her eyes to see Devik running into her bedroom with his claws out. Shocked, she gasped. Somehow she managed to turn off BB with one hand while grabbing the sheet and tucking it under her armpits with the other. She sat up abruptly, bringing her knees to her chest. *Just fucking great. BB's still in there and the balls are too big for me to close my legs. I've never been this embarrassed.*

"Devik! What the hell are you doing in here?" Emmy squealed.

"I heard noises like you were in distress as I was walking by and came in to save you." He retracted his claws and straightened. His eyes were a deep emerald, almost black.

She crossed her arms and rested her elbows on her knees. Dropping her head and hiding her eyes, she mumbled, "I'm fine. You can go. We never have to discuss this."

Emmy's eyes widened when she felt BB being pulled out of her core and heard the suction of her wetness trying to keep it in. Incredulously, she looked at Devik. *The bastard used his tail to pull it out.*

He transferred the vibrator to his hand, turning it this way and that. "Is this what a human penis looks like?"

"Only if a woman is lucky," she said quietly.

Devik tilted his head. "What do you mean?"

"In my limited experience, most human men are not as well-endowed as BB."

"BB?"

Fuck my life. I guess I can be even more embarrassed. "Big Boy."

Fangs flashing, Devik smiled. He accidentally turned on BB and some of her juices flew onto his face.

Oh my god! I don't know whether to laugh or cringe in mortification. She watched as he inhaled deeply, then licked his lips. *Why is that so hot? Shouldn't I be disgusted?*

Simultaneously closing his eyes and turning off the vibrator, he said, "Your scent is intoxicating, but your taste...your taste is addictive." He opened his eyes and gazed at her.

She shivered at the desire emanating from his dark eyes. "I don't know what to say, Devik."

He shook his head, his braids brushing his shoulders. "So human males do not have nodes?"

"N…nodes?"

Devik nodded. "Yes, Svesti males have three head nodes here." He pointed with a claw where the head met the shaft. "And a base node here." He pointed again.

Oh, fuck. Nodes. I didn't need to know that. Emmy's pussy clenched at the thought.

"Um, that's handy info to have. I guess."

He smiled. "Is this what you use to pleasure yourself every morning?"

She narrowed her eyes and glared at him. "What the hell is that supposed to mean?"

"I can tell you pleasure yourself in the mornings. Your scent is different."

"You can smell that?" *Just let me die now.*

"All Svesti can. Although some of us have better olfactory senses than others." He smirked.

"I think it's time you left, Devik." Emmy tried to look stern, but the whole conversation had her off-balance.

Devik dipped his head at her. "As you wish, Emmy. Where would you like BB?" He waggled the vibrator.

"Uh, on the nightstand is fine." Emmy put her head down on her arms again as she listened to him leave her quarters. *I cannot believe what just happened.* She looked at BB and just shook her head. *I don't think I can use that anytime soon.* She sunk back into the bed. *I should let the other women know the Svesti can smell arousal, but how the hell do I explain how I know it?*

Emmy groaned. *How do I face him tomorrow?* The sheer absurdity of it all hit her and she laughed until she cried.

Chapter 9

Devik forced himself to leave Emmy's quarters. His cock was as hard as tempered valadium. He made it to his quarters, seeing no one. He palmed, then adjusted himself through his pants. *Crek! I just reminded Vared today the females are meant for the nobility, not us. Now I need to remember that.*

Turning on the shower, he stripped and let the water hit his back. *I'm not ready to wash my face. I want her scent on me a little longer.* He licked his lips and groaned. Wrapping his hand around his engorged cock, he thumbed his sensitive head nodes.

When he'd heard what he thought was distress from Emmy's quarters, his heart had raced as he entered his security override to save her. He'd been ready to do battle. Then the sight of her splayed on her bed with her sex toy immobilized him. His tail had pulled the cock facsimile from her body before he'd even thought about it. He'd had to wrap his tail around his ankle afterward to keep it under control.

Devik's hand tightened on his member. Slowly, he moved his hand as he recalled her darkened skin and riotous brown curls. He only got a brief glimpse of her nudity, but her nipples were large and brown. Her skin was a bright pink where the scent of her was the strongest.

As he imagined teasing and licking her core, his movements grew in speed and intensity. He grunted at the thought of his cock taking the place of her vibrator. *Goddess, she'd be so tight and wet. Squeezing me as I pumped inside her.* His buttocks clenched as his orgasm built. His head fell back. Water pelted his face and ran down his body. His back bowed with the force of his pleasure. Ropey streams of his seed painted the wall as he groaned Emmy's name.

He tried to catch his breath. His head fell heavily onto the shower wall. *Goddess, guide me. I don't know what to do. I want to do the right thing, but I'm not sure what that is anymore. If I follow orders, I need to keep my hands and body to myself. But I'm not certain I can do that. There's something about Emmy that calls to me constantly. And knowing I arouse her, too, doesn't help. Crek.*

"The *Invictus* will be at Theron tomorrow. The females will be going to the station with a security team."

"Do you know what time? Will you be with them?"

"The shuttle will be leaving sometime after the morning meal. No, I will remain onboard."

"Good. Good. I will let our allies know."

"I must go now. Svesti always."

"Svesti always, Nephew."

Later that evening, Devik tried to focus on work and not on his desire for Emmy. He reviewed the scans he and Karid were running on XB9428B. Vared had been as interested as Devik and Karid about the decaying energy traces of a Frezzian freighter engine slowing down over the planet weekly, but never landing. They theorized the Frezzians were dropping supplies for a Zuvgran lab. They estimated there was another drop scheduled in two days. If the Svesti could track that freighter, they might learn more about the other labs. Maybe one would have the information they needed about the virus that killed most Svesti females.

The *Invictus* would arrive at Theron tomorrow for a resupply of their space cruiser before continuing to Costonia. Devik was concerned about taking the females to the space station, but Vared was correct. The females were guests, not prisoners. This might be their only opportunity to get off the ship before they reached the home world. *I hope nothing goes wrong.*

In the *Invictus* hangar bay the next day, Devik looked over the human females as Talia asked why they weren't porting to Theron. Vared informed them it was newer technology and only safe for three beings at a time. Theron maintained a scan-resistant defense which limited the ability to port. There was no way to ensure that a being wouldn't be ported into a wall or someone else.

Devik was glad to see the females were all wearing their nanosuits. Emmy had hers on under her regular clothing. It reduced her scent a little, but he could still smell her. He frowned when she avoided his eyes. *That won't do.*

Besides Devik and Vared, Karid, Ash'n, Jevax, and Brauvix were joining them to protect the females. Their head cook, Talen Previv, and their supply master, Leriv Volax, were there to purchase the needed supplies. The pilots, Gal'n Kalix and Brestov Xoriv, were already onboard the shuttle and would protect it while the rest of them were on Theron. Kalix and Xoriv were also part of Devik's security teams. He had the highest confidence in their abilities.

They boarded the shuttle. Emmy took a seat next to Lady Lin. Emmy's shoulders tensed as he sat on her other side.

Quietly, he said, "Did you sleep well, *milara*?"

Emmy glanced at him from the corner of her eye. "Yes. You?"

"Yes, I had interesting dreams last night." He smiled when she glared at him.

"I don't want to talk about it." Emmy crossed her arms and glowered. "I looked up *milara*. Are you really calling me a scared brown bird?"

Fangs flashing, Devik said, "You should've investigated more. While *milaras* can feign death, they are cunning birds. They set up false nests to keep predators away. When they fly, their brown chest feathers move to reveal the periwinkle and white underneath. They have those same colors under their wings as well to match Costonia's sky. When they fly near treetops, it is difficult to see them from above or below. They hide in plain sight."

"Is that how you see me? Hiding in plain sight?" She pursed her plump lips.

"In a way—you tuck yourself away from others. But I also admire your ability to assess personal danger to yourself and take action to redirect that danger." Devik leaned toward her and whispered, "And as I saw last night, you definitely hide much of your beauty underneath baggy clothes."

Emmy slapped his arm. "You're annoying me."

"Good." Devik grinned. "I'd much rather have you angry and speaking with me than embarrassed and avoiding me."

She closed her eyes and blew out a harsh breath. Softly, she said, "You scare me, Devik."

Just as quietly, he said, "No, I interest you, Emmy. In many ways. Partly because I do see you."

She opened her eyes and stared into his. "And that's why you scare me."

"If it makes you feel any better, you make me question myself and my beliefs. It's unnerving."

She laughed. "Well, so long as I'm not the only one confused."

Devik grinned at her. Her curls bounced as she shook her head in exasperation. She turned and began talking to Lady Lin.

I do see you, Emmy. I don't know why you keep yourself so contained, but I'm going to find out. Devik silently chuckled when his tail wrapped around her ankle. *Crekkin' thing has a mind of its own.*

Devik smiled as the human females took their first look at the Theron marketplace. Their faces shone with awe at five levels stuffed with stalls along the walkways. Storefronts were interspersed between them. He didn't understand Lady Natasha's comment of "retail therapy day," but the females all laughed.

They began their shopping at a weapons store. After that, they browsed for spices, fabric, and technology. *Interesting. Emmy bought a password decoder, electronic lock pick device, as well as components to build a computer. I wonder why.*

Lady Lin asked if they could look at stalls for a bit. Devik, Jevax, and Ash'n were watching over Emmy, Ladies Lin, and Natasha as they looked at more fabrics, while Ladies Rachel and Ava were with Karid and Brauvix at a food stall. Vared and Lady Talia were looking at jewelry. Devik eyed Emmy as she lingered over a dark blue silky fabric. *That color would look stunning on her.*

Devik's thoughts were interrupted as he heard Lady Talia scream, "Let me go!" and Vared's roar. He began to turn when he saw an orange arm grab Emmy's wrist. *Durelians!*

Drawing his dagger, Devik roared as another Durelian grabbed him around the neck from behind. From the corner of his eye, he saw Emmy use a move that Lady Rachel taught the females earlier in the week. *Good job, milara. You broke his elbow.*

Devik turned his head sideways. He was at an awkward angle to stab the Durelian in the torso, but he did it. It wasn't enough to seriously harm his attacker, but the Durelian loosened his grip on Devik's neck. Devik turned further and head-butted the orange alien. The Durelian released him, and Devik kicked him on the front of his knee shattering it. The Durelian screamed in pain as he fell to the grated metal floor.

From his comm, he heard Vared yelling for them to port the females or get them to the shuttle as Vared was following Lady Talia and her kidnappers. He looked around. Brauvix, Karid, Previv, and Lady Rachel stood over multiple three-eyed Durelians on the other side of the walkway, with Lady Ava hiding behind a crate. Jevax and Ash'n had disabled more attackers while Lady Natasha held Lady Lin. Emmy clutched her arm. Devik growled as he realized she was bleeding.

Devik stalked toward Emmy. "Let me see," he said. Gently, he took her arm. She hissed as he softly touched her wrist where a Durelian had grabbed her and moved the sleeve of her nanosuit up. Fortunately, she only had scratches on her exposed skin. He looked up when he heard Karid say, "Let's get everyone to the shuttle." He curtly nodded at his friend.

The Svesti surrounded the females and hurried back to where Kalix and Xoriv were waiting. On the shuttle's lowered ramp, Xoriv was standing with a blaster. Loaded maglevs were at the bottom. As their group approached, Xoriv said, "Kalix has the shuttle started. I stopped loading the supplies when I heard the Commander's orders."

Karid said, "Ladies, please go in and get ready to leave. Rivezt, go with them and heal the females. Tolvex and Jevax, keep watch with Xoriv. The rest of us will load the shuttle quickly." He looked at Xoriv. "Are we expecting any more deliveries?"

Shaking his head, shaved except for a center strip of braided hair, Xoriv said, "Not that I'm aware. Previv and Volax would know better."

Previv said, "I'll go check what's already loaded for food stores."

Volax was running toward the shuttle. "I got here as fast as I could, Lieutenant."

"Determine whether all the deliveries were made. If not, arrange for them to be delivered in an hour and a half. I'll have the *Invictus* send another shuttle to pick anything up, so we can get the females back to the cruiser now." Karid nodded at Volax.

"As you will, Lieutenant." Volax jogged toward the cargo bay.

Chapter 10

On the shuttle, Rivezt used the portable healing wand to treat Rachel's bruises. Emmy held her arm out to him when he crouched near her. He pulled items from the small med-kit to clean her wounds before passing the wand over them and her bruises. Warmth penetrated her skin. Beyond her arm being slightly reddened, there was no other sign she'd been injured. *Cool tech.*

Fingers tapping on her bouncing knee, Emmy looked around. Rachel was leaning forward, head bowed, with her elbows on her knees and clenching her fists. Natasha was holding Lin's hand, while tears ran down Lin's face. Ava had her eyes closed and was taking deep, measured breaths. The silence was deafening.

The rest of the Svesti males entered and took their seats. Low growls rumbled from their chests and tails flicked rapidly. *Damn, they're pissed.*

As the shuttle left Theron, Wurvez looked at Devik. "What do we know?"

Devik looked up from his tablet. "I cannot find Lady Talia's tracker. Durek's comm shows him leaving Theron."

"Don't lose the Commander and keep searching for Lady Talia," Wurvez said with a hard face.

For a long time, no one spoke except Wurvez when Commander Durek contacted him. Emmy's ears perked up when she heard the Commander was following Talia with beings called Wing Raiders but could not board the Durelian ship because of Zuvgran fighters. Wurvez seemed upset when Durek said Svesti from the ship were only backup.

"Who are the Wing Raiders?" Emmy asked Devik.

He looked up from his tablet. "They are Jalaxian mercenaries. I've heard they have an excellent reputation for getting the job done. All accounts say they are honorable warriors."

Emmy's knee bounced. "That's good, right?" She looked at the other Svesti nodding. Devik's tail wrapped around her ankle and her movements slowed.

Devik smiled. "Very good, Emmy. Durek has experienced warriors with him to help rescue Lady Talia."

Wurvez said, "Everyone did well on Theron."

"Not well enough," growled Previv. "Lady Talia was taken."

"No, Wurvez is right. It could have been much worse," said Rachel. She looked at Emmy. "I was pleased to see you get out of that wrist hold."

Emmy's back straightened. "I'm surprised I remembered how. And that it worked." Her teeth gnawed on her lower lip as her shoulders slouched. "I've never intentionally hurt someone before."

Rachel gave her a hard look. "It was us or them, Emmy. It was necessary."

Emmy ducked her head. "I know, but it doesn't make the feelings go away."

"At least you did something. I was terrified and useless," Lin said quietly.

Jevax said, "Lady Lin. You did as we instructed, even if you were scared. That helped."

Lin scoffed. "Sure."

"Jevax tells the truth. And you warned us when there were more Durelians behind us," Rivezt said with a smile.

"How does me following instructions help you?"

Rachel said, "Because they knew where you were at all times, Lin. They did not have to worry about inadvertently hurting you as they fought. They did not have to split their focus. And they had confidence that if they needed you to move, run or whatever else, they could expect you to do so. When you are guarding someone, being able to predict their movements is gold."

All the Svesti nodded.

"Lady Rachel explains it well," said Jevax.

"If you say so," Lin said. "What happens now?"

"We're almost at the *Invictus*," Wurvez said. "You females will go about your day, and our warriors will do their duties."

"Is there anything we can do to help with Talia's rescue?" asked Ava.

Wurvez shook his head, his ponytail brushing his shoulders. "No."

"Do we know how long it will take the Commander to rescue her?" Natasha asked.

"Unfortunately, until the Durelians land somewhere or rendezvous with another ship, we can't predict that."

"And then they'll have to assess the location and make a plan before they can extract her," said Rachel. "They can't just rush in without some intel."

Wurvez nodded. "Lady Rachel is correct. When I have better information to share, I will."

Natasha's brown eyes emanated sadness. "Sounds like it's a waiting game for us women." *I'm not so good at that.* Emmy's fingers tapped hard against her knee. *I want to do something.*

Rachel looked at the other humans. "Why don't we get together in my quarters for a bit when we get back?"

Ava shook her head. "I need to cook first."

Previv said, "We can handle the evening meal without you."

"No, I *need* to cook to work off some stress." Ava shrugged. "It's just something that helps me."

Natasha said with a smirk, "What if we go to the dining area and watch Ava make us goodies to take back to Rachel's quarters?"

Emmy laughed. "I like that idea. Especially if she can make some of her cookies."

The other women smiled. Rachel said, "I guess we have a plan."

Loaded up with plates of freshly baked cookies and snacks, Emmy and the other women headed back to Rachel's quarters. They sprawled out on the large Svesti-sized couches.

"I'm really worried about Talia," said Lin, grabbing a treat. "Can you imagine how her son and sister might react if she gets hurt?"

"We're all concerned," said Ava. "But right now, there's nothing to do but wait and trust the Commander will get her back."

"This sucks," said Emmy. *Goddamn knee keeps bouncing.*

Natasha frowned. "It's hard. I want to do something. Anything."

Rachel nodded. "We all do. Even with my security background, I have to concede the Svesti are better equipped to handle rescuing Talia. I'm not used to being sidelined."

The women sat quietly, deep in their own thoughts for a while.

"How did the Durelians know we were going to be on Theron?" Natasha said, standing. At the synthesizer, she asked, "Milk, anyone?" She counted the raised hands and began programming the machine.

Rachel narrowed her eyes. "Probably from the traitor onboard. That's the only thing that makes sense."

All the women nodded. Emmy sighed. "This traitor is cunning. We really need to be careful, just in case. It's a shame, really."

"What is?" said Ava, taking a glass of milk from Natasha.

"I'm finally liking the Svesti overall. Most of the time, I feel safer with them than I do with human men. But knowing there's someone working to hurt us because of politics just pisses me off."

"A bit like our governments, I think," said Rachel with a grimace.

"The hits keep coming. It's getting old," said Ava, munching on a pastry.

Rachel looked at Emmy. "Any luck finding out who switched the upload and put out the berries?"

"No. Devik noticed security cameras all over the ship had been moved." Emmy pursed her lips. "He's really angry about it."

"You seem to be getting along with Tolvex well," Ava said with a smile.

"He's been giving me a lot of access to the systems and teaching me more about their coding and technology," Emmy said. *Not to mention catching me with BB.* She shifted on the couch when her pussy pulsed.

The women teased Emmy some more about all her time spent with Devik, gushing over his abs and how calm he was in comparison to the Commander. Emmy might have taken it personally, but Natasha was also teased about her time with Rivezt in the med bay, Ava cooking with Previv, and Rachel working on a training program with Wurvez. By unspoken agreement, no one teased Lin about any Svesti—just her fascination with the plants in the aquiponics area. They chatted about Talia and Durek and made good-natured bets on when the two might sleep together.

Emmy stayed with the women for a few hours, trying to relax after the long, eventful day. They were all trying to keep their concern for Talia at bay. Despite their efforts, Emmy felt her anxiety rising again. She stood, grabbed a plate, and loaded it with a variety of the snacks.

"I'm off to my quarters now, ladies. It's been fun, but I need some rest." Emmy said.

"I was going to offer to have another sleepover here," Rachel said. "Like the one in Talia's room our first night, but without the hangovers." Everyone laughed.

Emmy shook her head. "I appreciate it, but I think I'm better off alone tonight."

Natasha's eyes were concerned. "Are you sure? We can divide up and I could stay with you."

"That's really nice of you to offer, Natasha, but I'm okay." Emmy hid her toe-tapping behind the couch where none of the women could see.

"Well, if you change your mind, you can rejoin us, or comm, and one of us will come to you," said Rachel.

"Okay, sounds good." Emmy waved as she tried not to rush out the door. *I really like them, but I don't want to get too close to them. It's easier in the long run.*

After Emmy showered, she pulled an oversized T-shirt over her head and padded barefoot to her living area. *I need something to focus on or I'm going to go batshit crazy.*

She pulled out the packages she'd bought on Theron and laid everything out on the table. Fortunately, nothing was damaged from when she dropped her bag fighting off the Durelians. Using her tablet, she looked up the computer components and connections to make sure she understood what was what.

She chewed on her lower lip as she thought. Nodding, she grabbed her Earth laptop and began disassembling it. She left the USB drive slots in the laptop shell. Humming softly, she rearranged everything on the table, putting aside the items she didn't want to use.

As Emmy picked up the first component, her hand shook. *Dammit!* She put it down and stood abruptly. Nibbling on a cookie as she paced, her mind spun in circles. All the unusual experiences of the last two weeks, culminating in Talia's kidnapping, rattled in her head bumping up against her other life experiences. *Maybe I need a drink. No, I don't want to need a drink.* Groaning, she plopped face first on the sofa and started banging her head in frustration on a pillow. *Why won't my mind shut off?*

Chapter 11

Devik strode down the corridor, the darkened walls indicating it was the night cycle of the ship. He glanced again at his tablet. Ever since the shuttle had returned earlier, he'd been obsessively checking the females' positions, but Emmy's most of all. They'd spent their time in Lady Rachel's quarters. Emmy's tracker showed she'd left over an hour ago. The kidnapping of Lady Talia after the previous incidents on *Invictus* had him on edge.

A low growl emanated from his chest. *That's the second time in a week when I should've been with Emmy, rather than doing my duty.* He hesitated in front of her door. *It's late, maybe she is asleep.* Then he heard a muffled groan. *Then again, maybe she's awake.*

Tail swaying, Devik waited for Emmy to answer the door chime. When the door opened, he took in her unbound curls and the shirt that said "Talk QWERTY to me." He wasn't sure what it meant, but knowing the female, it was probably some play on human words. He suppressed the rumble in his chest at the sight of her bare legs.

"Devik," she said. "It's late. Is something wrong?"

"No, Emmy. I wanted to check on you. May I come in?"

She thrust her hand through her hair. "Uh, yeah, I guess." Stepping back, she waved a hand for him to enter. "Would you like a cookie? I have some left over that Ava made earlier."

He smiled and nodded. "I'm not sure what a cookie is, but I'm willing to try it. I rushed through evening meal because of everything that's going on."

"You guys don't have cookies? You're missing out. There are thousands of cookie recipes on Earth. Something for everyone." Emmy smiled as she held out the plate to him.

Devik took a bite. "Mmm. This is very good. What is it?"

"I'm not sure what ingredients Ava used. I think it's supposed to be equivalent to an oatmeal raisin cookie. Oatmeal is a grain. Raisins are partially dehydrated grapes—a vine fruit that is also used to make wine."

He licked the crumbs off his lips. "Are all cookies like this?"

Her curls bounced as she shook her head. "No. Some are different flavors. They can be soft or hard and different shapes or colors."

"I look forward to trying others when they are available."

She shifted her weight from foot to foot. "So, um, why did you come by? Do we know more about Talia?"

Devik's smile faded. "She was taken to a planet. They're planning her rescue now."

Emmy sat on the couch next to him, leg bouncing. Wrapping his tail around her bare ankle, he felt himself relax for the first time in hours. She dropped her head forward, glancing sideways at him through her hair. "Can I ask you a question and have you tell me the truth?"

"I may not be able to tell you everything at times, *milara*, but I will never lie to you."

She drew in a deep breath, then exhaled sharply. "Do you think it makes me a bad person that I'm glad it was Talia who was kidnapped and not me?"

He took her hand. "No, Emmy. It's not unusual to feel relief that something bad didn't happen to you."

"It's not so much that, Devik. It's that I know she has a much better chance of rescue than I would."

His brows knit. "I do not understand."

"Talia won't ever be left behind. Not like me. I always get left behind."

His eyes perused her flushed face. "How do you mean?"

"Talia's got her son and her sister, even the Commander, who will fight to save her. Whereas me..." Her voice trailed off.

"You do know that if you were in Talia's place, we would be doing our best to rescue you, too?" Devik squeezed her hand.

"Devik, my father left when I was a week old. My mother died when I was four. I admit her leaving wasn't by choice." She bit her lower lip. "I was in and out of foster and group homes until I turned eighteen." She pulled her hand from his and clenched her fingers until they were white. "When I was ten, there was one foster family that was really good." She looked up at him, her brown eyes wide. "I thought they were going to adopt me. Then the dad got a job offer in Europe and they sent me back to the group home. They never even kept in touch with me. After that, I didn't try so hard in any foster home. Friends moved away and never contacted me again. Even the few boyfriends I had left me for something or someone better. Now I prefer not to get close to people, because I know they're going to leave me anyway."

Gazing into her sad eyes, he cupped her cheek in his palm. "Oh, *milara*, you are too young to be carrying such grief. I would never leave you behind if someone kidnapped you." *How do I make this better for her?*

Shaking her head, she said, "Yes, you would. All it would take is for the commander or the king to order you to do so."

His growl surprised them both. "No, leaving you would be more wrong than not following orders."

Emmy chuckled. "So Mr. Black and White can see shades of gray?"

He smirked at her. "Very funny."

They sat in silence for a long moment. Then she abruptly got up to sit on his lap facing him. She rested her hands on his shoulders, while his tail moved up to the center of her back to hold her steady.

"If I were on Earth, feeling this way, I would go to a bar and find a man to fuck," she said.

Devik stiffened. "Why are you telling me this?" *I do not want to hear about other males touching you.*

"Would you be willing to be fuck buddies? Friends with benefits?"

"I don't even know what that means, Emmy." He lifted her off his lap and stood.

"Pleasure each other sexually with no commitments. No expectations of anything permanent. When one of us tires of each other or meets someone else, we part as friends."

A deep growl emanated from his chest. "I have been ordered to escort you females to your Choosings. That implies no sexual contact."

"Really? Who was it that took BB from me and licked his face?" Her cheeks darkened and her breathing accelerated. She stomped away from him.

"I should not have done that," Devik said with a frown, following her.

Waving a finger, she spun back to face him. "Damn right, mister. I think you should leave." Lowering her voice, she mumbled, "I'll find someone else."

"You will NOT ask another to be your fuck buddy, *milara!*"

"You don't get to tell me what to do." He grasped her wrist when she attempted to punch him.

"Never try to hit me again, Emmy. Or I'll turn you over my knee and spank you." His voice sounded like gravel.

"Are you fucking crazy?" she said through gritted teeth. Her chest heaved.

Devik inhaled. *Oh, she likes the idea of a spanking.* His thumb rubbed circles on her tight palm until her fingers loosened.

"You naughty female. You want me to redden your beautiful, plump ass." He licked his lips. "I can taste your arousal in the air." He crowded her into the wall, bending his knees so his erection pressed between her thighs. "I would love to taste it from its source." *Goddess, her body feels perfect against mine.* He nibbled her earlobe.

"You're con...confusing me," she stuttered. "You don't want to be fuck buddies, but you're certainly acting like one." She moaned as he licked her neck.

"When I make love to you, Emmy, it won't be for temporary relief." His hand cupped her breasts. *They're so soft and heavy.* He leaned down to suck an erect nipple through her T-shirt. Through the cloth, he could feel it puckering even harder. His fingers rolled and pinched the other.

"That feels so good," she said in a husky voice.

"Yes, it certainly does, *milara*." Smiling, he knelt in front of her. "This will feel even better."

Devik lifted her T-shirt and groaned when he saw she wasn't wearing underwear. Her sex and thighs glistened with her dripping excitement. Parting her pink lips with gentle fingers, his breath caught in his chest. *So beautiful.* His tail tugged her knee over his shoulder. He licked her in a long, slow stroke from bottom to top. *Crek! She tastes even better than I imagined.* She jolted when his tongue touched the little nub above her core. He looked up. Her head dropped back and the stretch of her neck struck him as erotic.

"More, Devik." Her hands tugged on his braids. "Don't stop now."

He lightly nipped her inner thigh with his fangs, then kissed it as she sucked in a breath. Sliding his arm under her other leg, he moved his tail to support her under her ass. His fingers squeezed and kneaded her plump cheeks.

Dipping his head, he lightly licked around her opening. He felt her shiver. Stiffening his tongue, he plunged it inside her, lapping everywhere he could reach. He noticed her body go still when he touched a spongy area. He concentrated there and her thighs trembled.

Devik withdrew his tongue and replaced it with a finger, thrusting slowly. With his mouth, he began to play with her nub.

She gasped. "More. Right there, Devik."

He rolled and licked the nub, then suckled gently. Adding a finger to his thrusts, he curled the first one to caress that spongy area. Her breathing quickened and her moans deepened.

"Oh, my god. I don't know what you're doing, but..." Her voice trailed off as he added a third finger and thrust faster. Her wetness made sucking noises he loved to hear. The scent of her arousal filled his lungs. He nipped her nub with a fang and she screamed his name. Emmy's body froze, then shuddered uncontrollably. Her cunt gripped his fingers, trying to pull them deeper. *Goddess, that would feel amazing on my cock.*

Juices seeped from her core. Devik licked up everything, growling at the taste of her. Emmy orgasmed twice more. When her body went limp, he removed his fingers from her swollen cunt. He looked up again at her to see her hooded eyes, lazily satiated, gazing down at him. Smiling, he licked his fingers.

Breasts heaving, she drew in a breath. "That is so fucking hot, Devik."

Moving so she could stand on shaky legs, he rose languidly, rubbing his body against hers. He cradled her head in his hands, his fingers entwined in her curls, and kissed her for a long moment.

"Thank you for gifting me with your pleasure, *milara*." He put an arm under her knees and the other around her back. Carrying her to her bed, he said, "It's time for you to rest."

Emmy caressed his face and ran a finger over his lips before touching a fang. "Stay?"

Placing her on her bed, he said, "I think it's best if I leave. You really do need your rest." Smiling, he brushed her hair from her face before tucking her in.

"What about you? I didn't get you off," she said with a yawn.

"This wasn't about me, *milara*. I'll be fine." He kissed her forehead. "Sleep well."

Devik chuckled softly as she rolled to her side and promptly fell asleep. *I think she's well satisfied.* He adjusted his throbbing cock. *Shower and bed for me, too.*

Fortunately, he saw no one in the hall as he walked to his quarters. He frowned. *I hate that she feels she is less worthy than others.*

Chapter 12

Feeling more refreshed than she had in months, Emmy woke slowly. Rolling onto her back, she stretched, enjoying the relaxed, loose feel of her body. She smiled wickedly. *Devik's tongue should be registered as a lethal weapon.*

Sitting up, she frowned. *But he said he didn't want to be fuck buddies. I'm not sure what he's thinking. I can't believe I asked him to stay. I never, ever do that. I don't even fuck men in my own bed.* She got ready for the day quickly, synthesizing a quick breakfast. *I need to find out what's going on with Talia.*

When Emmy reached Devik's office, he stood and smiled.

"Good. You're here. Come with me," Devik said.

"Where are we going?"

"The War Room."

"Do we have any more information about Talia?"

His teal eyes were serious. "That's what we're going to talk about when we get there."

Rachel, Natasha, Wurvez and Rivezt were already seated in the War Room.

Wurvez said, "Let's get started."

"Aren't we waiting for the other women?" Rachel asked.

"No, that's part of what we need to discuss," Wurvez said.

Confused, the women looked at each other. Emmy shrugged.

"What's going on?" asked Natasha.

"Commander Durek and the Wing Raiders rescued Lady Talia from a Zuvgran lab several hours ago."

"Is she alright?" Rachel said.

"Yes and no," Rivezt said with a frown.

Arms crossed, Rachel said, "We want to see her."

"What we're about to tell you next is confidential. You cannot speak a word to anyone about it." Wurvez's gray eyes were steely as he met each woman's gaze. "I must have your word that you will keep this secret until we tell you it is safe to share."

Emmy glanced between Rachel and Natasha, silently asking what they wanted to do. After a moment, Rachel nodded.

"We agree," Rachel said.

"Lady Natasha?" Wurvez said.

"I agree."

"Lady Emmy?"

"I agree. Please tell us what's going on." Emmy's leg bounced. Her movement slowed when Devik's tail wrapped around her ankle.

"While in captivity, a Zuvgran scientist injected Lady Talia with a virus. It kills human and Svesti fertility," growled Wurvez.

Devik added, "The Commander was able to download data about the virus before we destroyed the lab."

Rivezt said, "From what we can tell, the virus is airborne."

"Lady Talia also said there was a Svesti noble who has been working with the Zuvgran," said Wurvez.

Rachel's brows came together. "Why would a Svesti be part of a plan to kill your race's fertility?"

Wurvez scowled. "From what Lady Talia said, the noble is unaware of the virus' effects on Svesti. The Zuvgran did not tell him that part."

"So a double cross." Rachel pursed her lips. "Not surprising."

"Please tell me that Talia and the commander are quarantined," Natasha said, her face concerned.

Wurvez nodded. "Yes. Fortunately, Lady Talia conveyed the problem before they left the planet. They are being towed on one of our shuttles, the *Intrepid*, until we can ensure the virus does not spread."

"That's good," Natasha said. She turned to Rivezt. "What do we know about it so far?"

"The most recent information and scans." Rivezt turned his tablet so Natasha could see it.

Natasha's eyes narrowed as she looked at the data. She looked at Rachel and Emmy, her brown eyes sad. "This virus is incredibly fast-acting. Even if we develop a vaccine, Talia will not be able to have her own children. Her eggs are being destroyed."

Emmy stiffened. *That's just fucked up!*

"Is there a chance of curing her?" Devik asked.

Natasha shook her head. "No. Human females are born with all their eggs. They don't develop any new ones during their lifetime. Human males constantly produce sperm; a cycle takes a little over two months, or *lunars*, as you call it. I'm not sure yet how this virus acts on that process." She looked at Rivezt. "We'll have to discuss similarities and differences to Svesti reproductive systems."

Rivezt nodded. "I would like to ask your assistance in developing a vaccine or cure."

"Of course I'll help."

Emmy straightened. "Well, now we know what Svesti faction our traitor is from."

Everyone looked at her. *Come on, guys, it's obvious.*

Wurvez said, "Explain."

"Think about it. The faction that wants to invade Earth and just take women wouldn't try to screw with our fertility. Only racial purists would think it was a good idea. If we're the only race so far that is compatible, if we can't conceive, they win by default."

Everyone took a moment to digest Emmy's words.

Rachel's lips tightened. "What Houses are most in favor of racial purity?"

"Houses Nuxar and Srotix," said Wurvez.

"Then we begin concentrating on those onboard who have close ties to those Houses," Rachel said.

"I can easily generate a list of personnel whose fathers are from those Houses." Devik frowned. "It will take longer to find those whose mothers are from Nuxar or Srotix."

"And then there's the whole cousin thing. There are a lot of ways to be related," said Emmy. "And there's no guarantee that the traitor is related."

"But it is highly probable. Someone from outside the House would not necessarily be as trusted," said Devik.

Wurvez leaned back and briefly closed his eyes before speaking. "Tolvex and Lady Emmy, begin generating those lists for Lady Rachel and myself. Also include an indication of those who were already on the suspect list because of their locations during previous incidents. We'll focus our search for the traitor on those personnel to start. Rivezt and Lady Natasha, obviously we need you to work on a vaccine or cure."

"If we can't tell anyone the truth, how are we explaining the absence of the Commander and Talia?" asked Rachel.

Rivezt said, "Lady Talia suggested we tell everyone she is traumatized from her experience and only trusts Durek near her. I will say that, for now, it is best to allow her to heal as she believes best."

Natasha nodded. "PTSD is a very real thing for humans. The excuse should work for a while."

Devik said, "Lady Talia also will disable video during her communications with the other women. She said it would allow people to imagine what might have occurred, but never confirm or deny it." His lips turned down. "She dislikes misleading everyone, but agrees it is necessary."

"We cannot let the traitors know we are aware of the virus or that it works," Wurvez stressed. "Lady Talia is the only known person to successfully receive the virus. We don't know if that information was shared beyond the lab. We need time to counteract the virus before the Zuvgran or the traitors try again." His face hardened. "The future of both our races depends on it."

Rachel said, "Talia was rescued from a Zuvgran lab overnight." She looked at the women gathered in her quarters.

"Where is she?" Lin asked.

"According to Wurvez and Rivezt, Talia refuses to be near anyone but the Commander since he's the one who rescued her. Talia and Durek are on a shuttle being towed by the *Invictus*."

Ava said, "PTSD?"

"Possibly. Or maybe she just needs time to feel safe," Natasha said.

"Is there anything we can do?" Lin's dark eyes looked miserable.

"Other than letting her know we've got her back, I don't think so," said Rachel.

I'll do my part in this charade. Emmy said, "Do we know what they did to her?"

Rachel shook her head. "No one told me anything."

Ava said, "Do they need anything? I can make some food to send to them."

"I don't know. Let me find out how the Svesti are handling it, but I think some of your cooking will definitely make her feel better," Rachel said with a smile.

"Maybe I can find a nice plant in the aquiponics bay to cheer her up," Lin offered quietly.

"I think that's a wonderful idea," Natasha said encouragingly.

"Let's give her a few more hours to settle in before we comm her. I'm sure she must be exhausted from everything yesterday,"

Rachel said. "I say we forego our time in the training area for today."

"That's a good plan. Maybe meet back here about an hour before evening meal?" Emmy said.

The women looked at each other and nodded.

Ava hopped up first to leave. "I'm going to the kitchen to start cooking."

"And I'm going to find that plant," Lin said as she followed Ava out.

Rachel looked at Natasha and Emmy after the door closed. "That went well."

"I wish we didn't have to lie to them," Natasha said.

"It's for the greater good."

"I know that, but it just feels wrong." Natasha's blonde hair fluttered around her face as she shook her head.

"At evening meal, we can discuss our conversation with Talia in the dining area and see who takes particular interest," Rachel said.

"Maybe we can narrow down our pool of suspects," Emmy said. "There are over three thousand people onboard. We need all the help we can get."

"Sounds like a plan," said Rachel.

Emmy walked the short distance to her quarters to work on assembling her new laptop. She felt twitchy. *I'm surprised at how much I dislike deceiving Ava and Lin. Maybe I'm getting too attached.*

"Talia? Can you hear us?" Ava said.

"Yes, I can," Talia said.

"There must be something wrong with the connection. We can't see you," Ava said with a frown.

"There's nothing wrong. I would prefer voice only," Talia said quietly.

"Oh," Lin said in a low voice. "Are you okay?"

"Just have a lot to process." Talia's voice hitched.

"Oh, sweetie. We're here for you. Whatever you need," Ava said.

"I appreciate that. I think I need some time, though. I'm not ready to talk about it."

Rachel said, "Do you need anything from your quarters? I can ask Tolvex to port something to you."

"Could I get a few notebooks and pens? I'm not sure how long I'll need to be here and writing will help me."

"Of course. We'll make that happen."

"Would you like some videos or books?" Emmy asked.

"Uh, I'm not sure. I guess if I decide I do, Vared can get them for me."

"But will he know what Earth chick flicks to get?" Emmy teased, and the women smiled.

Talia laughed softly. "You have a point. Feel free to send me anything you think will cheer me up."

"I'm going to send you fresh food daily," Ava said. "It'll help keep your strength up."

"That's sweet, Ava. I'm loving some of the stuff you've been coming up with using alien foods."

"I want to send you something, too, to cheer you up," Lin said shyly.

"I appreciate that. More than you know," Talia said. "Oh, anything you're porting to me, please send it through Tolvex. Vared said he coordinated a spot for ports so someone doesn't accidentally port boxes into our bodies or something." The women grimaced.

"I'm glad you said something," Ava said with a shudder. "I might not have thought of that."

"Anyway, thank you for calling me. I'm sorry to cut the transmission short, but I'm still exhausted," Talia said.

"We understand," Natasha said. "Listen to your body and please feel better soon."

The women exchanged goodbyes. Rachel disconnected the comm.

"What did they do to her that she doesn't want us to see her?" Lin's lips trembled.

"Try not to let your imagination run away with you," Natasha said. She hugged Lin.

"I agree," said Rachel. "We know she was hit and drugged on Theron. I'm assuming they restrained her or had her in a cell of some sort. Anything beyond that is speculation until Talia chooses to share."

Ava said, "She may never choose to share. We have to respect that."

"I think we're getting ahead of ourselves," Natasha said. "Let's allow Talia to lead her recovery."

"Yes," said Emmy as she looked around Rachel's quarters. "Are we ready to go eat?"

Everyone nodded and headed to the dining area.

The women were finishing up their evening meal when Jevax approached them.

"Ladies. I understand Commander Durek rescued Lady Talia earlier." Jevax looked at their group. "How is she feeling? Is she resting in her quarters?"

"Jevax," Rachel said. "Sit with us."

"Talia isn't onboard," said Lin with a trembling lip. "She's recuperating on a shuttle with the Commander."

"Recuperating?" Jevax's brown eyes were concerned. "Was she hurt?"

"We're not sure what happened," Emmy said. "I think she's suffering from PTSD." *I hope he's not the traitor; I like him.*

"PTSD?"

"Post-Traumatic Stress Disorder," said Natasha. "It's common for humans to suffer heightened stress responses after traumatic events. Nightmares, anxiety, moodiness, depression, and an inability to sleep are several possible symptoms."

Rachel said, "Right now, it sounds like Talia is experiencing increased anxiety near crowds, especially after being poisoned on the ship."

Jevax growled. "Is there anything we can do to help her?"

Ava shook her head. "She needs to cope in her own way for now, Jevax. Everyone deals with trauma differently."

"Would you pass along my well wishes for her recovery?"

"Of course," said Lin with a small smile.

Emmy looked up as more Svesti approached, including Sproid, Mantoor, and Rovex. Crulex and Brauvix appeared a few minutes later. The women repeated the story for everyone. *I'm not going to remember everyone who asked about Talia or the ones who didn't. I need to do something.*

Emmy stood. "Everyone, we have a custom on Earth called greeting cards. While many people use digital ones now, there are a lot of us who prefer paper. We send them to friends and family for different occasions, such as birthdays, weddings, and retirements. But we also give them for illnesses or difficult times. We call them get-well cards. I think we should send one to the Ambassador, but instead of signing it, we should include a picture of everyone to let her know we're thinking of her and we support her."

She saw a number of people nod. "If you'd like to be in the picture, crowd together near the back wall and I'll take it. We may have to move some of the tables and chairs so they're not in the way."

As most of the Svesti and the other women moved, Emmy grabbed her tablet and hopped up on a table on the opposite side of the room. *Shit! There's a couple hundred of them.*

"What are you doing up there?" Devik's low rumble sent tingles to her pussy. She looked down at him as he walked toward her.

"I'm taking a picture to send to Talia of people who want to send get-well wishes." She leaned forward to whisper. "I'm not going to remember all their names, so I thought this might be better to help keep track of everyone." She waggled her eyebrows.

Tail swaying, he crossed his arms. *Mmm, I want to lick those sexy biceps.* He sighed. "It sounds like a good idea, but please don't fall."

"If you're worried stay near, just in case."

"Well, what needs to happen?"

She turned back to the group. "Those in front, could you kneel on one knee, so we can see people behind you?" Emmy directed the group, trying to ensure she could see all the faces. As she was doing so, she covertly took pictures of the Svesti who forewent the picture.

Then she said, "Okay, everyone. Smile!" She snapped a few shots. "Now silly faces!" The Svesti looked confused, but then saw the women. Emmy giggled when she saw only a few of the males try. She took a picture. "You guys need to learn to lighten up. That's it. Now we have to put everything back. Thanks."

Devik's hands clasped her waist to lower her from the table. Emmy inhaled sharply as the warmth of his palms reached her body through her shirt. She rested her free hand on his upper arm, squeezing lightly. His head bent as he sniffed her neck. Then he straightened quickly. "Not here, Emmy."

"I know," she said as she patted his rumbling chest. She grinned and stepped back, perusing him. "But I do like a strong, hard body."

His fangs flashed as he smirked. "Hard is an understatement, *milara*. Stop teasing me."

She angled her head. "Or what?"

He leaned forward and whispered, "Or I'll retaliate."

Dampness flooded her panties. Devik sniffed and licked his smiling lips, before walking away.

Her grin widened, then she sighed. *He can be such a bastard, but I love it. And that tight ass is something to behold.*

Chapter 13

Crek! If we were on planet, I would think there's a full moon somewhere. Devik grumbled as he finally made his way to his quarters, tail snapping behind him. Four different altercations between warriors, several intoxicated males causing a disturbance, and Volax irate about some missing supplies had taken up his entire evening. Bypassing Emmy's door, he glanced at it wistfully. *It's late. I'll see her in the morning.*

Before morning meal, Emmy comm'd him to tell him she and Rachel were going to spend their time in the dining area spreading the word about Lady Talia. With so many warriors onboard, males cycled through their meals in shifts. The females wanted to be present for as many as possible. She apologized when she contacted him later to say they were going to do the same for the midday meal but hoped to have some more pictures for them to analyze.

Devik spent the morning contacting team leaders to get their warriors out of the brig and discussing their discipline. Then there were the reports to fill out. He eventually found Volax's missing supplies. They had been misidentified and were in the wrong cargo bay. By the time Devik made it to the training area in the afternoon, he was more than ready to take out his frustrations sparring with Karid.

The human females were practicing roundhouse kicks against the hanging bags with Rachel correcting or encouraging them. One moment Devik was admiring Emmy's kick—well, more her bouncing breasts, her leg muscles as they tightened and released, and the soft inner flesh of her open thighs during her kick, and the next moment he was gasping for the breath knocked out of him as his back hit the mat.

Karid chuckled as he reached down to help Devik up. "Which female distracted you, my friend? You should've seen that coming."

Devik wheezed, trying to reinflate his lungs. *Crek. He's right. I know better than to take my eyes off my opponent.*

"I don't know what you're talking about," he said.

Face alight with humor, Karid shook his head. "Devik, only a female could cause that much of a distraction. I've seen you stay focused while being shot at as plasma grenades go off around you."

Devik said, "I don't want to talk about it."

"If you're worried about the Choosing being a factor, I'm not so sure there will be one," his friend said as he handed him a water pouch.

Devik's braids whipped about his head as he turned to look at his friend. "What do you mean?"

"Vared said the king wants to meet the females before making a final decision. Especially with the news of Lady Talia. Not just the kidnapping, but also with Vared's attraction to her."

"There's been no official word, though?" Devik's tail swayed.

Karid leaned toward his friend. "I think the females will do what they wish and with whom they wish no matter what the Council wants. I also think if you're lucky enough to be a warrior that one of them wants and you feel the same, you should see where it goes."

Eyes narrowed, Devik stared at Karid. "I can't believe you're advising me to have a relationship with one of the females. Wait. Are you interested in one? Lady Rachel, perhaps?"

Karid's ponytail swayed as he shook his head. "I admire Lady Rachel, but don't have those types of feelings for her." His fangs were white against his reddish bronze skin. He gestured towards the females. "Just look at her. She'd beat my ass if I touched her the wrong way. If I wanted to fight in the bedroom, I'd take up with a male." He laughed.

"You have a point." Devik sighed. "Emmy fascinates me."

Karid said, "I'll tell you what I recently told Vared. Why not find happiness together? Our race has suffered so much. I'm starting to believe the Goddess meant us to find the human females." His face turned solemn. "And maybe it's the females who are more in tune with the Goddess' ultimate plans than the males. I'm sure the more pious among us would argue that point, but the Goddess is female, is she not?"

Devik coughed as he held back his laugh. "Please don't start any religious debates, Karid. Let's leave that for the more devout."

Karid slapped him on the back. "Well, I suggest you follow your heart...or your cock, whichever is leading you." He made a pained face. "You don't have to tell me which one, though. If there's a reckoning with the King, you can just say you were following the Commander's lead."

"So use Vared as flak protection? What a friend you are."

Karid waggled his eyebrows. "What's the worst that can happen? We all end up in the same cell. At least we'll have interesting stories to tell to pass the time."

"Has Ash'n developed feelings for one of the females?" *I hadn't noticed anything.*

"Not that he's said. You know him; he keeps such things to himself. Even when we visit erotica establishments or pleasure planets, he goes off on his own."

As Karid and Devik emptied their water pouches, they watched the females leave the training area. *I like seeing Emmy's strong legs in shorts. So much better than those baggy pants she wears.*

"So you and Lady Emmy?" Karid bumped shoulders with Devik. "Are you thinking of asking her for a troth contract?"

"It's still early yet. But thoughts of asking her to true mate with me have been hounding me, especially after Vared told us it might be a possibility."

Surprise lit Karid's face. "True mate? Have your fangs elongated?" At Devik's nod, Karid shook his head with a smile. "If you feel that strongly, don't worry about the King or the Council. We'll support you, Devik."

Devik frowned. "She asked me to be fuck buddies. She's not thinking long-term."

"Fuck buddies?" Karid clutched his belly as he laughed uproariously. "I love that term. And knowing you, my straightlaced friend, that angered you mightily if you're thinking true mate and she's thinking pleasure mate."

Slapping Karid's shoulder, Devik said, "You're a *crekkin' naroon*, Karid. But you're right. I was not happy."

With a sly smile, Karid said, "Well, I don't know how you'll do it, you being such a scrawny warrior, but try to pleasure her so much she can't imagine going without."

Devik laughed. "You just can't help yourself, can you?"

Karid's wide grin filled his face. "You wouldn't have it any other way." *No, I wouldn't, my friend.*

As Devik passed by Emmy's door, it opened and a hand yanked him into her quarters. He stumbled. With an open palm, she slammed the lock controls.

"Emmy, is something wrong?" Devik's eyes perused her, then her aroused scent filled his nostrils.

She pushed him back toward a couch. "I tracked your comm." Her hands were hot on his chest. "Sit."

What is she doing? She buried her fingers in his braids and kissed him ferociously. Crawling onto his lap, she sat and rocked against him.

"Every day in the training area, I see you all hot and sexy," she breathed as she licked his ear and his neck. "Your rock-hard abs and tight ass make me want so many things."

"Emmy?" *Goddess, I'm going to come in my shorts if she keeps this up.*

She leaned back. "If you're not interested, leave now." Her salacious smile caused his heart to skip a beat. "Otherwise, get naked and let me show you what thoughts go through my mind when you're training."

Sharply inhaling, he stared into her brown eyes almost black with desire. "I don't have the strength to leave, *milara*." His hands caressed her back.

"Good." Her fingers played with both his nipples.

His hips bucked, and he hissed when she pinched and twisted them at the same time. "Emmy, if you keep that up, I'm going to retaliate."

Seductively, she smiled. "I'm counting on it." Her fingers went to the front of his shorts. "How the hell do I open these?"

He clasped one of her hands and drew it behind him. "The fastening is in the back, so they're easy to put on or take off with a tail."

"I'd wondered about that." His shorts loosened and fell to the seat.

Standing, she undressed quickly. Her breasts heaved as she removed her bra. His mouth watered when he saw her nipples were already erect. He groaned low when she pushed her shorts and panties down in one fast movement. Her core was glistening with her arousal, her scent heavy in the air.

Dropping to her knees in front of him, she tapped his knee before grabbing the waistband of his shorts. "Lift. I want to check out your nodes." *What's a male to do when faced with such a bossy female?* His hips rose and his buttocks clenched when she squeezed his cheeks. *Her hands feel so good.*

He looked down at her. Licking her lips, she stared wide-eyed at his erection. "Oh my, Devik, you're so thick."

"Too much?" *Oh, please say no.*

She smiled wickedly. "I am looking forward to finding out."

Wetting a finger, she lightly traced it over his head nodes. *Crek!* His cock jerked.

"Are they sensitive? Do they make you feel good?" she asked as she pursed her lips and blew over his wet nodes.

She trembled when his voice dropped even lower. "Oh, yes, *milara.*" He caressed the small bumps that rose on her skin. "What are these?"

"Goosebumps. Your deep voice does it to me. Makes me all horny and shivery." Slyly, she looked up at him. "You mentioned a base node?"

He nodded, leaned back, and pointed. "Here."

"Let me check it out." She scooted forward and wrapped her breasts around his cock. Her nipples were hard points scraping against his skin. Dropping her head forward, her curly hair brushed his stomach and thighs.

"Oh, I see it now." Her hot breath caressed his sensitive skin. A drop of pre-cum escaped his cock when her tongue licked his base node.

Tilting her head back, she used her hands to squeeze her breasts harder against his member. She undulated back and forth, staring down at his engorged length as her lips pouted.

"You filthy female." Since she liked it so much, he kept his voice register low. "I think you like my cock anywhere on your body." Her scent turned spicier. "You like when I tell you how filthy you are, don't you, Emmy?"

She moaned. "I want to get so dirty with you, Devik." Her wet tongue swirled around his head nodes. She released her breasts and wrapped a hand around the base of his length. Her fingers couldn't reach the entire way. Her mouth trailed along his engorged member, licking and kissing, while pumping her hand.

When she opened her jaw wide to suck his cock, he groaned. He was so large, she could only fit the head into her hot, wet mouth.

With a shaky hand, he cupped her cheek. "Do you have any idea how beautiful you look with your lips around my cock? Your lips are going to be swollen later, all red and plump, and I'm going to know it's because I *crekked* your mouth." When she tried to nod her head, he placed his other hand on her other cheek to keep her head still. "Can you take more, *milara*?" Her cheeks hollowed under his palms as she sucked harder.

One of her hands drifted between her legs. He grasped it with his tail and pulled it to his mouth to suckle her fingers. *She tastes so good.* "Oh no, Emmy. Only I may touch your dripping cunt." She hummed around his cock, sending additional spikes of heat throughout his body.

"You look uncomfortable, Emmy. The couch is too tall for you." He patted the space beside him. "Kneel here and you can play some more. I'll make you feel good, too."

His cock slipped from her mouth and she gasped as she hurried to do his bidding. Resting a hand on one of his thighs, she lapped at his member. Her other hand played with his tail where it met his spine before rolling his balls in her hot little fingers. Her back arched as he ran his hand over her ass. She quivered when he extended his claws and scratched them lightly over her skin. Taking him into her mouth again, she groaned when his tail circled her clit.

"Tasting me makes you wet, does it? Are you a bad girl? Would you like me to spank this beautiful ass?" He squeezed a butt cheek, and she wiggled against his hand. Tenderly, he drew her hair from her face so he could see her working his engorged length. "Just a little heat, or do you want to feel it tomorrow?" Her moan reverberated around him and his balls tightened. Retracting his claws, he lightly slapped her ass, the sound echoing in the room.

He stiffened his tail between her legs, while keeping the tip playing with her nub. She closed her thighs around him, jerking with each slap. "Do you want me to come in your mouth?" Slap. "Or should I pull out and come all over your breasts?" Slap. Her body started shaking, and she took him so deep, he was afraid she wouldn't be able to breathe. He thrust his hand into her curls and pulled her off his cock. He reached under her to tug hard on a nipple while his tail slapped her clit.

"Oh my god, Devik!" Convulsing with her orgasm, her fingernails dug small crescents into his thigh.

"You are perfection, Emmy," he grunted as he pulled her upright and covered her chest with his cum.

Both breathing heavily, the hand in her hair tugged her closer to him. His tongue entered her mouth, and they lazily kissed. She crawled onto his lap, never disconnecting from their kiss. He plucked her nipple while his other hand caressed as much of her heated skin as he could reach. The aftershocks of her orgasm caused her to twitch intermittently. The smell of sex surrounded them. His chest became wet with the evidence of his pleasure as she writhed against him.

She broke off the kiss to rest her head on his chest. With a finger, she lightly traced his clan marking. She giggled. "We didn't even get to the main event."

He chuckled. "The night's still young, *milara*."

"Status."

"The female is onboard the *Intrepid* with the Commander. The Zuvgran lab on XB9428B has been destroyed."

"This is not what was planned." Displeasure laced the voice.

"I am aware. The Commander followed the female after the Durelians kidnapped her. He enlisted some aid from the Wing Raiders and rescued her."

"Is she infected?"

"Unknown. What little I have heard is that she is traumatized by her kidnapping and only allowing the Commander in her presence, which is why she is on the shuttle. The other females have expressed grave concerns about her emotional state."

There was a long silence before the reply came. "It is possible they suspect she was infected with something and that is why she is sequestered."

"That may be, Uncle."

"You must get her onboard the *Invictus*. If the Zuvgran were successful before her rescue, she must infect the other females before they reach here."

"I do not have that ability."

"Find a way." An angry growl filled the comm link. "We have worked too hard to have our plan fail now."

The male shook his head. "How do you suggest I do this? I am not high enough in the command structure to argue the point."

"Figure it out. Always Svesti."

The Svesti onboard the *Invictus* grumbled as the link was disconnected. *How does he expect me to follow his orders without exposing myself?*

Chapter 14

Who knew Mister Straight and Narrow would be so proficient at talking dirty? Or that he wasn't averse to a little light spanking in the bedroom? Emmy smirked. *It's always the quiet ones.*

Emmy practically purred as Devik shampooed her hair and massaged her scalp while showering. Efficiently, he washed their bodies. She pouted. *He could take his time. His hands feel so good. My lady parts are still tingling.*

He lifted her out of the shower. Climbing into the full bathtub, he arranged her between his thighs, her spine to his front. Her head fell back onto his chest. The hot water and his body heat relaxed her even further.

He cupped and squeezed her breasts before playing with her nipples. First, he lazily traced patterns on her areolas, then he pulled and tugged on the stiff flesh. Her breath hitched in her throat. *Damn! I can't believe how easy it is for him to get me ramped up again.*

Shivers ran through her when he spoke low in her ear. "Did you enjoy yourself, *milara*?"

"You couldn't tell?" Her sultry laugh echoed in the room.

Nipping at her earlobe, he said, "I only have one regret."

She frowned. "What's that?" Her hands drifted to his muscular thighs.

"I didn't get to taste you."

She wiggled and turned to face him. Leaning forward, she kissed him. "Like that?"

"No."

Cupping her breasts, she lifted them toward his mouth. "Here?"

Swirling his tongue around an engorged nipple while looking into her eyes, he licked and sucked. She gasped when he nipped it with his fang. She moaned as he took his time tonguing her other nipple.

Lifting his head, eyes hot, he said, "No."

She smiled seductively. "I'm just not sure where else you can taste me."

Hands under her ass, he stood and turned to place her on the ledge. His tail grasped her hands behind her back and he knelt in the water. Using his shoulders, he widened her thighs. He attacked her core with his tongue, lashing at her clit in rapid movements. The scruff on his chin rasped against the opening of her pussy. She wiggled impatiently, wanting the sensation harder against her core.

Her head dropped back. *I feel like I'm the all-you-can-eat buffet for a starving man.* Her hips bucked and twisted as her orgasm hit her fast and hard. He slowed his movements, then sped up again, nipping at her clit with a fang. *Holy shit. That feels fantastic.*

He slid a finger inside her and pistoned steadily. Her hips rose to meet him as much as she could manage. The tip of his tail lightly caressed the sensitive skin of her wrists causing shivers to travel down her spine. He groaned against her clit, mumbling. She had no idea what he said. *Doesn't matter. Feels wonderful.* Another finger in her channel wasn't enough.

"More," she demanded. A third finger filled her and she sighed as he increased the rhythm.

Her moans were loud over the sloshing water as he brought her to her peak two more times, finger fucking her all the while. Her body was a quivering mess, and she leaned against the wall trying to catch her breath. *He's really, really good at that.*

Devik stood and dried her boneless body with a towel. She curled into his chest as he carried her to her bed. Sated, she reached for him as he pulled the sheet over her. Smiling, he got into bed next to her. She burrowed into his side, her head resting on his shoulder. His warm lips kissed her forehead.

"Sleep well, Emmy."

"Mmm," she mumbled. Nestled in his strong arms, she drifted into sleep with his unique campfire scent surrounding her.

Emmy woke alone. Stretching like a cat in a sunny window, she smiled. *He's better than a sleep inducer. What a great way to fall asleep.* Padding to the sanitary facilities naked, she pondered his nodes. *I wonder what those will feel like inside me.*

Seeing her reflection in the bathroom mirror, she groaned. *I was so out of it last night, I didn't tell him to use the drying tube. Going to bed with wet hair was not a good idea. I look like a monster in a horror movie.* She tried running a comb to tame her curls. *Nope. Not working well at all.*

Chuckling, she took a quick shower. As she stood in the drying tube, she turned thoughtful. *I think last night was the first time I actually slept with a man, er, male. And to think it was with an alien.*

As she was finishing up with her morning routine, her stomach rumbled. *Shit. We never even ate dinner. I'm starving.* She hurriedly dressed and went to meet the women for breakfast.

In the dining area, Emmy carried her food to the table to join Rachel and Natasha.

"Morning," said Natasha. "We didn't see you at evening meal last night."

"I was tied up and got distracted," Emmy said. *Yeah, tied up by a tail and distracted by a talented tongue.*

"We got the last of the pictures you wanted," Rachel said. "I'll send them to you."

"Great. Hopefully, those will be a good start." Emmy leaned forward and quietly said, "How are they doing?"

Natasha smiled. "As good as can be expected."

They greeted Ava and Lin as they approached. Emmy sniffed and moaned.

"Please tell me those are cinnamon buns," said Emmy.

Ava grinned as she set her tray on the table. "My first attempt at them using Svesti ingredients. You guys are my guinea pigs." The women all grabbed a warm bun.

Emmy bit into hers and closed her eyes. "The texture is a little grainier than I'm used to, but the taste works well." She licked the icing from her lips. "I'd say these are a success."

The other women agreed with big grins.

"You really are talented, Ava," said Rachel. "I don't know how you do it. Making food that tastes like home without the same ingredients." She hummed as she took another bite.

"I agree," Natasha said. "These are so good."

Lin nodded and swallowed. "You know what I haven't seen here? Bread or bagels."

"You're right," said Ava with a frown. "No sandwiches or toast or anything like that."

"Or pasta," said Rachel. "I love pasta."

Emmy smiled happily. "I love the smell of freshly baked bread. There was this bakery in Canberra that made the absolute best sourdough bread I've ever tasted."

"I'll have to work on that." Ava polished off the rest of her bun. "I'm glad they have a spice that's close to cinnamon."

"Now you need cocoa," said Lin. "I miss chocolate cake. I love chocolate cake. And brownies." Her face was forlorn.

The women laughed.

"Sounds like Ava's got her work cut out for her," said Natasha with a grin.

"I'll see what I can do," Ava said, smiling. "I might have to start a list."

"How's Previv handling you in his kitchen? Any problems?" Rachel asked.

Ava shook her head, her red curls bouncing. "He's been great. We're both enjoying learning from each other."

Emmy smirked. "So you think you and Previv might become an item?"

Ava laughed. "No. I think of Talen as a protective older brother. One I wish I'd had growing up." Her face turned pensive. "I'd love for him to find a mate, though. He's a wonderful guy."

"Well, if he does, she'll definitely eat well." Rachel grinned. The women nodded in agreement.

As they finished eating, Lin said hesitantly, "Can I ask you guys something?"

Everyone looked at her. Natasha said, "Of course."

"How do you do it?"

"Do what?" asked Rachel.

"Be so fearless. We've had so much happen to us in such a short period of time. Just when I'm getting used to something new, another thing comes along that terrifies me." Lin looked uncomfortable.

Emmy tilted her head. "I can't speak for everyone else, but I know I'm not fearless. Sometimes I'm quaking in my shoes."

A chorus of "Me too" sounded from their group.

Lin's eyes widened as she took in their nodding heads. "To me, it seems like you're afraid of nothing. You're outspoken, and you don't cringe and cry like me." Her shoulders drooped.

Natasha took Lin's hand. "That doesn't mean we're not afraid. We just cope in different ways. For me, I like to observe and decide what I can do to make the situation better."

Emmy said, "I like to learn everything I can, even what people keep hidden. It helps me feel like I'm in control." *I can't believe I just admitted that.*

Rachel shrugged. "I rely on my training. It gives me confidence that I can react accordingly."

"I focus on what I can control. Like my breathing and my actions," Ava said quietly. "It doesn't take away my fear, but it makes it manageable."

Lin looked at each of them. "I just feel like I spend so much of my time afraid—even before all of this."

Everyone was quiet for a moment. Then Ava said, "Lin, you said you fought with your parents about an arranged marriage. Why did you fight? Weren't you afraid your parents would be upset?"

Lin looked down at the table. "I hoped I could find someone who loved me for me, not because it was advantageous for our families." She raised her head and stiffened her shoulders. "I was more afraid of being trapped in a loveless union and having no control of my life than I was of my parents' disapproval."

"So even though you were scared, you did what you had to?" Rachel smiled.

"Yes."

"Can you think of any other times you did or said something, even though you felt fear?" asked Natasha.

Lin nodded. "I went to college in the United States. My parents were against it. I would probably still be there if I hadn't received an exceptional grant offer back in China."

With a pensive look on her face, Ava said, "I think almost all fears have their roots in one major fear—involuntary loss of personal autonomy. It's probably why most of our coping skills focus on what we personally can control."

Emmy said, "I can see that for things like kidnapping, slavery, and even marriage, but what about something like a fear of heights?"

Ava laughed. "Gravity has control, not you."

Everyone giggled.

"Anyway, that's what I believe. Lin, it sounds like you have your hard lines where you'll fight for control for yourself. You may find other ways to cope with the other things that crop up, or maybe you won't. But don't get down on yourself if crying is your way to handle the stress. You're you—a kind, empathetic person who would rather everyone got along. That's really not a bad thing," Ava said with an earnest look.

Lin took in everyone, and her eyes filled with tears. "Oh, great. Now I'm going to cry because all of you are so nice."

Laughter broke out among the women, and they smiled.

"You do you, Lin," said Rachel.

After morning meal, Emmy went to Devik's office. He gave her a short kiss, then they worked on their respective tasks. She would be engrossed in her work and his tail would occasionally caress her arm or leg then a nipple or her crotch before retreating. When she looked up, he would be innocently tapping his tablet with a small closed-mouth smile. As she went to leave for midday meal, he pinned her up against the wall and kissed the ever-loving daylights out of her. Just as she was about to get them naked, he stepped back and deepened his voice.

"I'll see you at training this afternoon, *milara*."

Bastard is deliberately winding me up.

During training, Devik continued teasing her with scorching glances and stretching his hot body when he knew she was looking his direction. Emmy enjoyed his narrowed eye glare when she reciprocated by licking her lips and bending over at the waist and running her hands along the backs of her legs, ass in the air.

She casually sauntered up to where Devik was getting water pouches for himself and Rivezt. "Can I have some?"

Devik smirked and turned to get another for her. She stepped closer and ran her hand over the base of his tail before squeezing it. Startled, he jerked slightly before saying quietly, "You're playing with fire, Emmy."

She took the pouch from him and ran it over her face and upper chest, lips upturned as she watched his eyes glued on her motions. She whispered, "You started it." Turning to leave, she deliberately put an extra sway in her hips and grinned when she heard him growl. *Two can play at this game, mate.*

Later that evening after a shower, Emmy left the drying tube naked and went into her bedroom. She opened the compartment with BB and stared at it. *That's not what I want.* Slamming it shut, she huffed. She grabbed a tank top and boy shorts and roughly pulled them on. *Goddamn Devik. Getting me all horny and letting me stew in my own juices, so to speak. I thought he would show up after training.*

Frustrated, she headed to the main living area where her laptop components were still spread out. *Well, maybe it's time to work on this. Hopefully, it'll take my mind off Devik.* Using her tablet, she had it play some older Earth music while she worked. She hummed and sang along as she assembled the laptop with the parts she'd purchased on Theron. *Now to test the password decoder.* She set up a 64-character password and used the decoder to time how long it would take. Later, she'd set the password to change to her own designed algorithm and see if the decoder worked.

The door chime interrupted her. Barefoot, she padded to the door.

"Who is it?"

"Devik."

Opening the door, she crossed her arms. "Is there something I can do for you, Lieutenant Tolvex?"

He stepped in, forcing her backwards, his voice low. "I think there's something I can do for you." Her nipples pebbled.

Emmy shook her head and smiled. "No, I don't think there's anything I need." *Work for it, mate.*

The door closed behind him. His nostrils flared. He returned her smile, a devilish look in his eyes darkening with his arousal. "No? Perhaps I have something you want?"

She tapped her lips with a forefinger. "I'm not sure about that. I have ways to take care of all my wants and needs."

He chuckled darkly. Extending a claw, he traced the collar of her tank top, barely touching her skin. "So you do not want or need my hands on you?"

Breath hitching, she said, "No."

Lowering his head, he spoke over her erect nipple. "Then I guess you don't want or need my tongue or mouth on your body."

Emmy groaned. Arching her back, her breast lifted closer to his mouth, his hot breath sending shivers through her. She glanced down to see him watching her. She moaned when his tail pushed up to lightly trace between her legs.

"Or my tail?" Staring into her eyes, he licked his lips, his tongue just barely making contact with her tank top as he did so. "Oh, shit," she said as she pulled his mouth to her breast. "You win." Devik suckled her nipple through her top, then pulled away to breathe over the wet cloth. Goosebumps broke out on her skin as he said in a deep voice, "No, we both win, Emmy."

Chapter 15

With one arm behind Emmy's knees and the other behind her back, Devik lifted her and stood. Kissing her all the while, he strode to her bedroom. He tossed her onto her bed, smiling at her surprise and her bouncing breasts. Her curly brown hair splayed around her as he knelt on the bed to straddle her.

Leaning forward, he nipped at her lips. As their tongues played with each other, his hands wrapped around her waist. He caressed her satiny skin and slowly pushed her shirt up to expose her breasts. Pausing briefly to run his thumbs over her hard nipples, he inhaled as her scent thickened in the air. He drew back to lick a wet trail from her abdomen to the rounded underside of one breast. Scraping his fangs lightly over her skin, he moved to her other mound. Her sharp inhalation as he gently bit her skin made him smirk, especially when the smell of *tempika* berries grew heavier.

His hands continued moving her tank top over her head, forcing her to stop touching him. When he reached her wrists, Devik twisted the material to bind her arms and held the cloth with one hand. Gazing down at her, arms stretched over her head, plump breasts lifting their swollen buds in the air, he growled in appreciation.

"I approve of your kinky side," Emmy grinned mischievously.

"I'm not sure what kinky means, *milara*, but I do like seeing you like this." Devik's tail pushed under her waistband and tugged her boyshorts down. She lifted her hips to help him. He ran his free hand along the smooth curve of her hip and leg.

"I can smell your arousal. Spread yourself, Emmy, and let me see your needy cunt," Devik said with another growl.

She smiled licentiously as she brought her heels close to her ass and let her knees fall sideways. She licked her lips. *They look almost as wet as her beautiful cunt.*

"Emmy's pussy is now open for your dining pleasure," she said with a giggle.

Devik chuckled darkly. His tail lightly traced a path from her ankle to her core. Her eyes rolled back in her head and she groaned as it pushed into her.

"Oh, tail play," she breathed heavily. "Who knew it would feel so..." she squealed as his tail circled her insides before thrusting deeper. "Good." Her hips rose to take it deeper.

He bent to lick her clit with firm, long strokes, humming at the taste of her. Her moans filled his ears as she climbed closer to her peak. His tail focused on caressing the internal spongy spot that enhanced her pleasure. When she was close, he pressed a fang to her sensitive bud and growled. She trembled and shook, screaming his name. Removing his tail, he inserted two fingers into her rippling cunt. He continued to lap her pleasure center and scissored his fingers. *She's so tight.* As she loosened, he added a third digit and thrust.

Devik brought her to another climax when he turned one of his fingers to press her clit forward deeper into his mouth. He flattened his tongue at the same time, creating pressure on both the front and back of her clit. She let out a high-pitched wail as she bucked violently against his mouth. Slowing his movements, he lapped up her juices and withdrew his fingers.

Releasing her, he stood and removed his clothing quickly. He slowly fisted his engorged cock as he gazed at her flushed body. *Crek. She's gorgeous.*

"Are you ready for more, *milara*? Or do you not need or want anything further from me?" He grinned as she scowled at him playfully.

"You'd better not stop now, Devik. Or I might have to resort to BB." She raised her hands to caress his chest as he rejoined her on the bed.

"We can't have that, Emmy. My reputation could not handle it if I were to be supplanted by a sex toy." He sucked in a breath as she pinched his nipples.

"I want you inside me now, Devik," she hissed. "Stop making me wait."

"As you command," he said as the blunt head of his member breached her tight channel. Watching her eyes to ensure he wasn't hurting her, he cautiously pushed further. He stopped when her eyelids fluttered and she moaned.

"Keep going." She opened her eyes to stare at him. "I want all of you, Devik."

Bowing his back, he dropped his forehead to hers. "I do not wish to cause you pain."

"Oh, this stretch is the best kind of pain." Her teeth nipped at his neck. She raised her hips to take all of him at once. They both gasped as his base node slammed into her clit.

Crek! Her silken sheath was like a hot vise surrounding his cock. With a steady, even rhythm, he moved in and out, his head nodes rubbing the inside of her tight cunt. He twisted his hips with each downstroke to press his base node against her. He looked down at where they were joined. He grasped one of her legs and pulled it up against his chest, opening her further and lifting her ass off the bed.

"Oh, Emmy, your pretty cunt is gorgeous as it devours my cock. All wet and needy," he grunted.

"More," she demanded. "Harder. Faster." Her free leg wrapped around him, her heel against his ass.

His hips picked up the pace. His balls slapped her ass. The wet sounds of their joining grew louder—a counterpoint to their moans and heavy breathing. Sweat ran down his back and chest. His balls tightened and tension began rising at the base of his spine, spreading outwards. His tail played with her nipples before moving to her swollen nub. He watched her chest flush and heave with their exertions. She gripped his tail as her pleasure grew. His fangs elongated when her orgasm squeezed his cock so hard that he couldn't hold off his release. A riot of color sparked behind his eyelids. As his cum bathed her rippling channel, his movements became jerky, and he growled her name.

Sucking in harsh breaths, he gently dropped her leg and leaned forward to rest his weight on his elbows. Kissing her languidly, additional spikes of pleasure rolled through him as her aftershocks clenched his softening cock. He rolled onto his side, lifting her other leg over his hip to keep them connected. His fingers pushed her hair from her dewy face.

She gave him a sated smile as her hands trailed over his skin. "I'm glad I opened my door this evening."

He grinned. "Me too, *milara*."

She played with his braids and shot him a look from under her lashes. Her pussy clenched his cock. "So how long before round two?"

Hugging her, he laughed. "Not long at all."

Arms around Emmy, Devik listened to her soft snores as she slept. Their combined scent after he'd taken her two more times during the night surrounded them. *I need to have her in my quarters, so her scent is there.*

Unwrapping his tail and arms from Emmy, he cautiously slid out from under the covers. She grunted but didn't wake when he kissed her forehead. *I don't want to leave, but I need to get ready for the day.*

Hours later, Devik looked up as Emmy entered his office. He smiled as she strutted toward him wearing a T-shirt that said "I'm so lucky people can't hear what I'm thinking." *No one else knows about that tiny birthmark on her ass or how wild she is during mating.* Tapping a button on his tablet, he remotely locked the door to his office.

Swiveling in his chair as she rounded his workspace, he pulled her onto his lap with one hand buried in her curls to tug her closer for a kiss.

"How are you this morning, *milara*?" A lone finger traced her swollen lips. He suppressed a moan when she nipped it with her blunt teeth and then licked it.

"Well rested, which surprises me after last night." She smiled happily. "Someone kept waking me up."

"Should I apologize?" His hands cupped and kneaded her breasts.

"Don't you dare."

"Take off your shirt, Emmy."

"Oh, you think you can tell me what to do?" She smirked but arched her back to give him better access.

He released the fastening on her bra. "I think when our interests are aligned, you are very happy to follow orders."

"Hmm, you may be right." She pulled her shirt over her head and let her bra slide down her arms. "Is this what you wanted?"

Fangs flashing, he said, "It's only the beginning of what we both want."

He played with her hard nipples, rolling them and tugging. Leaning her even further back, he bent forward to trace his tongue around one, before enclosing it in his hot mouth. She squirmed against his cock. *Still too much clothing.*

Devik's tail teased her breasts after he released the nipple with a loud pop. He reached behind him to pull his shirt over his head from the back.

She grasped his tail and fisted it, sliding back and forth. His breath caught when she rubbed her chest against his.

"Devik, your skin feels amazing."

"Not as amazing as yours, Emmy." His hands encircled her waist. "I want you to ride me."

"What if someone comes in?" Her scent became heavy.

"Then there will be no doubt that you're mine."

She tugged on his braids. "Oh, you're an exhibitionist."

He shook his head. "No one else gets to see you like this. Only me."

Emmy's scent became heavier at his words. She stood and kicked off her shoes. Shimmying out of her pants and underwear, she gave him a heated look. "If you want me to ride you, you'll need to drop your pants."

Smiling, he removed his boots. He rose and crowded her back into his desk as he removed his pants. He enjoyed her involuntary moan as her nipples scraped his chest. His erect cock laid across his taut abs as he sat down.

He spread his arms. "Come here, Emmy."

Emmy bent forward to wrap her fingers around his member. His cock twitched when her thumb swiped the pre-cum around its head.

She frowned in annoyance. "Chairs are too damned tall."

He laughed. "Let me help." Her buttocks filled his hands as he lifted her to straddle him. Her knees stretched wide over his thighs. He gazed at where she was lowering herself onto him. She took all of him in one steady movement.

"*Crek!* Your cunt is so slippery and hot."

She moaned. "You fill me everywhere. So full. So good."

Holding his shoulders, she began to rise and fall on his cock. Her head fell back. He caressed her exposed neck and down between her mounds before his thumb found her clit. Applying gentle pressure, he circled her nub.

"Yes, Devik, just like that," she said.

He grunted as she moved faster and slammed herself onto him. "You're beautiful, *milara*."

"Help me. I need you deeper." Her thighs trembled.

Replacing his thumb with his tail, he moved both hands to her waist. He pulled her down hard on him while raising his hips simultaneously. Their flesh became slick the longer they moved in tandem.

Growling, he said, "Kiss me."

Her lips met his frantically. Their tongues dueled as their pleasure rose. When her body shuddered and her cunt clenched him, he swallowed her scream. He pumped into her several more times before his cum bathed her inner walls. Their movements became languid, and she broke off the kiss to rest her head on his chest.

"Damn, Devik," she breathed. "You're fantastic at that."

"We're fantastic together, Emmy." He nuzzled her hair.

After they cleaned up and redressed, Devik tapped on the initial list of potential suspects he received from Karid.

"Emmy," he said. She looked up from where she sat on the couch. "Do you think you can write a program to monitor and compare communication activity?"

She tilted her head. "What are you looking for?"

"Wurvez would like to determine if there's been unusual activity with Costonia since you females joined us."

"How far back should I go?"

"Six months? Do you think that would give enough data to compare?"

"I think so. But I imagine there would be an increase just with people letting their families know we're here."

"True." He nodded. "But, hopefully, our traitor is sending more frequent updates. We can cross check any names with the potential suspect list."

"Are the actual communications saved? If so, we could run some search terms."

"If they're not sent to or from a comm during scheduled work periods or any workstation, then they're considered personal. An individual has the ability to save it to their own personal files, but it would not be on the main ship's computers."

Emmy bit her lip. "Assuming our traitor is smart, he wouldn't save anything incriminating, regardless."

"I agree." Devik smiled as Emmy's brown eyes became unfocused as she thought.

"I believe I have some ideas on how best to do this."

"Good. Let me know what you come up with."

"Of course. Oh, I also had a question."

"What would you like to know?"

"Who would I talk to about getting a small power source for my laptop? I want to add one that will work out here in space."

"Our head engineer, Gat'n Wrox, should be able to help. I can ask him to come here or I can escort you to Engineering."

"That's not necessary. I can find it on my own." Emmy smiled and tapped her comm.

Devik chuckled. "Actually, it is necessary. You don't have access to that deck."

"Oh. Can I just comm him and ask him?"

"Yes, that would work as well."

"Okay, I'll comm him later and see if he has any suggestions." She bent her head and began working on her tablet.

Devik thought for a moment about Karid's list. He began tapping on his tablet. *I'll put Invisitraces on each of the suspect's passwords.* Devik set up parameters for what activity would send him an alert. *Maybe we'll get lucky.*

Leaving the dining area with a container after midday meal, Devik couldn't suppress his grin. He comm'd Emmy.

"Devik. What's up?"

"Emmy, sometime after evening meal, could you stop by my quarters?"

"Do you want to check my progress on that program?" *Hmmm. She must not be alone.*

"Yes, if you don't mind."

"Not a problem. I'll see you later."

"Thank you." Devik disconnected the comm and glanced at the container. *I was lucky I found these today. I'm going to enjoy later.*

Chapter 16

The new power source Wrox brought Emmy was working wonderfully. The engineer was kind enough to show her how best to make the connections, check its useful life, and recharge it. He also spent some time asking her questions about the hardware on her upgraded computer. At her request, he brought extras for the other women. *I'll have to find time to upgrade their laptops.*

She transferred the data from the tablet to the computer for the communications comparison. *It's so much easier typing on my laptop than on the tablet. Now I can finish up the program Devik asked me to code faster after I make one for my keyboard.*

I still don't know whether I should get all that info the Prime Minister demanded. I probably should have it when I go back to Earth.

Frowning, she chewed her lower lip. *I'm not as comfortable doing that as I was a few weeks ago. The Svesti, especially Devik, have treated me better than most humans on Earth have.* She shook her head impatiently. *I'll think about it later. We need to catch the traitor first.*

Setting an alarm so she wouldn't miss evening meal, she interlaced her fingers and stretched her arms with her palms facing outward. Then she got to work coding a personal program to convert her keystrokes to Svesti characters. Her fingers flew over her keyboard as she decided to add some macros to change certain English words to Svesti for the most used commands. The soft clicks of the keys were like music to her ears. *Yeah, baby, I'm back!*

At evening meal, the women chatted while eating what Emmy thought compared to a roast beef dinner. Thick brown gravy covered the meat and something like mashed potatoes. The vegetable looked like green beans but was a reddish-orange color. She silently hummed around her bites of the comfort-style food.

"You know what I'd like?" said Natasha.

"What's that?" Emmy took another bite. *Damn, this is good. Just a hint of hot spice in the gravy and beans.*

"A chicken Caesar salad," Natasha said. "The Svesti don't seem to eat as much salad as we do."

Ava tilted her head. "I'll talk to Talen and see what I can do. Even if it's just for us."

"Did you make the gravy?" Rachel asked Ava.

"It's not my recipe, but I helped make it." Ava shrugged.

Emmy pointed her fork at Ava. "You know what you should do? You should make a cookbook of Earth-type recipes using Svesti ingredients."

"That's a good idea," Rachel said. "You could also put Svesti dishes in there using Earth ingredients. I bet Talia could help you with publishing it."

Ava's brows knit together. "Do you think it's necessary?"

"I'd buy it," Natasha smiled. "You come up with great recipes, even with unfamiliar foods. When we're on Costonia, we might not all be living together. I'd like to be able to replicate some of the meals and snacks on my own."

Ava looked thoughtful. "Let me see what I can come up with for you ladies. I don't know about doing a whole book."

"You could probably do a whole series of books—comparable ingredients and adjustments, entrees, snacks, desserts—there's a whole lot of information most wouldn't take the time to figure out on their own." Emmy's fingers drummed on the table. "Assuming more human women eventually come from Earth, the Svesti might want to know what foods might appeal to them, too."

"Hmmm, you might be right," Ava said.

Emmy's fingers stilled as she looked at Lin. "You're awfully quiet this evening, Lin. Are you alright? You seem distracted."

Lin cheeks pinkened. "I'm fine. Just got a few things on my mind."

Natasha asked, "Is there anything we can help with?"

Lin coughed into her napkin. "No. I've got it. Thanks, though."

Natasha smiled. "Just let us know if that changes." She looked at everyone. "I've finally found some time to go through the fabric we got on Theron. Is there anything specific you guys want made with what you chose?"

"I'd like a camisole in that white shimmery fabric," Rachel said. "And maybe a short nightgown."

"A shirt of some sort with the green patterned one," Ava piped up.

"That green will look fantastic with your red hair," Lin smiled shyly.

"The blue fabric would be nice for formal dress for you, Emmy," Rachel suggested.

Emmy's lips puckered. "I'm not big on dresses."

"Well, last I heard, we probably have to attend some Court functions. We should probably all have something suitable to wear, just in case." Natasha frowned.

"Don't remind me," said Emmy. "I really don't want to participate in a Choosing."

"None of us do," said Rachel, her face hard.

"Why don't you ladies come by my quarters in the morning and I'll take your measurements. If there's a particular style you want something in, send me a picture. I'll see if I can make something similar," Natasha said.

"We could probably use the synthesizer to make clothes," suggested Emmy.

"Oh, I know. But sewing relaxes me." A big grin lit Natasha's face. "It reminds me of the time I used to spend with my *Babushka*—my grandmother—when I was little. She always had time for me and taught me a lot. And not just about sewing and crafts. She's gone now, but it keeps her close in my heart."

Lin smiled warmly. "That's beautiful, Natasha." Her lips turned down. "I don't have those types of memories of my grandparents."

Ava reached out and squeezed Lin's hand. "Me, neither." *Yeah, warm fuzzy memories of grandparents isn't something I have either.*

"If you really want to do it, I'm good with that." Rachel smirked. "About all I can do with a needle and thread is sew a button, maybe quickly baste a hem, and roughly stitch a battlefield wound."

"Battlefield wound?" Emmy asked. "Is that something you see a lot of in security?"

Rachel smiled mysteriously. "A woman needs her secrets, Emmy."

Everyone laughed. *I'll bet she's not just in security.* Emmy was surprised she wasn't twitching to try to find out what Rachel was keeping from them. *That's strange. Normally, I'd be all over finding out everyone's secrets.* She looked at all of them. *Oh, shit. Somehow, I think I made friends when I wasn't paying attention.*

Emmy perused the contents of her small bag one last time. *Tablet, check. Clothes, check.* She drew in a deep breath. *I'm not sure why I'm nervous. I'm just headed next door to Devik's quarters.* She walked the short distance and pressed the door chime.

Devik's smiling face greeted her when his door opened. "Good evening, Emmy. Come on in."

She glanced around his main living area and realized she hadn't been in his quarters before. The layout was similar to hers, but his couches and chairs had long open spaces where the backs met the seats. Deep, jewel tone colors drew her eye to the throw on one chair. Holographic pictures were displayed on a wall.

"This is nice," she said as she walked toward the pictures. She pointed to one with Devik and four other males. "Is this your family?"

Devik nodded and drew closer. "Yes, the older male is my father." He pointed to each male. "That's Solen, my oldest brother. Pex, who is six solars younger than Solen. And Rassix, who is four solars older than me and two solars younger than Pex. My sister and mother died from the virus."

"Was your sister older than you?"

"Yes, she was. She was two years younger than Solen."

Emmy calculated in her head. "So Solen is twelve solars older than you? And you're the baby?"

Devik chuckled. "Your math is correct, although I'm not sure I qualify as a baby."

"I can see the resemblance between all of you. Your father appears pretty stern in this picture. The rest of you look happy and relaxed."

Devik's face grew solemn. "My father changed after we lost our females. In his grief, he became very rigid and controlling."

She placed a hand on his forearm. "I'm sure it wasn't easy on you and your brothers."

Sighing, Devik pulled her into his embrace and kissed her forehead. "It wasn't, *milara*, but my brothers took it upon themselves to look after me as best they could."

"Are you still close to them?" Emmy's hands trailed over his pecs, his skin warm against her palms.

"Yes. I think you would like them and they you." His fingers played with her hair. "Have you eaten?"

"Mmm. Yes," she murmured distractedly when he sucked her earlobe into his hot mouth. She arched her neck to give him better access.

"Dessert?" Goosebumps raised on her skin when his breath ghosted where her shoulder and neck met.

"Huh?" Her eyes closed when his hands cupped her breasts. *Too much clothing.*

"Did you have dessert, Emmy? I've been waiting for mine." His fangs nipped her skin.

"No," she exhaled, thrusting her fingers into his hair. *Less talking, more touching.*

Her eyes popped open when he grasped her buttocks and lifted her. She wrapped her arms around his neck and her legs around his torso. She kissed what skin she could reach. He walked them to his bedroom before gently setting her back on her feet. She began to lift her T-shirt but stopped when he growled.

"Let me," his voice rumbled low. Callused hands caressed her body as he drew her shirt over her head. With one hand, he unclasped her bra and pulled it down her arms. "Beautiful."

Emmy loved the contrast of his darker skin against hers. She squirmed as he removed her shoes and the rest of her clothing.

Her curls touched her shoulder blades when her head fell back as his tongue scorched wet trails on her body. Her ankles, calves, knees, and inner thighs all received his dedicated attention. Occasional scrapes of his stubble caused her to shiver. She grunted when he bypassed her pussy and sucked the curve of her hip.

Devik rose to his feet and stripped quickly. "Lie back on the bed, *milara*."

She sat on the edge of the mattress and scooted back. The satiny feel of his sheets were cool against her body. Her lids at half-mast, she watched him take a container from his bedside table. He pulled out what looked like a fruit-filled pastry.

"What are you doing, Devik?" Her eyes narrowed.

He broke the pastry in half, the green filling oozing. Deliberately, he dribbled it over her breasts and down her torso before pushing most of the remains into her pussy. She squirmed at the coolness of the dessert on her skin. When he lifted his eyes to hers, they were almost black with his desire.

"Your scent is like the *tempika* berries in the tart. I want to taste them together and compare." His voice was gravelly. Shivers ran through her body.

Her moan was low and continuous as he began licking the fruit from her body. *No one has ever done anything like this to me.* Every cell in her body sparked like fireworks from his thorough attention to finding every bit of his dessert on her skin. When he finally got to her core, his fangs pulled the crust from her. He chewed it with his face against her pussy, sending tremors into her limbs. Some of the filling dripped down toward her rosette and his tongue followed. Her hips twisted in surprise. *Oh my god. I can't believe how good that felt.*

Devik returned to her core. His agile tongue thrust inside her, seeking and teasing. Her pleasure kept rising higher and higher, her moan becoming ragged gasps. His tongue lapped from her swollen pussy to her neglected clit. He circled it in barely-there licks, then closed his mouth over her engorged nub to suck hard. She screamed his name as flashes of color exploded behind her eyelids and hot, tingly pleasure streamed like quicksilver throughout her body.

She groaned when he pushed his cock into her pulsing pussy in one swift movement. Buried deep inside her, he rested his forehead on hers.

"Feels so good, *milara*." His voice was strained.

"Move, Devik. Fuck me hard."

"I'm too close. I need a minute."

She tightened her pussy on his cock. He groaned. He lifted his head to gaze into her eyes.

"So impatient, Emmy. Good things come to those who wait."

Smirking, she clenched again and was gratified when he started moving.

"Harder. Don't hold back."

"As." He bottomed out inside her. "You." He pulled out most of the way. "Command." He drove deep and fast, balls and base node grinding against her clit.

"Yes," she groaned. "More. Just like that." Her hips rose to meet each of his thrusts.

Her pussy fluttered, then deep spasms rippled, clutching his cock. Her back bowed, her nails bit into his backside, and she gasped for air.

He grunted her name as he released jets of hot cum into her soaked pussy, prolonging her orgasm. Together, they shuddered, breathing heavily. His full weight pressed her into the bed for a moment before he rolled them onto their sides.

When she could breathe again, she pushed his sweaty hair back from his face and traced the lines of his ear and jaw. She returned his grin.

"I have to admit, dessert was a great idea." She kissed him, tasting the *tempika* berries. "So how did I compare?"

He chuckled. "No comparison, *milara*. You taste better. The fruit was a nice addition, though."

She giggled. "A little sticky and messy."

"That's what showers are for." His tail wrapped around her ankle and pulled her leg over his hip. His hands lazily stroked her body, while his nose nuzzled her neck.

Their breathing slowed. She leaned back slightly to trace his clan marking.

"This is your father's House? House Vramel?"

"Mmm," he said. "The circular outline is my mother's. House Binova."

"That's the same House Wurvez is from, isn't it?"

"Yes."

"Is there a lot of difference between the Houses?"

"The Houses are more for the distribution of seats on the Council. But each House is known for different things."

"Like what?"

"While House Vramel has many occupations, we are predominantly educators and warriors. House Binova has a lot of merchants or traders. House Yula, the one Ash'n is from, is well-known for its healers."

"Are there class distinctions within a House?"

"Mostly between nobles and everyone else," he said.

She grimaced. "So rich versus poor?"

"No, everyone is cared for, *milara*. Some nobles like to think they're better than those they represent because their family lines are the longest. Perhaps they are the richest, too. But I think most try to do their best for those within their care." He looked thoughtful. "The Houses are more cautious with their people's survival now. We lost so many to the virus. We can't afford to lose more. That's why finding human females are compatible brings us great hope for the future."

She frowned. "I don't like the pressure of being a race's salvation, Devik. It seems like a lot of responsibility on us, especially for a race we've only just met."

He cupped her cheek, his thumb rubbing over her skin. "I understand, *milara*." He sighed. "I think now that we've met and gotten to know you, we have to adjust our thinking. Yes, collectively you are our hope, but we can't take away your individual rights for our own gain."

Emmy smiled gently. "It means a lot to me that you believe that, Devik." She kissed him.

"Enough of this seriousness, Emmy. What was in the bag you brought with you?"

"Oh, my tablet. I have that program you asked me to code for you to look over. And a change of clothes so I don't have to take the walk of shame in the morning."

"Walk of shame?" His brows pulled together.

She laughed. "An Earth expression. It means returning home after a night of debauchery in the same clothes as the night before. Many times it signifies a one-night stand." When she saw his confused look, she continued. "One-night stand is usually sex with a stranger you don't plan on seeing again."

Grunting, he said, "Have you done this walk of shame much?"

She slapped his shoulder. "That's an impolite question to ask."

He swiveled his hips against her. His cock twitched where they were still connected. "I would know the answer, Emmy."

She bit her lip. "Truthfully, Devik, I rarely had sex with the same man twice. Everyone leaves me, remember? It's easier that way."

He rolled onto his back, taking her with him. His tail played with her clit while his hands squeezed her ass. His claws pricked at her skin. He smiled up at her.

"So I'm special? To have had the pleasure of you more than once?"

She clutched at his pecs and began riding his stiffening cock. "Oh, you're special, alright." She laughed. "You know, on Earth, special can be an insult."

"Insult me more, then, *milara*. If this is the result. I can take it." His fangs gleamed.

Moaning, she pushed down as his hips rose up. "Oh yes, take it, Devik. Take it all."

Back in her quarters the next morning, Emmy comm'd Talia to update her on the search for the traitor. *She looks better than she did, but she's still not herself.*

In the hologram, Talia's brown eyes were serious. "I'm really worried, Emmy, that the traitor is going to find a way to have me infect everyone on the *Invictus*. I just don't know how. It's driving me crazy."

Emmy's foot tapped a restless rhythm. "You think that's his next move?"

"It makes sense, doesn't it? If he suspects I'm infected, then he would want to ensure all of you are, too. If the virus doesn't spread, it's basically useless."

"You're right." Emmy chewed on her bottom lip. "Let me think on it. Maybe I can figure something out."

"I hope you do. I don't want any of you to go through what I am right now. At least I'm a little older and I already have Joshua. None of you have kids yet. I'd hate for you to lose the option."

Emmy nodded. "I don't know if I want children, but I know I want it to be my choice, not someone else's—especially someone with an agenda." She hitched her breath when a vision of a young Svesti girl with butterscotch skin, teal eyes, and curly black hair crossed her mind. *Really? I'm thinking of a possible child with Devik? I must be insane.*

"I'm mostly worried about you women. There isn't much else that the traitor can do to me, but my situation puts all of you at higher risk." Talia looked angry.

"We'll get him, Talia." Emmy looked at her. "Do you need anything? More notebooks, movies, anything?"

"No, not yet. Thanks." Talia smiled.

"How are you keeping busy?" *If you're sleeping with the Commander, he must not be any good, because you don't look happy.*

"I've been putting together some ideas for a treaty. King Sovex wants me to work with Durek to come up with something."

"Well, I guess all that Svesti law in your head will do some good." Emmy laughed.

Talia smirked. "Yeah, maybe something positive will come out of that experience."

Chapter 17

Ash'n was in his med bay office when Devik entered.

"What did you need, Ash'n?"

"Let's wait for Natasha and Lady Emmy. They're on their way."

"Okay. Have you made much progress on a vaccine?"

"Some. Natasha has some good ideas. Earth had a flu pandemic about twenty years ago where their medical community needed to develop vaccines quickly. We're testing in the lab now." Ash'n looked hopeful.

"That's good," Devik said. "The more we can protect our two races, the better." A growl rose in his chest. "*Crekkin'* Zuvgran make me angry with their relentless experimentation."

Ash'n nodded. "I agree." He looked at Natasha and Emmy when they arrived. "Ladies, please come in." He locked the office door.

"So what did you need us for?" Emmy asked.

"We need to conduct full body scans on the Commander and Lady Talia, but we do not want to port over a full med bed," Ash'n said.

"Is there any way you can modify a handheld scanner to have a wider range?" Natasha said as she picked one up from a shelf.

"To do a full body scan, the handheld would have to be much larger and would likely be too heavy to hold," said Devik with a frown.

Emmy said, "Can we modify it to expand the scan area a little more, then write a program to 'stitch' the scans together for a complete image?"

Oh, milara, I love how you see solutions, not problems. Devik smiled. "I think your idea would work." He took the device from Lady Natasha and began programming the handheld's outer scanning limits.

Emmy's face lit up, then she scrunched her nose. "Anatomy isn't my thing. Natasha, do you have time to sit with me to figure out which points are the most easily identifiable to make the holographic jigsaw?"

"Of course," Natasha said.

Devik gave the scanner to Ash'n. "Take a look at this. Are you losing any detail with the new scanning area?"

Ash'n scanned Devik, then looked at the screen. "It's difficult to tell on the scanner. Let me send the results to my computer." A few moments later, he said, "It looks good. I don't think we can go any further, though, without losing cellular structure information."

Natasha looked at the display. "I agree. With the new scanning range, I think we might be able to do three top-to-bottom scans, front and back, and have all the data we would need."

"Emmy, why don't you work on this here with the healers? You can write the program to put it all together to display wherever they want the information," Devik said.

"Do you want to review my code before we try it?"

"I believe you'll be fine on your own for this project. If you are uncertain about anything, just comm me. I'll be spending the next few days on recurrent training with my security teams," Devik explained. "Truthfully, it won't be long before your programming skills exceed mine. Maybe I'll ask for your assistance for the next round of training scenarios."

A blush rose on Emmy's cheeks. "Thanks." She ducked her head and her hair covered her face. Devik's chest rumbled. *I dislike how uncomfortable she is with compliments.*

Ash'n said, "Ladies, please start without me. I need to talk to Tolvex about something else."

As Devik followed Ash'n into the larger med bay, he heard Emmy say, "Do you port the samples here?"

"No, we port them to a separate, much smaller med bay that is self-contained. It's on the other side of the storage area down the hall," Natasha said as Devik tapped the door closed behind him.

"What did you need to speak with me about?" Devik asked as they walked to the other side of the med bay.

"How long have you and Lady Emmy been intimate?" Ash'n said.

Devik's tail flicked. He crossed his arms. "Why do you ask?"

Showing his fangs, Ash'n grinned. "I'm curious, my friend."

Devik sniffed. "Are you and..."

Ash'n cut his words off with a quick gesture. "It's too soon to see where that may go. I'd rather not speak of it now."

Devik laughed. "Oh, you can be curious about me, but I can't reciprocate? Hardly seems fair."

With a smile, Ash'n smacked Devik's shoulder. "You have a valid point." His eyes turned solemn. "How do you think the King will react?"

Devik shrugged. "I don't know." Laughing, he added, "Hopefully, we'll keep all our parts intact. Karid told me to blame it on Vared's example."

Ash'n chuckled. "Sounds like something Karid would say."

Devik said, "Karid believes the human females will do what they wish. If Emmy's behavior is any indication, I have to agree with him." He paused. "She can be very persuasive."

Smiling, Ash'n nodded. "I know what you mean. Are you considering a troth contract?"

"Given how I feel about her, I'm hoping to true mate with her in the future."

Blue eyes widened. "True mate? Congratulations."

Chuckling, Devik said, "I think it's a little early for felicitations, Ash'n. She isn't thinking in those terms." He sighed. "There's something special about her. She brings out instincts and feelings I didn't know I had."

"I've decided human females have an impressive internal strength. They may not have natural physical defenses, but they are fierce warriors in their own unique way." Ash'n smiled. "So what about Karid? Is he also becoming close to one of the females?"

"I asked him about Lady Rachel, but he says he doesn't care for her in that way. He hasn't mentioned anyone else. Have you noticed anything?"

"No, that's why I asked you."

Devik tapped out the last few lines of his proposal for a program to cross-train warriors for various positions. *I think it's ready. If it works well, perhaps we can expand the idea to other specialties, not just security.* Satisfied, he sent it to Vared for his approval.

He walked to the special security training area, which looked like a converted cargo bay, to conduct a last minute check before he started running his teams through the course. Tail swaying, he pushed on the twelve-foot high interlocking panels arranged to simulate a Zuvgran lab facility to ensure they were steady.

Humming one of Emmy's Earth songs under his breath, he confirmed the placement of the small holo-emitters. With those, he was able to program different beings, as well as change the look of the panels. The panels would register simulated blaster hits and tabulate which shot the proper targets and where. They would also keep a record of wasted shots or those hits that took out innocents rather than combatants.

Starting the latest program, he smiled in satisfaction as it ran through. The panels now looked like white walls, instead of gray. The holo-emitters placed doorways, equipment, Zuvgran warriors and scientists, as well as cells with other beings requiring rescue. *Let's see if my teams catch the few surprises I put in there for them.* He enjoyed inventing new scenarios to push his teams to improve their skills.

Devik climbed some stairs to a balcony that overlooked the entire training area. Workstations were on his left and right—some to view each team member's recordings, while others kept track of individual performances. Cameras built into the panels also sent feeds to the workstations. He reset the program to the beginning, paused it, and left it in standby mode. He went back down to wait for the first team.

Kalix and Xoriv arrived first, followed shortly by Krivez Tesix and Slaiv'n Westov. All wore nanosuits and had their weapons sheaths full. Devik nodded.

"Please verify all your gear is in training mode."

Xoriv slapped Westov on the back. "Yes, we do not want to blow a hole in the walls with a blaster. That's pretty dangerous on a spacecraft."

Westov bared his fangs in a mock grimace, his sea green eyes filled with humor. "That is a vicious rumor, you *naroon*. I never did that."

Everyone chuckled as they checked their gear.

"Your objective for this session is to secure a Zuvgran lab and rescue survivors." Devik handed them each identical items. "These are simulated data discs. Just adhere one to a workstation wall next to a computer. If there is at least one minute left in the training exercise, it will count as a full download. However, you must be present while the fictional download is occurring for it to count."

Tesix said, "We should secure the facility first, then depending on what we find for survivors, one or two of us should do the downloads. That's the most efficient use of our resources." His teammates nodded in agreement.

Not surprising Tesix took command. He's got a strong tactical background.

Devik said, "Last-minute intel suggests there are four scientists, two guards, and six captives inside. A Zuvgran warship is expected to arrive within two hours to relocate the lab and beings."

"How reliable is the intel?" asked Tesix.

"It's last-minute. That's all I know," said Devik.

"Well, that means it's probably *crekkin'* useless," said Kalix. "We'll be lucky if we don't encounter a battalion of Zuvgran warriors."

Westov said, "If we're pressed for time, is there any data more valuable than the rest?"

"Nothing stated."

"If it's a lab, then I believe the scientific information takes priority. We'll need to be gone before the warship can detect our presence," said Tesix.

The males nodded.

Devik stepped back toward the stairs. He tapped his tablet and the program began running. The area's lights dimmed. The outside of the panels now appeared to be a stone building surrounded by a tropical forest at night. Intermittent animal and bird noises added to the atmosphere. The scent of wet dirt, leaves and animal dung rose in the air. *Those new odor emitters are working wonderfully.* He saw noses twitch and could swear Xoriv shook his head and chuckled low.

As he climbed up to the workstations, he watched the males approach the building stealthily, using tree trunks as cover. Splitting his attention between overlooking the area and the screens, Devik observed the hand signals. Kalix took out a guard by slitting his throat and dragging him behind a tree.

Westov crouched in front of the building entrance with the other males keeping watch. He took out a piece of equipment to hack the electronic lock. Devik smiled. *Good time. Took him only eleven seconds to open the door.*

The males entered the building as a group, each watching a quadrant. They communicated with hand signals as they checked behind doors, one by one, silently taking out guards and scientists. The last guard, who had a prosthetic arm, surprised Tesix, who needed a few extra moments to extricate himself from the neck hold before he overpowered his adversary. *Surprise number one.*

They reached the dark cells at the rear of the building. Ten locked cells, with nine visible beings, ranging from Frezzian to human. Westov decoded the main lock and overrode all the doors simultaneously. A Durelian rushed out of a cell, his three eyes filled with hate, and tackled Kalix. *Surprise number two.* They grappled for a bit, with Kalix whispering harshly, "We're here to rescue you, you *naroon.* Knock it off."

The Durelian continued to fight. Xoriv smacked the Durelian's head with the butt of his blaster, knocking him unconscious. Xoriv held out a hand to Kalix to help him up. *That was efficient, even if the Durelian will wake up with a headache.*

"Now's not the time to play with your food, my friend," Xoriv said as he grinned.

Kalix grunted. "He wasn't supposed to be food." He looked at the other captives. "Is anyone else planning on giving us trouble? Please speak up now."

The bruised and battered captives, male and female, all shook their heads. The human female had her arms wrapped around her waist as if she were cold.

Westov walked to the last empty cell. "Why did they have this one locked?" He fell to the ground as a large, black arachnid dropped on him and attempted to sting him with its tail. Xoriv shot it as it left the ceiling, and it went limp. *Surprise number three.* Devik grinned. *That's not something they've seen before.*

Westov hissed, "A little help, please. This *naroon* is *crekkin'* heavy."

The Svesti males chuckled as they lifted the spider-like being off him.

Westov clasped Xoriv's arm. "Thank you. I did not see that coming."

Xoriv's fangs flashed. "I'm a pilot, we always look up."

Devik said into the earpieces. "Zuvgran warship within range. You have ten minutes to get to your ship before they'll be able to see you."

"*Crek!*" said Tesix. "That wasn't close to two hours."

"What did I say? Useless intel," said Kalix.

"How many computers did you count?" Tesix said.

"There were six where we found the scientists," said Westov. "Another two in what looked like a security room."

"Kalix, Westov, go download the six. Xoriv and I will get the captives to the shuttle." The males jogged out of the cell area.

"Did anyone see a maglev or stretchers? The Durelian and the arachnid beings are heavy," said Xoriv.

The Frezzian female said shakily, "They have them in the next room. They used them to transport us after some experiments."

Tesix nodded. "Thank you, female. Xoriv?"

"Getting something now."

Tesix said, "Can everyone walk? Preferably run when we're out of the building."

The captives nodded. The human female said, "If it means getting rescued, I'll walk on hot coals."

"No need for that, female. Just floors and wet dirt until we get to the shuttle."

Xoriv returned with two maglev stretchers. He and Tesix lifted the two unconscious beings onto them. Xoriv restrained both, including the arachnid's tail.

"Just in case they wake in a bad mood." His fangs flashed in the dark area when he grinned.

Tesix shook his head. "Let's go. You lead." He pointed to two of the captive males. "You each take one stretcher and push it. I'll bring up the rear."

The group moved out single file, moving as fast as they could with the captives slowing them down.

Devik turned his attention to Westov and Kalix. They were retrieving all the data at once from the six computers.

Westov said, "You go do the other two. I'll stay with these."

"Will we have enough time?"

"The instructions were that we had to stay for the entire download—one minute. We're doing all six at once. That means one minute total, not six." Westov smirked.

"Good point. I'll meet you on the way out," Kalix said.

Westov nodded. After the allotted time, he gathered the discs and ran to Kalix, who was just finishing up. They caught up to the ragtag group close to the shuttle.

Devik ended the training exercise. The overhead lights came on, and the holograms disappeared. The Svesti males blinked at the sudden change.

The team approached Devik as he walked down the stairs, pulling out the data discs. They handed them to him when he held out his hand.

Xoriv grinned. "The latest upgrade to the holo-emitters is amazing. The beings had form and substance. Much more realistic."

"And painful," said Westov, lips twisting.

Devik smiled. "How do you think you did?"

"Overall, we accomplished our objective," Tesix said, but he frowned. "Although we could improve."

"How so?"

Westov said, "I think opening all the cells at once when we were outnumbered was a poor decision on my part. If I had kept it to two or three at a time, the Durelian might not have attacked."

Everyone nodded. Tesix smirked. "I also learned our scans should include looking up, not just around us." Snickers and chuckles echoed in the large space.

Westov grimaced. "Oh, I bet that somehow that was my fault."

Kalix said, "You made up for it by downloading all the computers simultaneously, saving us enough time to get all the data." Westov looked happier.

Devik smiled. *This is a good team. They learn from their mistakes and give constructive feedback.*

"That last Zuvgran guard shouldn't have been an issue," said Tesix. "I don't know how I missed him."

"He was lying in wait behind the door," said Kalix. "I thought I was going to have to shoot him."

"Intel was bad. Their numbers were incorrect. We should've had a larger group to infiltrate." Xoriv grumbled.

Devik grunted. "I learned on my first mission not to rely solely on the intel provided." *That mission went bad in so many ways— from the ambush to the explosion that trapped Vared in the rubble.* "I believe you learned what you needed to."

"Can we run it again? I'd like to see how our performance improves," said Tesix.

"And see if the holo-emitters hold up," Xoriv added with a grin.

Devik looked at the other males. They all nodded.

"Give me a moment to change a couple things, then I'll restart the program," Devik said.

As he watched the males run through the program three more times, Devik grunted in satisfaction. *I didn't have to suggest they repeat the exercise. They were motivated to do it on their own. I hope the other teams are as ambitious.*

Chapter 18

When a hand waved in front of her face, Emmy jumped in her chair.

"Geez, Natasha, you scared the shit out of me." Emmy glared at the blonde.

Natasha laughed. "I've been trying to get your attention for a couple minutes now. It's time for midday meal."

"Already?" Emmy rolled her head in a circle, hearing her neck crack. "Ouch. I guess I have been focused."

"Come on. Let's eat, then you can continue programming."

"Can you take me by the sterile med bay on the way?"

"Sure. Why?"

"Talia mentioned being worried about the traitor using her to infect all of us. I'm thinking of setting up a porting program. It would redirect anyone from the *Intrepid* to the sterile area."

"Do you really think he might do something like that?" Natasha's lips compressed.

"I don't know, but I'm trying to cover all the bases, just in case." Emmy shrugged. "It only costs me some time. And it would give her, and me, some peace of mind."

"Well, I'd feel better knowing there's a plan in place. I hate not knowing what's going to happen next. We need to catch the traitor." Natasha led the way to the sterile area.

Emmy looked around the space and saw a med bed and some other equipment on the other side of the room. "How do you keep the samples contained?"

Natasha walked halfway across the room. She put her hand up and touched an invisible barrier. "There's a force field. Behind it is the quarantine area."

"Oh, that's incredible." Emmy reached out to touch the force field. "It doesn't hurt."

"Not unless you walk into it," Natasha smirked. "Not that I've ever done that." She shook her head while rubbing her nose. "Nope, not me."

Emmy laughed. "I believe you." She tapped her tablet. "Let me get good coordinates for inside the sterile area, then we can go have lunch."

Yeah, this should work. I'll set it up so that anything with biological matter from the Intrepid comes here. As an added safety measure, I'll put some lines in case Talia's tracker or Durek's comm is used.

Now where should I send us women if the traitor tries to send us to the Intrepid *instead?* Emmy thought for a bit, then smiled. *Yes, that is a good idea. Sometimes I surprise myself.*

As she walked with Natasha to the dining area, her mind kept working. *I wonder if there's a way to catch the traitor in the act?* A huge grin broke out on her face as a solution came to mind. *I need to talk to Devik.*

Emmy worked late into the evening to finish up the scanning program for Natasha and Rivezt. With exception of meals and bathroom breaks, she pushed hard to get it done. It took her mind off the fact that Devik was busy elsewhere. *Besides, the docs need every bit of information as quickly as possible so they can develop a vaccine. I'll start on the other one for Talia tomorrow. That program is going to be much more complex.*

She stood and stretched her arms and back. Rolling her ankles, she felt the increased blood flow refresh her a little. *I need to get some running in soon. I haven't kept up with it since I got here.*

She uploaded the program into the scanner, then scanned herself as best she could. She checked her laptop. *Looks good. Natasha and Rivezt gave me some good reference points to put the scans together. A bit like putting together a panoramic photo.* She snorted. *Just need to test it on a Svesti to make sure I got that right.*

When her comm chimed, she was happy to see it was Devik. He asked if she'd like to join him in his quarters. She tossed the scanner, tablet, and laptop into a bag already packed with clothes. *Not that I expected to see him tonight. Just hopeful.* She shook her head. *Stop lying to yourself. You were going to start looking for him soon.*

As soon as Devik's door closed behind her, she dropped her bag. They reached for each other, kissing frantically. Their hands tugged at each other's clothing. Panting, Emmy pulled away long enough to tug her T-shirt over her head and toss it over her shoulder. Devik hissed when he realized she wasn't wearing a bra. His hands slowed to skim over her waist to the underside of her breasts. He extended his claws and squeezed her mounds. He dropped his head to suck on an erect nipple, kneading her other breast.

"Oh," Emmy sighed. "Yes, that feels good."

He murmured as he licked his way to her other breast, "I missed you today."

Her fingernails bit into his shoulder when his fangs gently scraped her hardened nipple. "Missed you, too. I was just getting used to spending most of my day with you."

Devik sucked on her nub and pulled back, elongating it. Then he released it, grinning at its reddened state. "I need to taste more of you." He dropped to his knees, butt resting on his feet. His unfastened pants slipped to his hips. Tugging on her shorts, he bared her to his hot gaze.

Eyelids at half mast, she looked down at him. She moaned when his tongue teased her opening. Lifting her leg, she draped it over his shoulder. Her hands dug into his long hair and gripped his head.

Her voice rose to a squeal when his lips surrounded her clit and sucked. Growling, he shook his head. Her orgasm took her by surprise. Her fingers tightened in his hair, while her thighs clutched his head. Her body shuddered with exhilarating pleasure. She floated back to awareness as he slowed his movements.

Shaking off his pants, he stood and lifted her up. Walking to a couch, he set her down next to it while his tongue invaded her mouth. She tasted herself on his lips. He turned her and bent her, stomach down, over the padded arm of the furniture. Her feet left the floor. *Damn couch is too tall.* She turned her head and rested her cheek on the seat.

Nudging her thighs apart with his knees, his hot hands grasped her hips and tugged her toward him. His tail wrapped around her ankle and spread her wider. She gasped when his fingers entered her to scissor and thrust inside her pussy.

"Are you ready for me, *milara*?" His voice rumbled low. Tingles chased down her spine to her limbs.

"Yes! Give it to me, Devik," she panted. One of her hands slid through the back opening to grab the seat, while her other hand gripped the front of it.

His hot cock inched into her wetness. They both moaned. He moved his hands to hold her thighs. His tail slid under her to play with her clit.

"So tight," he grunted. His hips retreated, then pounded forward while his hands pulled her thighs to his body.

"I'm so full. Fill me more." Emmy's eyes closed as a warm buzz of pleasure built with each drag and push of his wide girth and head nodes. Her pussy rippled and squeezed.

"Your cunt is stretching and sucking at my cock, Emmy, trying to pull it in deeper." Devik let go of one thigh to caress her back and knead one of her ass cheeks, tracing her birth mark with a claw. "So *crekkin'* beautiful."

Emmy made happy noises, but no coherent words were coming out of her mouth. She had no traction in this position. All she could do was hold on and take whatever he dished out. She let go and enjoyed the ride.

Both hands back at her hips, he increased his pace. The wet friction burned hot. Long moments of dazzling pleasure became frenzied, needing an outlet.

"I'm going to come soon," she gasped.

"Yes," he said behind clenched teeth. "Give it to me. All of it, *milara.*"

He hammered into her even harder and faster. Her breath caught and waves of bliss flowed through her. Not having much room to move caught her in a vortex of escalating pleasure. A second climax, on the heels of the first, engulfed her. Devik stilled as his cock erupted, spilling into her spasming sheath.

Chest heaving, he bent forward to kiss her neck. His campfire scent surrounded her.

She mumbled, "Too hot. Can't breathe."

Chuckling, Devik pushed up and stood. They groaned as his cock left her. He picked up her limp body and carried her to his bedroom.

"Let's rest for a bit before we clean up, Emmy."

"Mmm, hmm."

Emmy raised her head from Devik's chest. "I finished the scanner program. I want to scan you later to test my code with a Svesti body."

Devik grinned mischievously. "My body is at your disposal." He licked his lips and his eyes darkened. "For whatever you need."

She giggled. "I have a question."

"Mmm?" His fingers played with her curls.

"Why are your couches different? That space in the back made it easier for me to hold on, but the design is unusual." Her face heated.

"All our couches and chairs have the ability to retract part of the back. There is usually a switch to change it from an open back to a solid one. The openings make it easier to sit with our tails." His tail caressed her spine.

"That makes sense." Emmy bit her lower lip. "Oh, I also need the coordinates for a cell in the brig."

His forehead scrunched. "What for?"

"A program I'm working on for Talia, in case we have an opportunity to catch the traitor red-handed."

"Red-handed?"

"In the act of committing wrong."

"I can get those for you. I really enjoy working with you, Emmy. You are bright, motivated, and your mind is always thinking many steps ahead." He brought one of her hands to his mouth and kissed her lax fingers. "And you're unfailingly sexy."

Goosebumps ran down her arms. *What is it about this guy that sends my body and mind into overdrive?*

His eyes turned serious. "*Milara,* I want you to stay with me."

What? "You mean the night or move in with you?"

An earnest expression lit his face. "Don't take part in the Choosing. Don't return to Earth. Be mine and I'll be yours."

Her body stiffened. "Devik, it sounds like you're asking for a commitment. I don't do those. Everyone leaves me, remember?" *Don't do this.*

His teal eyes softened. "Emmy, I have no intentions of leaving you. I know you've had some heartbreaking experiences, but you can't shut yourself off to the possibility that what you and I have is different. More compatible and enduring."

Her eyes watered. She blinked. *You had to go there, didn't you. Shit!* Suddenly chilled, she sat up and rubbed her forearms. "I thought we were fuck buddies."

He rose to a seated position, his muscular torso exposed. "You were never that for me, *milara.* I would not have taken the chance of angering the King for transitory sex. I'm happiest when I'm with you. Is that not true for you, also?"

She hopped up from the bed and looked for her clothes. *Damn. Everything is in the living area.*

"This is too much for me, Devik. I need to go." Her breathing quickened.

Despite her best efforts, his nakedness drew her gaze when he stood. *Why does he have to look so delicious?* "Please stay, Emmy. Let us talk about it."

She shook her head frantically. "No. You want more from me than I'm capable of."

"You're not unable, *milara*, just unwilling to trust in us." He growled in frustration.

"I told you upfront—no commitments, Devik," she hissed angrily over her shoulder as she left his bedroom. "Why do you need it to change it? Can't we just enjoy whatever this is?"

"I do enjoy it, but I'd enjoy it more if you were mine." His tail flicked in short bursts as he followed her to the door. His eyes saddened. "I thought you felt the same way. Obviously, I was wrong."

She pulled the scanner from her bag and tossed it on the couch. "Scan yourself and check the program. If I made an error, I'm sure you can fix it." He ignored the scanner.

"Running away won't solve the issue," he said, his lips thinning.

"It always has before," she mumbled under her breath as she hastily dressed. Louder she said, "I think we need a break from each other. I don't doubt you'll eventually be glad I didn't commit."

"*Milara*, please," he pleaded. Reaching out a hand, he took a step toward her.

"No, Devik," she said as she bolted from his quarters carrying her bag and her shoes. "Just no."

Emmy tossed and turned. *Why did he have to ruin a good thing? I thought he understood me.* She punched her pillow in frustration. *How can he expect me to commit to anything*

anyway? We haven't even been sleeping together a week yet. Hell, I've only known aliens exist for less than a month.

I'll just ignore him. I'll work on Talia's program. That should keep me from thinking about him for several days. He's smart. He'll get the hint—professional behavior only.

Rolling over, she caught a whiff of the other pillow in her bed. Burying her face in it, she inhaled Devik's campfire scent. When she couldn't hold it in any longer, she let her tears fall. *Damn. I already miss him.*

Emmy spent the next four days avoiding Devik. Fortunately, he was conducting some sort of training with his security teams. He did send her the coordinates for the brig she had asked for before their relationship blew up. *That was my fault. I ran like I always do.* Huffing, she chastised herself. *Yes, and that's why I'm not sleeping or eating well. A big part of me can see trying to make it work with Devik.* She shook her head. *Well, what happens when he leaves me? Everyone leaves me. That's why I leave first.* She stilled. *Crap. That's what I do, isn't it? I leave before I have to feel the pain of someone leaving me.*

She pondered that revelation for a bit. *But I feel pain now. I miss him. Not just the sex, although that's out of this world...universe...whatever. I just miss being with him.*

She had changed her morning schedule to run in the aquiponics area, then hang out with Lin for a bit. Sometimes Ava joined them while she gathered herbs. Emmy kept hoping the increased exercise would help her sleep better, but so far, she was still restless at night.

Most of her time, though, was spent working on the program for Talia. She finally finished it. She rechecked her code. *I'm confident this will work.* Nodding firmly, she uploaded the program. *I'll tell Devik about it in the morning.*

I really blew it with him. She chewed on her lower lip. *I guess I should have a plan in place for going back to Earth.* Her fingers hesitated over her keyboard before she squared her shoulders. It took her a while, but she hacked deep into the Svesti database and began downloading the information the Prime Minister demanded. As she typed, her mind raced. *I don't know what Earth will do with this information. I can't betray the Svesti completely. It's just wrong.* She sighed deeply. *Great. Now, I'm starting to sound like Devik.*

Chapter 19

The next several days after Emmy left his quarters in a panic, Devik oversaw all of his teams go through the recurrent training scenario. He was pleased every team chose to redo the training multiple times to improve. But his mood stayed discontented. *I was looking forward to showing Emmy the holo-emitter technology. She would have liked it.*

He asked Karid to be in the regular training area when Rachel was teaching the females. Overseeing the recurrent training was Devik's excuse for not doing it himself, but he could have easily rescheduled the security teams at that time. *She's running from what we have. I need to give her space and hope she misses me as much as I miss her.*

Frowning as he left the special training area after the last team finished, his tail flicked rapidly behind him. *Maybe she doesn't miss me.* He rubbed his chest and his frown deepened. *I wonder if this is what the heartbreak Lady Talia mentions in some of her books feels like.*

As he passed by Emmy's quarters, he inhaled the faint traces of her scent. *Crek. Another night without her.*

In the morning, he was happy to see Emmy's name when his comm chimed. *Crek. It's voice only. I wish I could see her.*

"Hello, Emmy."

"Devik. I sent you a copy of the program I uploaded last night."

He frowned. "What program?"

"Remember when I told you Talia was worried about the traitor using her to infect everyone? I thought he might try to port her to the *Invictus*, or us women to the *Intrepid*." The words poured out of Emmy in a rush. His tail flicked in rapid movements. "I wrote a program to redirect Talia or the commander to the sterile med bay, and us women somewhere else. I also put in some code to port whomever was at the workstation that initiated the port to send them to the brig at the coordinates you sent me. If he does try something, maybe we can catch him."

"I'll check the code when I can, but you should not have uploaded it without telling me first. If there are errors in your code, someone could get hurt."

"Give me some credit, Devik," she bit out. "I didn't touch any code for the mechanics of the port except the destination. I wouldn't put anyone at risk."

He grunted. "I know you wouldn't hurt anyone. But it is only prudent to have someone else check the work."

"I'm sorry. I can take it out." *Oh, she's really upset.*

"No, that's fine, Emmy. Leave it alone." He lowered his voice. "I've missed you, *milara*. How are you?"

Her breath caught. "I'm fine."

"Good." He drew in a deep breath. "If you want to talk, I'm here."

"Devik, don't. I'm not ready."

"As you wish, *milara*. Was there anything else?"

"No."

"Then I won't take up more of your time." Devik disconnected the comm and rubbed his chest. *I wish she could see herself the way I see her.*

The Svesti male worked at the console at the edge of the cargo bay. Ever since Theron, he hadn't been able to do anything else to scare the human females. They were more cautious and rarely alone.

He didn't know why the Commander and the kidnapped human female hadn't rejoined the *Invictus*. His uncle was insistent that if there was even a remote chance the Zuvgran infected the female before her rescue, she needed to infect the other females. He'd thought long and hard about how to make that happen.

He typed the last few lines of code into the console. *That should do it.* He whistled tunelessly under his breath as he walked away. *Now, to ensure my alibi.*

Devik's tablet alerted him. *Emmy's program. Crek!* He looked at the information and ran toward the sterile med bay. He checked the security cameras for the brig as he hurried. *Crek! No one there.* Vared comm'd him to tell Devik what he already knew—Lady Talia was on the *Invictus*. Devik told him he was on his way to check on her and dissuaded his friend from following her. When he knew more, Devik would comm Vared.

When he got there, Lady Talia was behind the force field. Emmy was with Ladies Ava and Lin on the other side of the room. He locked the door behind him.

"Lady Talia, are you okay?" he asked.

"Yes, Tolvex, but I'm confused."

"Devik, was anyone in the brig?" Emmy asked. *She looks tired, but beautiful.*

"No, no one is there."

"Damn, damn, damn. Let me see what happened." Emmy tapped on her tablet.

Lady Ava crossed her arms. "Would someone tell us what the hell is going on?"

He looked at Lady Talia, who nodded. He said, "This is confidential information, ladies. When Lady Talia was with the Zuvgran, she was injected with an airborne virus that kills human and Svesti fertility."

"What? Are you okay?" Lady Ava asked Talia.

"Yes, but that's why Vared and I have been on the *Intrepid*. We're hoping they'll develop a vaccine to keep everyone safe. But I don't know if you're all infected now."

"No, we shouldn't be," said Emmy. "When we spoke a few days ago, you mentioned being worried about the traitor using you to infect the *Invictus*. I thought about the ways he could do it. The primary way was to port you onboard. So I wrote a program that overrides any porting between the two ships so that you end up here, since this is where Natasha and Rivezt port your biological samples. The traitor tried to port you to the dining area, but my program redirected you here. You're in a self-contained isolation area—not even air recirculates to the main ship."

"Traitor?" Lady Lin bit her lip. "The traitor again?"

"Oh, there's so much we need to catch you two up on," Emmy said. "For now, don't discuss this outside of our quarters. Devik, Rivezt and Wurvez might conduct a meeting about it elsewhere. They'll let us know if it's safe to talk. We're the only ones onboard that know about it. Publicly, we have to keep pretending Talia is suffering from PTSD."

Ladies Ava and Lin looked at each other and shrugged.

"Okay, whatever you say," Lady Ava said. "But we want the whole story as soon as you can tell us."

"Rivezt and Lady Natasha are on their way," Devik said. "Why was no one in the brig?"

"I'm trying to figure it out, mate." Emmy's impatient snort sounded loud over the tapping on her tablet.

Oh, milara. I've missed your attitude. His comm chimed. "Tolvex."

"Is Talia safe?" Vared's growly voice filled the space.

"Yes. The traitor tried to port her into a main area of the ship, but Emmy's program sent her directly to an isolation area."

"Thank the Goddess. Ask her why she's not wearing her comm."

"Tell him I didn't think I needed it."

"You will wear it from now on, *kirani.* I need to be able to contact you."

"We'll discuss it later, Vared. Right now, there are more important things we need to know. Like why someone should be in the brig." Lady Talia looked at Devik.

"Emmy's program should have immediately ported whomever was initiating the porting process to the brig so we could catch the traitor. But it seems it did not work." Devik frowned. *I know I didn't have time to review it all, but the code I saw was good. It should've worked.*

"It worked just fine, mate," Emmy countered. "The bastard put the port on a time delay, so there was no one standing near the station when the port began."

"If he weren't a traitor who needed to be caught, I'd be impressed with his ingenuity," Devik grumbled.

"When is Talia being ported back?" Vared asked.

"We're waiting on Rivezt and Lady Natasha to give the all clear."

Ash'n spoke to them via a speaker. "Tolvex, I need you to get blood samples from the females and yourself, so we can ensure none of you are infected. Also, an air sample to see if any of the virus made it outside the isolation area. Everything you need should be in the storage area."

Devik moved to collect what he needed. "Should we port Lady Talia back now?"

"Actually, since she's here anyway, I would like to get another full body scan and blood sample," Lady Natasha said over the speaker.

"Did you hear that, Commander?" Devik asked.

"I do not like it. How long will it take?"

"Less than an hour, then we can send her back," Ash'n said.

"Comm me before you port."

"As you command."

Devik helped the females collect their samples. He suggested everyone sit while they waited. Ash'n and Lady Natasha conducted a full body scan remotely. When they extracted some of Lady Talia's damaged eggs, he looked away, uncomfortable at being present for something so personal. It did not matter that she remained fully clothed. *Vared should be with her. All I can do is keep her safe until she returns to him.*

When Devik asked if she would like to port to the *Intrepid*, Lady Talia asked him to wait until they had the results back. Once they received the good news that no one else had been infected, he ported her to Vared.

He unlocked the room and Ladies Ava and Lin left. Emmy trailed slowly behind, intent on her tablet and muttering to herself.

"Emmy," he said. She stopped but didn't turn around. "Your program worked well and you saved all of us from contracting the virus."

"Thank you," she said quietly.

His tail wrapped around her ankle. "I miss you, *milara*."

"I don't know how to do this, Devik. I care about you, but I have to protect myself."

"I will always protect you."

She spun to face him. "You say that now, but you'll change your mind. I know it."

Frustrated, he ran his hand through his hair, catching his fingers on his braids. "I can't see me doing that."

"But I can." Her eyes looked watery. "I have to go. Please release me."

Reluctantly, he unwrapped his tail. "As you wish."

He watched her hurry down the corridor until she was out of sight and sighed. *Oh, milara, how do I make this better for both of us?*

Crek! As far as the Svesti male could tell, the human female never made it to the *Invictus*. *What happened? The coding was sound.*

The traitor punched the training bot hard enough that it tipped over. Growling low, he turned it off before yanking it upright. As he cooled down, his thoughts circled the problem. Then he smiled.

If I can't get her here, maybe I need to reverse it. In a much better mood, he left the training area. *It'll take a day or two to arrange it, but perhaps it will be worth it.*

Later that evening, Devik finally had an opportunity to check the Invisitrace logs. As he perused the data, Emmy's name caught his eye. *That's right. There is an automatic Invisitrace for all new users who are given more than general access to the databases.* As he read the information she'd downloaded in the past day, he clenched his teeth and growled. His tail whipped furiously behind him. *What the crek does she need that data for?*

He checked her tracker. *She's in her quarters. Good.*

At her door, he activated the chime. Emmy answered the door with a scowl.

"I told you to leave me alone."

"I am not here about us. I need to talk with you about a ship matter."

She frowned. "Can it wait until morning? I can meet you in your office."

He crossed his arms. "No. We must discuss it now. If you prefer, we can go to my office."

Sighing, she moved out of his way. "If it's that important, you may as well come in."

"Thank you." He paced away from her, then back again. Short flicks of his tail whipped in time with his feet. Running a hand through his hair, he stopped, and then faced her. "Tell me why you were downloading confidential Svesti military information last night," he said through clenched teeth.

She froze and her skin paled. The guilt on her face crushed his battered heart. *Oh, milara, what did you do?*

She sat on a couch, her arms wrapped around her stomach. Her head fell forward as she said quietly, "How did you find out?"

Devik sat across from her, fists clenched on his knees. "It doesn't matter. I need to know why and what you plan to do with the information."

A bitter laugh left her lips. "You want to know why? My government forced me on this trip. It was either do this or spend the rest of my life in prison. If I return to Earth without something, they will arrest me."

"Prison? I don't understand."

"On Earth, I'm what's known as a hacker. I get in and out of computer systems without leaving a trail."

"You're a criminal?" His body tensed even more.

"And there he is, Mr. Black and White." She threw her hands into the air. "Most of the time, the companies who own the computer systems hired me to test their security. But I've hacked into others, because of the challenge."

"For money?"

"Not for the challenge hacks. Information."

He growled. "What did you do with the information?"

She tilted her head. "It depended. If I found evidence of a crime, I made sure law enforcement received an anonymous tip. Otherwise, it was just for me."

"So the Svesti military data you downloaded is just for you? I doubt that," he bit out.

"You know what?" She pulled her laptop toward her and started typing, fingers banging angrily on the keys. "You can see for yourself what I planned to do with it." She shoved the laptop at him. "I changed the password to make it easier for you to find everything. It's now Fuckoff123." She opened a drawer and pulled out the flash drives. She shoved them across the table at him. "Here are all my storage drives, too. Take them all."

He picked up the laptop and drives. Grief tinged his voice. "I trusted you, *milara*. I wanted to ask you to true mate with me." Rising to his feet, he shook his head sadly. "You should have come to me and told me the truth."

"What part of 'I don't trust anyone' did you miss? I think I was pretty upfront about that all along." *I've never heard her voice so lifeless.* "For your edification, trust has to go both ways. You obviously didn't trust me if you were tracking my movements."

Frustrated, he growled. "It is an automatic function when someone new is given access to sensitive systems. I didn't even look at the logs until I was checking for what our numerous suspects had been doing."

He turned to go. "I'll make a determination of your status once I finish my investigation." *Crek. That hurt to say. I don't know if I can put her in the brig.*

When he was at the door, he heard her say, "I told you that you'd be glad I wouldn't commit."

In his quarters, Devik logged into Emmy's laptop. Tail drooping, he saw the long list of the files. *She downloaded more than I thought.* He opened one and frowned as he began reading. *That's not right.*

Checking more files, he realized all of them had inaccurate information. He tapped on his tablet, pulling up the corresponding files on the Svesti system. *Oh, she's devious. She changed the data to show Svesti capabilities as better than they are.*

Even the star charts and technology schematics are garbage. Fascinated, each file he checked revealed a convolution of facts mixed with falsehoods. If you didn't know the truth, the data appeared reasonable.

Hours later, he sat back, feeling his muscles cramp from being in the same position for so long. *Yes, she accessed what she shouldn't have, but her loyalties were with the Svesti, not the humans.* Stretching, his heart lightened. *She did not betray my trust the way I believed.*

He grimaced. *It seems I have some apologizing to do.*

Chapter 20

After Devik left, Emmy prowled her quarters like a caged animal. Her mind raced. *So stupid, Emmy. Of course the Svesti have some way of monitoring computer activity. Why did I think I could get away with it? Just because I slept with Devik? Am I really so arrogant?*

Exhausted, she collapsed on her bed, burying her head in her pillow. *Damn, I can still smell him.* Inhaling deeply, she curled into the fetal position, hugging the pillow. *I'm no good at this relationship stuff. I didn't want to care, but somehow he snuck into my heart. What the hell did he mean by true mate? I screwed everything up.*

He looked so hurt and disappointed. She sniffled. *And what did I do? Did I explain everything? No, I got angry at him, because that's easier than being vulnerable. I just keep pushing people away. I thought it was better that way, so I wouldn't feel the pain of someone leaving.*

Tears flowed down her face. *Well, that's not working out so well, is it? Because I hurt more than I ever thought possible.* For the second time in days, Emmy cried herself to sleep.

In the morning, Emmy grimaced in the mirror when she saw her swollen eyelids, blotchy face, and red nose. *Not a good look for me.* She showered, letting the hot water pelt her body. *Time to put on my big-girl panties. I need to apologize to him. I deserve whatever he decides. I hate to admit it, but he's right. I did betray his trust.*

After getting ready, she checked her tablet to track Devik's comm. *Okay, he's still in his quarters. Suck it up, and get it over with.*

When he answered his door chime, he looked surprised to see her. She frowned. *He looks exhausted. I did that to him and not in a good way.*

They stared at each other for a long moment, then both said, "I'm sorry."

She shook her head. "No, you did nothing wrong, Devik. No matter what my reasons were, I shouldn't have betrayed your trust."

He took her hand and pulled her inside. "You did and you didn't, Emmy. I went through the files last night. You changed everything from the originals. Why?"

Her fingers ran through her curls. "My government gave me up for the Choosing without my consent. With the exception of the traitor, the Svesti have treated me with respect and honesty. Spying for my government would be wrong. They threatened me to get the information, but no one said it was supposed to be accurate." She smirked. "I dislike being forced to do anything. And I really hate being lied to."

Devik's teal eyes were sad. "I understand why you did what you did, but it hurts that you didn't talk to me about it. I would've understood."

"Maybe. Maybe not, Devik. But when you started going on about commitment, I knew I would be going back to Earth. The only way to stay out of prison was to have something to give them." She shrugged uncomfortably. "I didn't like doing it, but I felt I had to protect myself."

He pulled her into his arms and hugged her close. Resting her head on his bare pecs, she absorbed his scent and warmth. She wrapped her arms around his waist. *I missed this.*

"Emmy, is it really so difficult for you to give us a chance at a future?" His chest rumbled beneath her cheek calming her even as his words made her stomach clench.

She sighed heavily. "I don't know how to let people in, Devik. I've been hurt so many times."

"I've been miserable without you these past days," he admitted. His warm lips kissed the top of her head.

Sniffling, she said, "Me, too." She drew her head back to look at his face. "You said something last night I didn't understand." She squared her shoulders. "What did you mean by true mate?"

A small smile graced his lips. "True mating is a biological urge for the Svesti. Our fangs elongate and we bite each other. Unlike a troth contract, true mating is for life."

"Oh, so like a destiny thing?" Her brows creased.

"No, that would be fated mates. We haven't had a fated mate pairing in a century. It is believed the Goddess blesses us when we find the one person in the universe meant to be ours. It's as if two halves of the same soul finally connect. True mates are committed to each other by choice."

"You wanted me as your true mate?" She shook her head. "I can't understand why. I'm nothing special."

He growled. "I dislike when you don't acknowledge your worth. You are intelligent—brilliant in fact—beautiful, and as much as you try to hide it, very loving and caring. Not just with me, but I've seen how you work to protect the other females."

"I think you see what you want to see, Devik. I'm not so altruistic."

"Really? Did you not tell me last night that when you found illegal activities during your hacks, you let law enforcement know?"

"Well, yes. It was the right thing to do. Some of the things I found were truly disgusting—selling people, including children."

His hair tickled her nose when he shook his head. "*Milara*, we might not always agree what the proper way to do things is, but your heart and mind try to do what is morally best. Your actions make that clear, not just with those hacks, but with how you tried to protect the Svesti by changing the data and how you work so hard to catch the traitor."

"You really believe that, don't you? I'm afraid you'll be disappointed when you discover I'm completely ordinary." Emmy chewed on her lower lip.

His thumb gently rubbed her abused lip. "What happens when you discover I was right about you all along?"

A surprised laugh burst from her. Smiling ruefully, she said, "You are persistent."

Fangs flashing, he grinned. "I know you are worth fighting for, *milara*. I don't make it a habit to give up when it's important."

Her hands caressed his face. "I wasn't lying when I said I don't know how to do this, Devik. Long-term relationships—hell, any relationships—are not in my wheelhouse. I know I'm going to mess this up again."

Turning his head, he kissed her palm. "I'm not perfect either, Emmy. I jumped to conclusions last night. I should have handled it differently." His teal eyes gazed into hers. "We will both make mistakes. We need to trust in each other, not run and hide when we're uncertain." He tucked a stray curl behind her ear, then rested his hand on her nape. "This is new to me, too. There are very few females on Costonia and I'm a warrior. It's not like I've had relationships myself."

"So we figure this out together?" Emmy lips turned up slightly. "All I can commit to right now is to try. Nothing more." *I can do this. I think. I hope.*

"Trying is good." His fangs gleamed. "I can be patient. You are worth it." As he leaned down to kiss her, his hand gently pulled her head closer.

She closed her eyes as his lips caressed hers with soft pressure. He nipped her bottom lip, then his tongue laved it. Opening her mouth, her tongue met his. His tail stroked her back, while her hands moved restlessly over his body.

Warm hands cupped her face as he drew back. Gazing into her eyes, he asked, "Stay?"

She nodded. "Yes."

A huge smile on his face, he dropped his hands to cup her ass and lift her. Squealing in surprise, she wrapped her legs around his waist and laughed.

When Devik reached his bed, he turned and fell backwards onto it with Emmy still in his arms.

"Oomph," she huffed. "A little warning next time would be nice." She leaned down and kissed him. "You're lucky I like you."

Grinning, he said, "Yes, I am."

She playfully slapped his shoulder, then sat up. Drawing her shirt over her head, she tossed it aside then unhooked her bra. The evidence of his arousal twitched under her ass. She wiggled as she threw her bra aside.

His teal eyes darkened. His hands moved to her breasts, thumbs teasing her hard nipples.

"You have the most beautiful breasts, Emmy. So soft and full and heavy." He licked his lips. "They make me want to taste them."

"I'm not stopping you," she said breathlessly.

His abs tightened and he sat up, dislodging her. As she fell backward, his tail slowed her body to gently hit the mattress. He rolled toward her, pinning her with his body. Wet heat surrounded a nipple as his mouth sucked. His tongue flicked at it sending tingles to her clit. He took his time lavishing attention to both breasts, occasionally nibbling at her flesh with his fangs.

Her fingers clenched in his hair. Her hips wanted to move, but his weight kept her in place. She tugged. He looked up at her, mouth open, tongue just barely licking her engorged nipple. *That is so hot.*

"Too many clothes, Devik," she gasped.

His seductive eyes held hers as he licked a path down the center of her abdomen. When he reached her pants, he used his teeth to unbutton them. Unable to look away, she moaned. His tongue and mouth never left her skin as his hands drew her pants and underwear off her legs. He kept watching her as he moved back up to her core.

Spreading her thighs, his eyes closed when he inhaled. When they reopened they were almost black with desire. Thrusting his tongue into her, his hands squeezed her ass. She lost track of what his hands and tail were doing. Every particle of her being was focused on his mouth and tongue. Her eyes drifted shut as small waves of pleasure grew into a tsunami of ecstasy throughout her body.

Coming back to her senses, she opened her eyes to him smiling down at her. His large palms framed her face as he lightly kissed her flushed skin.

"*Milara*, I hate to tell you this."

"What?"

"I am on duty in ten minutes. I have to go."

"You can't be late?" She reached down and palmed his erection through his pants. "I could take care of this for you."

Resting his forehead on hers, he grunted. "I wish I could." His hips bucked when she squeezed. "You are such a temptress."

Grinning, she released him. "Well, then you better finish getting dressed." She pushed him to his back and gave him a quick peck on the lips before rolling away in the other direction. She got out of bed to find her clothes.

"You could've tried convincing me some more." He pouted.

Laughing, she said, "We should pretend we're responsible adults. I have to meet the girls for morning meal anyway."

Sighing, he got up. When they were dressed, he pulled her into his arms for a hug and another kiss.

"At least I'll have your scent on me all day," he said as he dropped his arms.

"You are such a perv." She shook her head as they left his quarters.

Chapter 21

As he walked to his office, Devik's balls felt heavy, but his heart felt light as air. *She's willing to try to make our relationship work. I'm glad she chose to protect Svesti sensitive information. I don't know what I would have done if it were otherwise.*

His day seemed interminably long. All he wanted was to spend time with Emmy and reconnect more fully after their separation. When he finally got to her quarters after evening meal, her smile as she opened the door brightened his soul. *Mine.*

The next morning, Devik and Karid met with Ash'n and Natasha in the med bay.

"We think we have a vaccine," Ash'n said.

"That's good news," said Karid. "Have you tested it?"

"That's the problem," said Lady Natasha. "We need to go from the simulations to a live test. The question is who do we test it on?"

"What does the vaccine do?" asked Devik.

"It won't correct the damage that has already occurred, but a vaccinated being should be resistant to the virus and won't spread it. That's if it works the way we believe it will," said Ash'n. "I volunteer to be the test subject."

Devik shook his head at the same time Karid said, "No. We need our healer. I will test it."

This time it was Ash'n who shook his head. "No, you are needed to command the *Invictus*, especially if this doesn't work as we hope."

Devik said, "It should be me."

"Why?" said Lady Natasha.

"The only ones who know of the virus are the human females and us." Devik gestured to his friends. "Testing on a female is too risky. I have three older brothers who could continue my family line if it doesn't work. And of the three of us, I'm needed the least on the *Invictus*."

Karid frowned. "Don't discount your worth."

"I'm not, Karid. But with Vared mostly unavailable, you are the best to command *Invictus*. Ash'n will be needed to continue work on the vaccine if this is unsuccessful. I'm the best choice."

"You are all forgetting one thing," said Lady Natasha. "I don't think Talia or the commander will approve testing on anyone."

Nodding his head, Karid said, "You are correct, but as acting commander, I could order it."

Shaking his head again, Devik said, "No, you could damage your friendship with Vared. We need to involve the king."

"*Crek!* Vared is going to be furious." Karid grimaced, then he grinned. "But I will be out of reach." He slapped Devik's back. "You will be the one on the *Intrepid* with him. Hopefully, he'll cool off before he gets back here."

Devik grumbled. "Great. I'll be the one who takes a beating." Then he sighed.

"Only fitting, my friend. It was your idea." Karid waggled his eyebrows. "Let's speak with the king and get this over with."

After contacting King Sovex for his approval, Ash'n administered the vaccine to Devik.

"How do you think we should handle this?" Ash'n asked.

"I think I should port over while you're telling them about it and surprise them," Devik said. "He's going to be angry no matter what. It's best to face him with it already done."

"You know he is probably going to rearrange your internal organs?" Ash'n said. "Should I send over a med bed?"

Devik grunted. "I'll handle his anger."

Ash'n squeezed Devik's shoulder. "You're a good male, Devik. I hope this works."

"I hope so, too."

Via an earpiece, Devik listened to Ash'n and Lady Natasha as they conversed with Vared and Lady Talia. As they discussed the vaccine, Devik tapped out his commands at a workstation to port himself. He initiated the port when he heard Ash'n say, "The only way to test it is to expose someone to you before you receive the vaccine."

Rematerializing within the cargo hold of the *Intrepid*, Devik walked to the main areas of the shuttle. He turned off his earpiece when he heard Vared's growl in front of him.

"We cannot expose anyone else," Vared said.

"Too late," said Devik. "I'm already here."

"Why would you do this, Devik?" Vared yelled at him.

"Because I am the logical choice, Vared," Devik said calmly. He enumerated the reasons for the decision to his friend and Lady Talia.Lady Talia said, "Why weren't we involved in this decision?"

Lady Natasha said, "Because we knew both of you would disagree."

"Last I heard, I was still the Commander of the *Invictus*." Vared's angry roar echoed off the walls.

Devik nodded. "Yes, you are. That is why we went over your head to the king."

"You did what?"

"This vaccine better work. I don't know if I can handle the guilt if you become infected, too, Tolvex," Lady Talia said quietly.

"Lady Talia, I trust the healers, and I believe it will work. But if it doesn't, it is my honor to sacrifice my fertility for both our worlds. Guilt is unnecessary. My life is not in danger, and it is my choice." He looked at Vared, his face hardening. "I'll say it again, Vared. It's my choice."

After some long tense moments, Vared blew out a harsh breath and said, "My friend, I am going to take pleasure in causing you great pain when we spar."

Laughing, Devik clapped Vared on the back. "I look forward to it."

The healers instructed them to inoculate Vared, but not Lady Talia. Lady Natasha told the males what blood and sperm samples the healers required. *I hope this works as we all hope.*

Devik stood by Vared as they drank from their water pouches. Vared had worked off his anger while they had sparred. *I thought I was going to end up with broken facial bones—at the very least a broken nose. Vared's right, though. We should have told him about the plan before talking to the king. I'm sorry he felt disrespected.*

Vared said, "I have no problem sending you into battle, Devik, but the thought that you could lose your chance at young upsets me." *Ah, my friend, you have always had a good heart.*

"Because the virus is an enemy that our skill and determination can't fight, Vared. Our warrior skills mean nothing to it."

They spoke for a bit about Vared's relationship with Lady Talia, before moving on to other subjects. *He loves Lady Talia and is willing to move to Earth to be with her. Would I do the same for Emmy? Crek. Yes I would if it were the only option that let me be with her.* Stunned, Devik lost track of Vared's words for a short time. *I should tell him about Emmy.*

Devik's thoughts came back to the conversation when Vared asked about the new holo-emitters. As he told his friend about the recurrent training for the security teams, he realized the moment was lost. *I'll tell him about Emmy tomorrow. I'm not sure how he's going to take it, especially when I inform him of her downloading military data. I don't want to have to spar with him again a second time today.*

Emmy was too quiet when Devik comm'd her that evening to tell her he was on the *Intrepid.*

"*Milara?* You seem upset," he said.

"You should have discussed this with me before you did it."

"It was my choice, Emmy. It was the right thing to do." He frowned.

"I'm not arguing that, Devik. I'm saying you should've talked to me beforehand," Emmy bit out through gritted teeth.

"I'm telling you now," he said, tail flicking.

"Too little, too late."

"I don't understand."

She sighed. "I know. That's the problem. I need time to think, Devik. So do you. I think we should keep our communications to only those that are necessary while you're on the *Intrepid.*"

"It is necessary to keep in touch with you."

"No, Devik. Ship's business only for now. Maybe when you understand why I'm upset, I'll change my mind." Emmy's eyes were sad.

"Just tell me, so I can fix it," Devik pleaded.

She shook her head. "I'm not sure how to articulate it yet." She swiped at a lone tear running down her cheek. "Damn. I hate crying." She sucked in a breath. "I hope the vaccine works. Goodbye, Devik." She disconnected the comm.

Crek! Why is she upset with me? He tried to comm her again, but she refused the connection. His shoulders and tail drooped. *How do I make this right?*

During the midday meal the next day, Devik debated with Lady Talia about intent versus the written word in the draft treaty. *I wonder if all human females are as intelligent and passionate about their beliefs as the ones I've met.* When she and Vared agreed that an addendum to the treaty explaining the intent of each section was a good idea, she began writing and mumbling to herself.

When Devik asked Vared about Lady Talia's actions, Vared laughed indulgently. He told Devik that Lady Talia often focused so intently on her work that the outside world no longer existed for her. Vared also told him that handwriting her thoughts before typing them digitally worked better for her.

"Have you read any of her fiction?" Devik asked.

"No. Have you?"

Devik informed Vared he had searched for Lady Talia's books after one of the Wing Raiders had mentioned them after the rescue.

"They are surprisingly good stories. The characters feel believable, even in unbelievable circumstances. And there are warriors," Devik said.

"Then why do you look uncomfortable?" Vared asked.

"There are a lot of detailed descriptions of mating in the books, much more so than in our literature. However, I do feel I've learned a lot about human anatomy when it comes to mating." Devik laughed. *Also, I have some firsthand experience. I think it's time to tell him about Emmy.*

"Really?" Vared smiled. "Send me the titles so that I may read them and see if there is anything I should learn myself."

"I'll do that." Devik squared his shoulders. "I have things to tell you, Vared. They may anger you."

Vared frowned. "Let's leave Talia to her musings and go elsewhere while you tell me."

They walked toward the training area. Devik informed Vared about Emmy's predicament with her government and her subsequent actions. Vared growled.

"So the files on her laptop were not accurate?"

"No, she changed them all to protect the Svesti interests."

"But you did not put her in the brig for downloading the information initially? Did you inform Karid?"

"No and no." Devik stopped and faced Vared. "If you want her confined, you will have to find someone else to do it, Vared. I can't."

Brows drawn together, Vared said, "Would that be because you are intimate with her?"

"How did you know?"

"Your scent when you came onboard yesterday. You're not the only one with a nose," Vared smiled. "How serious is it?"

"I was thinking of asking her to true mate, but she's upset with me right now and I don't know why." Devik's tail made short, irritated movements.

"True mate? When you were reminding me the females were meant for the nobles?"

Devik said, "I was trying to advise myself at the same time as you. It seems to have worked as well for me as it did you."

Vared laughed. "These human females are definitely changing things for us."

"Yes, they are. I'm happiest when I'm with her, even if she's not happy with me." Devik shook his head. "I wish I knew why she doesn't want to speak with me."

"Is it because you are testing the vaccine?"

"Possibly. She agrees it was my choice but said I should've spoken with her first."

"You didn't tell her before you did it?" Vared's scar turned white.

"No, the decision happened fast, then I was here. I told her last night."

"Does she want young?"

"She's never said one way or another. Her childhood wasn't ideal." Devik's shoulders tensed.

"So you made a decision that potentially affects her future and you didn't discuss it with her," Vared said with a sigh. "That could be the issue. I don't even want to think what Talia would do to me if I did something similar." He mock shuddered.

"*Crek.* That is what I did, isn't it?" Devik frowned. "How do I fix it?"

"I'm not sure, but I imagine some groveling will be involved," Vared grinned. "And you should've informed Karid about Emmy's actions. You didn't follow the chain of command...again."

Devik sighed. "You're right." His face brightened. "Maybe he'll go easy on me because I took the brunt of your anger about the vaccine."

Vared clapped him on the shoulder. "I doubt that. But feel free to hope."

Devik's lips twisted and Vared's smirk became a loud laugh. *I'm glad he's amused and not angry. It's much easier on my body.*

Later in the dining area with Vared and Lady Talia, Devik tapped his comm to connect to the healers on the Invictus. Ash'n and Lady Natasha informed them that Vared's samples showed the virus was inert in his blood and Devik showed no signs of being infected.

"We'd like you to give Talia the vaccine now. You'll be able to..." Lady Natasha's words cut off as she was ported unexpectedly.

"What the hell?" Talia exclaimed.

"Devik, where is she?" Vared growled.

Devik tapped his tablet. "I'm searching for her tracker now." His comm chimed. "Emmy is attempting to contact us."

"Encrypted channel," Vared ordered.

"Devik. The traitor is at it again," Emmy said. "He attempted to port all the women to the *Intrepid*."

"Where are you now?" Vared asked.

"In Talia's quarters. I set up the program to port us here, since we knew no one would be in the way." *I like that she tries to be one step ahead.*

Emmy informed them the traitor again used a time delay on the ports. Devik comm'd Karid to have him join in the conversation. They discussed options for dealing with the situation—from guards with the human females to allowing the traitor to believe he was successful. Both Vared and Karid were concerned the traitor might not give them another opportunity to catch him if he thought the human females were infected.

Rachel said, "I think there's another way to try to flush him out."

"We're listening."

"Emmy and Tolvex adjust the logs to show us ported, but no destination. Then, in an hour, show another port to our quarters on the *Invictus* without an origin point. We women don't say anything about it at all. We see if anyone asks where we were and just answer that we've been sworn to secrecy, which would be the truth. We note anyone's interest in our whereabouts and follow up with more investigation."

Vared nodded slowly. "I like this idea. Are you females willing to assist us in the manner Lady Rachel outlined?"

"Yes," they all answered.

"Devik, Lady Emmy, are you able to adjust the logs?"

"I'm working on the initial port now," said Emmy. *I enjoy the look of concentration on her face.*

"I'm setting up the return ports," Devik said as he tapped on his tablet. *She and I make a good team.*

Ash'n instructed them to give Lady Talia the vaccine and arranged for blood samples to ensure the vaccine didn't need adjustments for human biology. He told them he was already synthesizing the vaccine for the Svesti and would tell the other healers it was for a human flu virus he'd discovered.

During the discussion, Devik focused on Emmy. *Does she look tired?* She avoided looking directly at him for most of the conversation. He frowned as they disconnected the comm. *She was too quiet. I don't like it.*

Chapter 22

Emmy looked at the other women. They all seemed to be overcoming their shock at being unexpectedly ported. *I'm glad the program worked.*

"This traitor is a real pain in the ass," said Rachel. She sat on one of the couches in Talia's quarters. The other women followed her example.

"He's smart," said Emmy. "Between moving cameras and time delays, he's been practically a ghost."

"Have you had any luck narrowing your suspect list?" asked Ava.

"Not really. With three thousand warriors onboard and twelve Houses, there are a lot of males related to Houses Nuxar and Srotix." Rachel grimaced.

"Is there anything we can do to help?" asked Ava.

Rachel shook her head. "Not right now."

"How's work going on the vaccine?" Emmy asked Natasha.

Natasha smiled. "It seems to work on Svesti. Tolvex's samples came back with no trace of the virus at all. So we can start inoculating the males onboard. Talia should be getting the vaccine today. If it neutralizes the virus so she can't spread it, we can do us next." Her eyes were serious. "We're going to wait, though, until everyone onboard the *Invictus* is vaccinated before letting Talia and the commander return. It'll only be a matter of days, but both Rivezt and I want to ensure everyone is protected, just in case."

"It seems very fast," said Lin. "I mean, it's only been two weeks since Talia was infected, and you already have a vaccine."

Natasha nodded. "Compared to what we could do on Earth, I agree. The Svesti capabilities to run simulations are light years ahead of anything we know. I even ran simulations testing on each of the human blood types and whether cancerous cells would affect its efficacy on humans."

"Wow," Lin said. "I want to see that setup. It might make a difference when I'm testing plants for healing properties."

"You know what I wish?" Rachel said.

"What's that?" said Emmy.

"I wish Ava had been holding a plate of cookies when she was ported." Rachel grinned.

Everyone laughed.

Ava said, "I can get us something from the synthesizer while we wait."

Shaking her head, Emmy said, "I don't know if there's a record of usage. If there is, Talia's synthesizer being used when she's not here might tip off the traitor."

Rachel pursed her lips. "That's a good point. I don't think I would've thought about the possibility." She smiled. "Nice work, Emmy. Especially with redirecting the ports."

"It was nothing."

Natasha shook her head. "It's not nothing. You saved everyone on this ship from becoming infected."

Emmy's knee bounced and she rubbed her hands on her pants. *You can do this. Just talk to them.*

"Can I ask you ladies something?" Emmy chewed on her lower lip.

"Sure."

"Have any of you been in a serious relationship?"

Everyone nodded.

"Why do you ask?" said Rachel.

"How do you know?"

"Know what?" Natasha said.

Emmy sighed. "Know whether it's worth getting your heart broken."

"You don't," said Natasha with a small smile.

"Then why take the risk?" Emmy's fingers tapped rhythmically on her thigh.

"Connection and the hope that it will work," Lin said quietly.

Rachel leaned forward. "Yes, it's a gamble taking a chance on someone. He's also taking that risk. You might be the one who breaks his heart. Or maybe you'll both realize it's not working and part amicably. Or maybe—just maybe—it will be the best thing that ever happened to you two." She gently laid her hand on Emmy's forearm. "We don't know your story, but we're willing to listen and help if we can."

Emmy's body stilled as she looked at their concerned faces. *No one seems to be judging me. Should I?* She held her breath, then let it out slowly.

"I don't know if you've noticed, but I make it a point not to let people in." She tapped her chest above her heart.

Ava said with an encouraging smile. "I figured you had your reasons." The other women agreed.

"I grew up in foster care—mostly group homes. Every relationship I cared about ended badly for me." She dropped her eyes to stare at her hands. "I eventually decided that it wasn't worth being vulnerable to anyone. It always ended in pain for me."

Lin said sadly, "Oh, Emmy. I'm sorry you had to go through all that."

Natasha said, "What's changed?"

Emmy waved her hand around. "Being here. All of you. Devik."

Chuckling, Ava said, "That's not very enlightening."

Emmy laughed softly. "I guess not. Being here is well outside my comfort zone."

"I'd say that's the case for all of us." Rachel smiled. "From where I sit, it looks like you've adapted very well so far."

"If we were on Earth and I knew I had to spend all this time with you, I would've investigated each and every one of you." Emmy frowned. "I haven't done that, not only because I literally can't access anything that wasn't on the public internet when we left, but because I don't want to."

Natasha frowned. "I don't understand."

Rachel's face was pensive. "On Earth, was it because you wanted to know everyone's secrets?"

Emmy nodded, her curls bouncing. "Knowing your secrets would give me insight on how to interact with you. Or even if I would want to." She felt some shame. "Saying it out loud makes me sound awful."

"Maybe," said Rachel. "You've been hurt and you wanted as much information as you could to decide how trustworthy people are." She gave Emmy a stern look. "I'm not saying it was the right thing to do, but it's understandable."

Ava's forehead wrinkled. "You said you don't want to investigate us now. Why?"

"All of you accepted me immediately, even when I told you I was a hacker. No one judged me." She looked each of them in the eye. "None of you have done the catty-bitch thing to anyone—trying to put down someone else to make themselves look or feel better. I feel like I would be violating your trust if I investigated you now."

Natasha laughed. "The catty-bitch thing. I can relate to that. I knew a few people in medical school and the hospital who were experts." Everyone nodded.

"Sounds like you may have already let us in a little," said Ava with a smile.

Emmy's lips tipped up. "Yeah, I think I have. I have to be honest, it's scary for me."

"It can be scary for all of us," said Lin.

Rachel said, "Initially, we were all in the same position. In a situation that none of us had even considered. Well, except maybe Talia. She writes fiction." Everyone laughed. "It's easier to bond under those circumstances. People tend to show their true colors under stress. It strips away a lot of the public personas we routinely show others."

"That makes sense," said Emmy.

Ava wagged her eyebrows. "Now let's get to the good stuff. Devik? You and Tolvex? Tell us more."

Emmy's face heated. "Uh, a couple of weeks ago, I suggested to Devik we become friends with benefits."

"Oooh, go on," said Ava with a grin.

Fanning her face with a hand, Emmy said, "The sex part is beyond satisfying."

"So what's the problem?" Rachel said.

"He wants more and I don't know how to make it work. Or even if I should."

"Everything has been going well?" asked Natasha.

"Well, not exactly."

"What does that mean?" Lin said.

"I downloaded some sensitive information to give to my government and he found out." Emmy bit her lower lip. "I had changed all of it to protect Svesti interests, which is probably the only thing that saved me from all of you visiting me in the brig."

"If you were going to change it, why download it at all?" Rachel said with a frown.

"I panicked. Devik pushed for more of a commitment, and I knew it was going to end badly for me—it always does. So I had to have something for my government to stay out of jail when I go back." Emmy's eyes watered as she looked at the solemn faces around her. "I'm not proud of it. I tried to do what was best, not only to protect myself, but to keep from completely selling out the Svesti. They've treated me better than humans ever have."

Natasha sighed. "You know, Emmy, underneath all the prickly parts you like to show people, you have a really good heart."

"Um, thanks." Embarrassed, Emmy continued. "We sorta got past that, then he went and took the vaccine without talking to me about it. I'm upset, but I can't figure out why. It's not like we've totally committed to each other. I only committed to try." Exasperated, she threw her hands up. "I'm not even sure why I did that much. I couldn't help myself."

"That's a lot to unpack," said Rachel. She looked at the other women. "What part should we start with?"

"I also worry because we're so different." Emmy frowned.

Natasha pursed her lips. "How so?"

Emmy waved her hand. "He's all 'right is right, wrong is wrong,' whereas I..." Her voice trailed off.

"Operate in gray areas?" Rachel smirked.

"Yes."

"Well, if he understood why you downloaded the info and didn't arrest you, I'd say he's willing to at least consider the gray areas," said Rachel.

"And he might be good for keeping you from going too far astray," added Natasha with a smile. "How does Tolvex normally treat you?"

Emmy smiled. "Usually, very well. He's kind, considerate, sexy as hell, and for some reason thinks I'm better than I know I am."

"Hmm, maybe he sees you more clearly than you see yourself," said Lin. "How do you feel when you're with him?"

Emmy closed her eyes. "Freer. Calmer. More excited." She opened her eyes. "That doesn't even make sense when I say it. Everything is better when I'm with him."

"Sounds like he's worth taking the risk for," said Rachel with a smile.

"Why am I so upset he didn't talk to me? It's not that I don't believe it wasn't his choice to volunteer. I actually agree he was the best choice to test the vaccine."

"Do you want kids? Is it the possibility he might become infertile?" asked Natasha.

"I always assumed I'd never have them because I wasn't going to get close enough to anyone to go that route. So whether or not he's fertile makes no difference to me." Emmy shrugged.

"Well, speaking for myself," said Ava with a thoughtful expression, "I believe I'd feel disrespected. He made a big decision that could affect both your lives without even discussing it first with you." She looked at everyone. "I think I would feel like an afterthought, not a priority. And if he's the one pushing for more commitment, I can see why it would upset you."

Emmy stared at Ava, letting her words bounce around in her head. "Thank you, Ava. That feels right. Afterthought, not priority." She took a deep breath. "I feel better understanding why I feel what I feel."

"That's a lot of feels," Natasha said with a grin. Everyone laughed.

"What should I do?"

"Well, maybe make him suffer a little first before you forgive him," said Ava with a grin.

"You need to tell him what is bothering you and why," Lin said with a shy smile. "If you can't communicate with each other honestly, then there's no point in taking the risk. You both need to respect each other and make changes to support each other's feelings, even if you don't always agree."

All the women looked at Lin with wide eyes.

Rachel's blue eyes narrowed. "You've been holding out on us, Lin. There's a big brain in that little body."

Lin stuck her tongue out at Rachel. "Just because I'm as small as a child doesn't mean I am one." The women laughed again.

Natasha hugged Lin. "We're just teasing you. You're so quiet most of the time, I think sometimes it surprises us when you speak up so eloquently."

Lin glanced at Emmy. "It's hard for me, too, Emmy. You're not alone in that."

"I'm really glad I talked to all of you. I'm feeling better."

"We're glad. We're here for you," said Ava.

"Now that I know why I'm upset, I have an idea to illustrate it to Devik. But I might need a little help," Emmy said.

"What's your plan?" Ava said.

Emmy outlined her idea to the women.

Natasha nodded. "I can make that happen. We might piss off more Svesti than Devik, but it's doable."

"Thanks." Emmy bit her lip. "Uh, there's one other thing I think you should know."

"What's that?" asked Rachel.

"The Svesti have really great olfactory senses." Emmy's cheeks heated. "Like they can smell when we're aroused."

"Oh, shit," Ava said with wide eyes. "Are you serious?"

Emmy's head bobbed rapidly. "I would've told you all sooner, but I didn't know how to bring up the subject without letting you know about Devik."

Natasha frowned. "None of the healers have mentioned Svesti enhanced senses to me."

"They might not have thought it was important. It's normal to them, right?" Lin's face was pink.

"Lin's probably right," Rachel said.

"I wonder if there's a way we can mask our scents," said Natasha. "I think I feel exposed knowing any of them could smell something like that."

Emmy shook her head. "I don't think so. At least it wouldn't work on all of them. Devik said some have more highly developed senses than others."

"Well, that's disconcerting," Natasha said. "Thanks for letting us know, Emmy." She grimaced. "Although, it might've been nice to stay blissfully ignorant for a while longer."

Emmy grinned. "Anything for my friends."

"Is it done?"

"Unknown," the Svesti male grumbled. "I've attempted porting the females to each other twice, but do not know if the ports were successful."

"What do the females say?"

"They are not speaking about any of it, and I cannot ask without drawing attention to myself."

"You must take greater risks, Nephew." A growl echoed through the comm.

"Do you have any suggestions, Uncle?"

"Kidnap the lone female and ensure she returns to the *Invictus*."

"I will be caught."

"There may be a way, nephew, to have another do your bidding. We've been testing a way to use implants to control others. We haven't perfected it, but perhaps a field test is in order."

"What do I need to do?"

"You'll need an upload device."

As the Svesti male listened to the detailed instructions, he cringed inwardly at the thought of mind control. While it may be effective for achieving goals for their cause, his warrior's honor felt abused by using such tactics.

"Uncle, why are you researching mind control at all?"

"If we wish to keep the Svesti race pure, we must use every means available to us." His uncle growled through the comm. "Do you have a problem following orders?"

"No. I will do as you instructed."

"Be aware that most test subjects went insane when forced to go against their belief systems. It is best to give short, concise instructions and align them as closely as you can with their own beliefs. In this instance, making a warrior believe he needs to save a female in danger should work."

"How long does it take to work?"
"A couple of days for something simple like this."
"I will do as you instruct."
"Always Svesti."

Chapter 23

Devik smiled at the hologram of his brother, Solen, noting the laugh lines around his eyes had deepened since the last time they'd spoken.

"Happy birthday, Solen," Devik said.

"Many thanks, brother." Solen's wide smile lit his face. "It is good to hear from you. I hear rumors that you may be home in another month or so. Can we expect to see you?"

"I don't know how long the *Invictus* will remain on Costonia, but I hope long enough for a visit to see you." Devik's grin matched his brother's.

Solen tilted his head slightly. "You look different."

Devik's brows knit. "How so?"

"I'm not sure yet." Solen leaned forward and lowered his voice. "Is it true? Human females are coming to Costonia?"

Devik laughed. "Where did you hear that?"

"Oh, here and there. What are they like?"

"I haven't met many, but they are physically smaller than Svesti. Wide range of skin, hair, eye colors, and personalities."

"Are they pleasing?"

"Some more than others."

Solen's blue eyes widened. "I know that look. It's been so long since I've seen it on a Svesti male's face. You care for one."

Crek. Devik sucked in a breath. *What do I say? I can't lie to my brother about something like this.*

"Tell me, Devik."

Devik sighed. "You are correct. There is one I deeply care about."

"Does she feel the same?"

"She cares. I think more than she is willing to say. She has her reasons which I understand, but it is frustrating." Devik pushed his hand through his hair. "I made it worse when I volunteered for a special assignment without telling her beforehand."

Solen chuckled. "I was only mated for a couple years, but I do remember when a female is displeased, it is very uncomfortable."

"She's refusing to speak with me and until my assignment is complete, I can't do much about it." Devik frowned. "I miss her and it's been less than two days."

Fangs prominent, Solen grinned. "You have it bad, brother."

"I know." Devik shrugged sheepishly. "What do I do?"

"You apologize profusely. Perhaps a meaningful gift. Oh, and lots of hands-on attention." Solen wiggled his eyebrows.

Devik chuckled. "How is it you are the oldest? You act like a youngling at times."

"Levity has served us well." Solen's expression turned solemn. "We had so much grief and sadness for too many solars, Devik. We needed to learn how to enjoy life again."

Nodding, Devik said, "I am beyond grateful for you, Pex, and Rassix."

Solen waved his hand. "We are family." He paused. "Well?"

"Well, what?"

"Tell me more about your human. I will get to meet her when you get here, yes?"

Shaking his head, Devik said, "I'm sure you'll meet her, regardless of what happens with us. I'm assuming the king will hold a reception at some point." He proceeded to tell Solen about Emmy.

Solen smiled. "It sounds like she will keep you from becoming complacent."

"I hope to true mate with her, Solen. If only I can convince her to let go of her fears."

Happiness shone from Solen's face. "I cannot wait to meet the female who can make you feel uncertain. Life should hold surprises. I hope it works out for you, Devik. You deserve it."

They chatted for a while longer, Solen sharing news about their other brothers as well as gossip from the home world. Disconnecting the comm, Devik sighed. *Thank the Goddess for Solen and his perpetual humor. That's probably why Karid and I became friends. Karid's personality is similar.*

He frowned. *Now how do I get Emmy to talk with me?*

Three days later, Devik's frustration levels were high. Although he was enjoying his time on the *Intrepid* with Vared and Lady Talia, he missed Emmy terribly. She wasn't answering her comm. If he left a message, she sent him a text message answering anything having to do with security, but there was no personal interaction. *I really upset her. I have to find a way to fix this.*

Despite his problems with Emmy, it had been a long time since he had spent an extended period with his friend Vared without all the trappings of work. Vared was happier and more relaxed than Devik had ever seen him. Even though they were confined to the shuttle, it felt more like a mini-vacation. *I'm happy for him. Lady Talia brings out his best qualities. I only wish Emmy could be here, too.*

Lady Talia asked him to read over the draft treaty and give his opinion. Devik was pleasantly surprised at how thorough and innovative some of the sections were. He offered his input willingly and suggested that Lady Talia also ask the human females what they thought. She smiled and said she'd already sent them a copy.

Devik's comm chimed. He drew in a breath when he saw it was from Emmy.

"*Milara*, it is good to hear from you." His eyes drank in her appearance. *Was she thinner?* "How have you been?"

She nodded. "Fine, Devik. I just needed time to think."

He frowned as he took in more of the background. "Are you in a med bay? Did the traitor do something else?" His heart raced, his claws extended, and his tail whipped furiously behind him.

Her curls bounced as she shook her head. "No to the traitor. Yes to the med bay."

"Are you alright? What happened?" *I should be with her.*

"I'm fine. I'm in isolation."

"Why?"

"I volunteered to have Natasha give me the vaccine to ensure there were no side effects for humans."

"What? Why would you do that?" Devik's voice rose. "You could lose your fertility or become ill."

Her full lips thinned. "Talia's results looked good. I'm the best choice. I can still program and research on the computer from isolation. The other women can't do what they need to from here."

"Why would you make this decision without speaking with me?"

She cocked an eyebrow. "Really? You are seriously saying that to me?"

Devik's heart thumped as he stared at her. His tail began to slow and his claws retracted.

"Is this how you felt when I told you I took the vaccine?"

"I don't know. How do you feel?"

"Upset. Very upset."

"Why?"

"I feel..." He frowned. "I'm not sure how to explain it."

"Let me help you. Maybe you feel like an afterthought, not a priority in this relationship. If you were important to me, then I would have at least spoken with you about my decision before going ahead with it."

Remorse filled Devik. "Oh, *milara*. Intellectually, I understood why you were hurt and why I was wrong. But experiencing it for myself, I am more sorry than I can say." He hung his head. "I am not worthy of you."

"Devik," she said firmly. "Look at me."

He raised his sorrowful eyes.

"If we are going to try to make whatever this is between us work, we both have to adjust how we do things. I was wrong to download the data without talking to you and you made a mistake by not talking to me." She smiled sadly. "I'm trying my best here, Devik. I don't have any good examples to follow. I'm making it up as I go along. A lot of the time I feel like I'm floundering."

"You are correct that we both need to adjust, Emmy." He gave her a sad smile. "Can you forgive me?"

"Yes. And there's something else you should know."

"What's that?"

"I haven't taken the vaccine yet. But I will after we finish our conversation."

"I thought you said..." His eyes became unfocused as he reviewed their conversation in his head. "Oh, you never actually said you'd already taken it, just that you volunteered."

She nodded. "This was an object lesson for you, Devik. But I wasn't going to do what you did to me intentionally."

He shook his head with a smile. "You are devious and wise, *milara*. You proved your point. Now that I am calmer, please tell me why you think you're the best choice."

"Natasha is needed as a healer. Lin works in aquiponics, Ava in the kitchen. Talia is already accounted for and Rachel is our de facto leader with Talia on the *Intrepid*. I can easily do what I need to from isolation. Natasha says there's no chance I can lose my fertility from the vaccine. The worst that might happen is it might not work to neutralize the virus if I come in contact with it later." She shrugged. "Logically, I am the best choice. If I can do my part to protect the other women, it seems like a low-risk way to do it."

Devik gazed at her. "Surprisingly, I agree with you. I dislike that it's you, but I can't fault your logic." He looked concerned. "Did Lady Natasha say how long you would be in isolation?"

"She thinks I'll be able to leave in the morning. She just wants to observe overnight to ensure there are no unusual side effects."

"Good. Will you answer my comms now?" His face was hopeful.

She laughed. "Yes, Devik. We're good." She looked down then back at him. "Truthfully, I miss you much more than I thought I would."

"And I you, *milara*. I dislike that duty takes me away from you as often as it does."

"We'll figure it out. You'll be back as soon as everyone on the *Invictus* receives the vaccine."

"Plan on some alone time when I get back, Emmy," he growled. "It's been too long since I've tasted you."

She shivered. "I'm really looking forward to that, Devik." Her eyes dropped as he adjusted his engorged cock in his pants. The desire in her eyes as she raised them to his seared him. "It can't be soon enough." She shifted in her chair.

"Are you wet for me, Emmy?" His voice rumbled low.

"Oh shit, Devik, don't." She squirmed. "Natasha is going to be here soon and I really don't want to explain why I'm fidgety. Or have Rivezt smell me wanting you."

His growl deepened. "You and your arousal are mine, Emmy."

Her chest rose with her deep inhalation. "Get back soon and remind me, Devik. I'll be here."

"Emmy, are you ready?" Lady Natasha's voice sounded as if it were approaching.

"Yes, Natasha." Emmy smacked her lips in an exaggerated kiss. "Later, Devik." She disconnected the comm.

Devik chuckled even as he maneuvered in his chair to get comfortable. He sat back and palmed his crotch. *Soon, milara, soon.*

Devik's happiness increased over the next several days. Emmy suffered no ill effects from the vaccine, and the human females were vaccinated. Emmy asked if there was a database onboard that might have images of the warriors' clan markings. He told her to ask Rivezt if the healers kept one, as he did not. It was something Devik planned to rectify when he returned to the *Invictus*. Her plan was to run image searches on such a database to ensure they didn't miss any potential suspects.

He and Emmy comm'd regularly, sharing more of their childhoods. As much as he disliked it, he believed the enforced separation was good for them. They talked more about myriad subjects. He loved how her mind worked and her humor. He could feel them draw closer emotionally as she slowly dropped more of her self-imposed walls.

Although his cock was hard most of the time, connecting with Emmy soothed his soul. He also enjoyed teasing her, dropping his voice low, and watching her face flush with desire. *Maybe tonight I can convince her to do more.*

"I miss you, *milara*. I want to touch you."

Her eyelids closed partway and her mouth parted. "I miss you, too, Devik."

"Maybe your hands could be my hands, Emmy." He licked his lips.

"What are you suggesting?" She smirked.

"Run your palms along your stomach and cup those beautiful, luscious breasts for me."

She hummed low as she followed his instructions.

"Squeeze them, tug on those nipples through your shirt." His voice deepened.

"Like this?"

"Oh, yes. I want to feel your warm, smooth skin under my fingertips. Bare those breasts for me."

Crek! She was naked under her shirt. "The Goddess could not be more beautiful than you, Emmy. Lick your fingertips and circle those hard nipples. They're begging for my attention." Her moan caused his cock to twitch.

"Devik, I want you."

"I want you, more than you know."

They both startled, sat straight up, and stared at each other when they heard a scream.

"That's Talia!" Devik stood abruptly, claws extended.

"Go help her, Devik," Emmy said as she threw on her shirt. She grabbed her tablet. "Let me see if I can find out anything from here."

Devik ran from his quarters toward the dining area and found Lady Talia attempting to hold up a bleeding Vared. There was another Svesti behind his friend stabbing him as Vared sliced with his claws. He arrived at the group just after Vared's knees gave out. He disabled the attacking Svesti and restrained him. *Nerid Mantoor?*

He helped Lady Talia lay Vared on his side and comm'd Ash'n. "The Commander has been attacked. Stab wounds. Difficulty breathing. Just lost consciousness." *Crek. There's a lot of blood. Goddess help him.*

After Ash'n ported to the Intrepid and checked Vared, he said, "I need to get him to a med bed now. Override Lady Emmy's program and port us, Tolvex."

Devik ported Ash'n, Vared and Lady Talia directly to the med bay. He comm'd Karid and informed him of the situation. Karid ported Devik and Mantoor to the brig area where Kalix, Westov, and Tesix took custody of a mumbling Mantoor. Devik's tail whipped furiously throughout it all.

"He goes nowhere and has no visitors without the approval of Lieutenant Wurvez or myself," Devik ordered. "He is not to be left unguarded for a single moment, understood?"

"As you will, Lieutenant." Kalix said. "You should go get cleaned up. We will ensure your orders are followed."

Devik looked down at his bloody hands, before turning and walking towards the med bay. When he got there, the healers were operating on Vared with Lady Talia stroking his friend's head. Ash'n looked up briefly and mouthed, "It will be hours before we know." *That's not good.*

Devik nodded. As he headed to his quarters, he silently prayed to the Goddess to help his friend. His tail alternated between furious slashes and drooping sadly as he walked along the darkened corridors. His emotions were in turmoil.

Emmy was waiting in his quarters. She hissed as she took in his bloody state. "Is any of this yours?"

He shook his head. "Mostly Vared's. Some Mantoor's."

She bit her lip and took his hand. "Come, let's get you in the shower."

He tried to pull back his hand, but she held on tightly. "I'm a mess, Emmy. You're getting blood on you."

"I don't care. Now strip and get in the shower." He followed her instructions and rested his head on the wall as the hot water pelted him.

Her arms wrapped around his abdomen from behind and she rested her head on his back. She said nothing, just held him for a long time. Then she soaped her hands and began washing him. He turned when she tugged on his arm and watched her as she ran her soapy hands over his chest.

His arms wrapped around her, forcing her to stop as he absorbed the feel of her warm body against his.

"What can I do to help?" she whispered against his chest.

"You're already doing it, *milara*. Just let me hold you."

She kissed his pec, then peered up at him with concerned brown eyes. "For as long as you need, warrior."

After they dried off and got dressed, she led him to a couch and sat next to him. She dragged his arm over her shoulder and snuggled into his side.

"Can you tell me what happened?" She stroked his hand softly.

"From what I could tell, Nerid Mantoor ported to the *Intrepid* and began repeatedly stabbing Vared from behind. Vared was able to inflict some damage, but he collapsed. Lady Talia was there."

"Was she hurt?" Emmy's voice shook slightly.

He shook his head. "I saw no wounds, but there was a lot of blood. The healers are operating on Vared now. Ash'n said it was going to be hours before he could update us."

"The healers are good at what they do and Durek is strong. We have to believe he'll be okay."

"From your lips to the Goddess' ears, *milara*. I hope so. He's one of my best friends."

"Where's Mantoor?"

"Guarded in the brig."

They sat in silence, one of his hands rubbing her upper arm, the other drawing patterns on her hand. Finally, after a long while, he sighed. "I'm going to have to go to work and investigate."

"I know." She looked up at him. "Do you need more time before you go?"

His large hand cupped her cheek. His thumb smoothed over her skin. He leaned down to kiss her softly. "I want more time, but no, I don't need it." He blew out a breath. "This isn't how I imagined seeing you again, Emmy."

She smiled. "I know. Let's get through this, then we'll take some more time for us."

He kissed her again before he stood. "I hate leaving you like this."

"Go. You have a job to do. If there's anything I can do to help, just comm me and I'll do it. I'm going to check and see if I can figure out how he ported there." Emmy reached for her tablet, then looked at him encouragingly. "Durek will be fine, Devik. Grumpy and pissed off, but fine."

Devik involuntarily snorted. He smiled. "How do you know the right thing to say?"

"Talent, I guess." She smiled back at him as he turned to leave. *This proves to me beyond a doubt she is the one I want by my side.*

Devik was with Karid in the on-call room when Ash'n comm'd.

"Ash'n, how is Vared?"

"He made it through surgery and is heavily sedated. I don't expect him to regain consciousness until late tomorrow—maybe." Exhaustion laced his voice.

Karid said, "But he'll make it?"

Ash'n shook his head tiredly. "I honestly don't know. He took a lot of damage."

The three friends were quiet.

"Another reason I comm'd you is Lady Talia said she thought something was wrong with Mantoor," said Ash'n.

"Obviously, something's wrong. He attacked his commander," said Karid angrily.

"She mentioned mania or a fugue state. Devik, can you meet me at the brig so I can assess him?"

"Of course. I'm on my way." *Mania?* Devik's brow furrowed. *Should we have seen signs that Mantoor required a mind healer?*

"I'll go with you," Karid said.

At the brig, Ash'n was waiting for them with a med kit.

Devik asked Tesix, "Has anyone attempted to see the prisoner?"

Tesix shook his head. "No, sir. He mumbled incoherently for hours, and finally passed out a little while ago."

"Healer Rivezt will be checking him out. Lieutenant Tolvex and I will join him," said Karid.

"Yes, sir."

Devik and Karid watched as Ash'n healed several deep claw wounds on Mantoor's torso and arm. Ash'n frowned as he ran the scanner over Mantoor's head.

"What the..." Ash'n pulled out an upload device and pressed it behind Mantoor's ear. "Devik, there was an upload in his head." He handed the device with the upload to Devik.

Karid frowned. "There is no medical reason to leave an upload in place, is there?"

Ash'n shook his head. "No. I can't imagine why. As far as I'm aware, he hasn't had any uploads from medical at all."

Karid jerked his chin at Devik. "Find out what's on there and let us know." As Devik left to check the upload, he heard Karid say, "Other than that, what is his condition?"

When Devik found the repeating subvocal audio clip on the upload, he worked until he found the frequency range to decode it. He hissed in anger through his clenched jaw when he listened to it. It was short, but the repetitive words were "Durek dishonorable. Must save the female. Protect her on the *Invictus*." He immediately comm'd Karid and Ash'n to let them know. Both growled at the news.

Ash'n said, "I've never even heard of using uploads like this before. I'll have to consult the Master Healers on the home world."

Karid reminded him, "Go through the king, Ash'n. He will definitely want to know about this."

After they finished, Devik went to the med bay to check on Vared and Lady Talia. Lady Ava left just as he walked in.

"Tolvex, is Mantoor the traitor?" Lady Talia asked. *She looks exhausted.*

"I don't think so. Rivezt found an upload in his implant. It appears the traitor was brainwashing Mantoor to attack the Commander and bring you to the *Invictus*."

"The implants can be used to control people?" Her hand on Vared's head stilled.

Devik frowned as he said, "We've never seen anything like this before. If the traitors are experimenting with implants this way, there is great potential for misuse."

Lady Talia said, "No one should be experimenting with mind control. People are dangerous enough on their own. They don't need others messing with their free will."

Chapter 24

Emmy fell asleep in Devik's bed waiting for him to return. She roused slightly when he slid into bed. Rolling over, she threw her arm over his stomach and felt his legs intertwine with hers.

She murmured, "Are you okay?"

He kissed the top of her head. "I am now. Go back to sleep, *milara*. We can talk in the morning."

She nuzzled his chest and inhaled his unique scent. His warmth surrounded her as she drifted back to her dreams.

Hours later, she lazily awoke to find herself wrapped in his arms, her back to his front. She arched her spine slightly when one of his hands burrowed under her shirt to knead her breast.

"Are you awake, Emmy?" His breath was hot in her ear.

"Mmm, no, just having a wonderful dream." She groaned low when he tugged her nipple.

He nipped her earlobe, then licked it with his tongue. "Tell me about your dream."

"Some hot male is making me wet." She smiled and pressed her ass back against his erect cock. *Gotta love morning wood.*

His tail tugged her panties down, then drifted back to play with her clit.

"Anyone I know?" He kissed her nape and she shivered.

"Nah, some stranger." His fangs scraped her neck. She gasped when he pinched her nipple.

"Only I am allowed to make you wet." He lowered his voice register and she sighed.

"What are you going to do about it?"

He lifted her leg over his. The tip of his cock teased her opening from behind. She tried to push back against him, but he held her stationary.

"Make you scream my name so you don't forget," Devik growled.

"Promise?"

He slammed his hips forward and buried his cock deep in her pussy. She mewled at the sudden fullness. His tail wrapped around her calf, holding her leg up. His fingers played with her clit as he pumped with a steady rhythm.

Her head fell back and his mouth traveled back to her ear. "Who's making you wet, Emmy?"

She moaned. "You are."

"Say my name." He moved faster, his base node hitting her perineum just right.

"Ahhh..."

He rolled her clit between his fingers, increasing the pressure. His breath was loud in her ear. She had trouble catching hers.

She screamed his name when he pinched her clit. Her climax shook them both and she shuddered more when he orgasmed inside her. He wrapped her in a tight hug, his cock still filling her.

"I missed you, Emmy."

She raised a hand to his cheek and turned her head sideways to kiss him.

"I missed you, too." She smiled. "What a nice way to wake up."

He chuckled. "I agree."

She covered his arms with hers, lacing their fingers together. "How's Durek?"

Sighing heavily, he said, "Still unconscious. Ash'n said there was a lot of damage. Vared might not make it."

"He'll make it." Emmy squeezed his hands. "You came in late."

Devik grunted. "I had to take care of the *Intrepid*. I took images of where the attack happened and packed up all of our belongings to return here. Then I programmed the cleaning bots to remove all the blood."

Frowning, she said, "You should have comm'd me. I would've helped you."

"I know, but I needed to do it myself. If I had been there..."

"No." His cock slid from her core and her hands slipped out from his as she turned to face him. "Don't do that to yourself. You had no way of knowing any of that would happen."

He rested his forehead on hers. "In my head, I know that, but Vared is one of my best friends. I consider him a brother. We've been together since our warrior training. I can't help but wonder if I could have prevented it."

Her hand caressed his cheek. "None of us considered someone porting to the *Intrepid*. There was no warning. This is not on you. The traitor is the one who should feel guilt."

Emmy tossed on her "Everyone was thinking it, I just said it" T-shirt and tied her sneakers. Putting on her comm, she looked to ensure she hadn't forgotten anything. *It's amazing how much of my stuff has moved into his quarters in the past couple days.* She smirked as she pulled her hair into a ponytail. *Maybe I can do this relationship stuff. At least with him. We're adjusting really well now.*

She headed down the hall to the lift and took it to the aquiponics area. Taking a deep breath, she inhaled all the fresh scents. *I really do like this part of the ship.*

"Hey, Lin, how's it going?"

Lin looked up from where she was kneeling tending to a plant and smiled.

"Hi, Emmy." She giggled. "I love that shirt."

"Thanks."

"Going for a run?"

"Yes. A few laps around this huge space always makes me feel better." Emmy began stretching. "Anything new happening?"

Lin sat up on her heels and arched her back. "I haven't heard anything other than the commander left the med bay yesterday."

Emmy smiled. "It was a relief to find out he is going to be just fine. I know Devik was really worried."

"We all were. I think Talia moved in with him."

"Really? That doesn't surprise me. Their chemistry has been off the charts since day one." Emmy laughed.

Lin grinned. "I agree. She seems happy."

"She deserves it."

Emmy jogged along the wide pink gravel path that wound along the outside edges of the aquiponics area. She enjoyed the crunch of the small stones as she set a steady pace. *I still can't believe how huge this space is. Four decks tall. Gotta accommodate the trees.* She shook her head. The greenery-covered walls were shaped like an upside-down wedding cake, expanding outward the higher you looked. Ladder-like contraptions and steps interrupted the plants at regular intervals. Lin had told her they were so the food could be harvested easily, as well as for maintenance of the automatic watering and lighting systems.

Through the foliage on her left, she occasionally saw Jevax doing his training forms. *It looks like a form of tai chi.* By the third time she passed Lin with a wave, a layer of light sweat had formed on Emmy's body. Her muscles felt warm and loose. She smiled wickedly as she passed some *tempika* bushes on her left. *I have some good memories of tempika berries. I wonder if any of the women have any chocolate bars. I could return Devik's creativity with melted chocolate on his body.*

Fifty feet later, Emmy's foot caught on an unseen obstacle and she fell forward with a startled scream, scraping her palms and face. She heard the air whistling and then a number of stings on her arms and back. *What the fuck?* She looked at her forearm and it looked like there were eight-centimeter-long needles sticking out of her. *Shit!*

Slowly she moved her hand and tapped her comm and said shakily, "Devik, I need help in the aquiponics area. Bring Rivezt."

"What's wrong?"

"I'm not sure, but I think the traitor is at it again." She drew in a long breath.

"On my way."

Rapid footsteps sounded on the gravel from both directions.

"Lady Emmy, I heard you scream. Are you okay?" Jevax squatted next to her. He growled. "What are those?" He gestured to the metal sticking out of her.

"I don't know, but don't touch them. I already comm'd Tolvex to come with a healer."

"Stay still, Lady Emmy. There are more on your back."

"Emmy? What happened?" Lin's voice sounded behind her.

"Stop, Lin! I think there's a tripwire on the path. Be careful where you step," Emmy called. *Please don't let her get hurt, too.*

"What?" Lin's footsteps slowed.

Jevax's thighs bunched as he stood and walked toward Emmy's legs. He carefully placed his feet as he searched for the trap. He squatted again and pushed aside some leaves before finding an end.

"I see one side. Some of the needles are still embedded in the source."

Pounding boots on gravel sounded behind Lin.

Jevax said, "Slowly. There's a tripwire that shoots something from it."

Growls sounded as the pounding tapered off.

"I see it," said Devik angrily. Moments later, he knelt next to Emmy. "Are you alright, *milara*?" His chest rumbled. The air moved around her from his swishing tail.

"I might've twisted my ankle, but I've got these things sticking out of me," Emmy said in a rush.

Rivezt crouched on her other side. "Don't move. Let me scan you first and get these out of you."

Emmy grimaced. "Good plan." *Damn this gravel is starting to feel really uncomfortable. Funny how I didn't notice until he told me I couldn't move.*

"Do they hurt?"

"They sting like paper cuts...a whole crapload of them."

Rivezt said, "I need a sterile container to collect these to ensure they weren't coated with anything."

Lin said, "I'll be right back with my bag."

Rivezt scanned Emmy. "Your right ankle is sprained, but not broken." He pulled something that looked like long curved tweezers out of his med kit.

Lin said breathlessly. "Here. I have collection bottles in different sizes. Which do you need?"

Rivezt used the tweezers to pull out a needle and hold it up. "Do you have one that can hold something this long?"

"Yes." Lin said as she rustled in her bag. Out of the corner of her eye, Emmy saw Lin hold the bottle while Rivezt released the needle from the tweezers. The tinny clink sounded loud to Emmy. She suppressed a shudder when she saw her blood coating the tip.

"Lady Lin, if you could hold the bottle while I remove the remainder, it would help."

"Of course." Lin knelt next to Emmy and gently touched her hand. "How are you doing?"

"Fine. Just uncomfortable." More clinks filled Emmy's ears.

"This shouldn't take long," said Rivezt.

"Lieutenant," Jevax said. "Assuming the configuration was the same as what is left on this, twenty-seven needles were released from here."

With a low, steady rumbling emanating from his chest, Devik leaned close and spoke softly in her ear, "I want to be here for you, but I also need to investigate. What do you need from me?" *He's such a good male.* Emmy relaxed as she inhaled his scent.

"You'll be close. Please find out what happened, Devik." *It's better to keep him occupied while Rivezt does his thing.*

Devik checked out what Jevax had found and took images. Emmy heard him move to the other side of the path and growl when he found a similar thing there.

"We're looking for a total of fifty-four needles."

"I've removed fifteen so far," said Rivezt. "I do not think all of them impacted Lady Emmy."

"I see some on the gravel," said Lin.

"Don't touch them with your bare hands. We don't know if they're safe to touch," said Devik.

"Was it a tripwire?" Emmy said, her cheek scraping the gravel.

"Yes."

After Rivezt finished removing a total of thirty-three needles from Emmy's body, Devik, Jevax, and Lin found the remaining ones either on the gravel or embedded in nearby plants, which were put in a separate container. Lin put on gloves and gently removed impacted plants and placed them in other collection containers. She took off her gloves, leaving them inside out, and put them in her bag.

Emmy sat up and Rivezt treated her scrapes and ankle. Devik used some of Rivezt's sealant on his hands, then detached the tripwire at both ends and put it in another of Lin's containers.

Jevax said, "Tolvex, does it seem to you that there have been too many incidents involving the human females? I think someone is trying to harm them."

Devik nodded. "It appears that way. We're investigating." He leveled a stare at the male. "Do not speak of this to anyone, Jevax. We have our reasons for not making it widely known."

"As you command, Lieutenant." Jevax nodded. "If you need any assistance, I am happy to volunteer. I do not like knowing someone is trying to hurt females." An angry rumble emanated from his chest and his tail flicked in short movements.

"I'll inform the commander," said Devik.

"Uh, about that. I'd rather Talia didn't know about this, Devik," Emmy said.

He turned to her. "Why not?"

"She and the commander have had a couple of rough days and he was just released from the med bay. I really don't want to cause her any more stress right now." Emmy said with a frown. "They've been through a lot recently."

Devik nodded. "I'll brief Wurvez and let him know your concerns."

"Let's get you back to the med bay, Lady Emmy, so I can treat you properly," Rivezt said.

"I'm not sure I can walk."

"Hold on to me," said Devik as he picked her up. "Jevax, check the remainder of the path to ensure there aren't any more traps."

Jevax nodded. "If I find anything, I will notify you."

Rivezt and Lin toted the containers to the med bay, while Devik carried Emmy. A near-constant growl from his chest and flicking tail concerned Emmy.

"I'm fine, Devik."

"You were hurt."

"I've fallen before. Rivezt said it was just a sprain."

"You could have been seriously injured from those needles. We still don't know if they were coated with anything that could harm you."

"But I wasn't and I feel fine." She reached up a hand and caressed his jaw. "Save the anger until we know what's what."

He leaned into her palm and whispered, "You are my everything, Emmy. I can't stand the idea of anything bad happening to you."

Emmy blinked at the sudden tears in her eyes. *Damn, he's so sweet.* She nuzzled his neck and whispered, "I've never been anyone's everything."

Turning his head, he kissed her. "You're mine."

In the med bay, Rivezt tested the needles for harmful substances. Emmy was relieved that nothing was found. The healer had her change into a medical gown and he cleaned each site before using a healing wand. Devik's growls grew less as Rivezt healed the scrapes on her face, hands, and ankle. After she changed back into her regular clothes, Devik hustled her to his quarters.

Lifting her up, he pinned her to the wall and kissed her voraciously. Extending his claws, he tore her shorts from her body and lifted her with his hands under her ass. *Oh, that's hot.* She groaned as he plunged into her with one smooth motion. His tail played with her breasts under her shirt. She kicked off her sneakers and wrapped her legs around him, resting her stockinged feet on his ass. His buttocks flexed as he pounded into her wet core.

In time with his thrusts, Devik chanted in her ear, "Mine. Mine. Mine." Emmy felt her climax building as her hips met his over and over. Their heavy breathing and thuds from each time she was pressed against the wall filled the room. As she gasped for air, his campfire scent filled her lungs. His tail dropped to her clit and she bit on his shoulder to keep from screaming as fireworks burst throughout her body. His fangs scraped her neck and she clenched her inner muscles harder. He came so hard, she felt the warmth spreading deep within her. She rested her head on his shoulder when her body relaxed.

"Wow, Devik," she whispered. She ran her hands along his taut back muscles.

Through gritted teeth, he said, "No one will hurt you again. Ever."

Chapter 25

"I'm sorry," Devik said. *I'm such a naroon.*

"For what?"

Devik smoothed the crease between Emmy's brows with the pad of his forefinger.

"I should be caring for you after your ordeal, not using your body so roughly."

She smiled. "I think you cared for me quite well." Her expression turned serious. She placed her palms on his cheeks and stared at him earnestly. "Devik, I may not be confident about emotional intimacy, but I am about physical interactions. If I am unwilling or not enjoying myself, I have no problems speaking up for myself."

He rested his forehead on hers, inhaling her scent.

"I don't deserve you."

"No, you deserve better, but for some reason you want me." She kissed him. "I really am fine. Great actually, after being fucked so thoroughly."

Chuckling, he carried her toward the sanitary facilities. *Crek. Walking with my cock in her cunt is distracting in all the right ways.* When she squeezed her inner muscles around his shaft, his stride faltered.

"So naughty, *milara.* Do you want me to drop you?"

She giggled, then moaned when he squeezed her ass, claws pricking at her skin. "No, I just couldn't resist."

He turned on the shower, then lowered her so she could stand on her own. Her groan matched his as he slipped from her wet heat.

"I like seeing my seed run down your inner thighs."

"Caveman." She caressed his pecs.

Leaning down, he kissed her.

"I'm a lucky male."

She looked up at him through her lashes as she took off her socks. "Play your cards right, warrior, and you'll get lucky again." Pulling off her shirt, she laughed as she entered the shower.

He grinned as he undressed and joined her. *I would follow her anywhere.*

"At least we have good security footage of everyone who entered and exited the aquiponics area," said Karid.

"True, but we don't know how long the tripwire was there," Devik said with a frown. "Emmy said she had already run two laps without an issue."

"What about the moisture in there? Did it affect any parts of the tripwire?" Vared said.

"The needles were tempered valadium, so there would be no rust. The tripwire itself was a clear plastic. Again, no rust," Devik said.

"So how far back do we go? If we can thin out our suspect list, it would help," said Karid.

"When did Lady Emmy start running in there regularly?" asked Vared. "I would think that would be a starting point. I doubt the traitor would be trying to hurt Lady Lin in that way. Her movements, testing, and harvesting, are slower and more measured. It would not be as likely she would encounter the trap."

Devik tapped out a message to Emmy. He looked up at his friends. "She says she started running regularly almost three weeks ago."

"Then find out who has been in and out of there since then and when," Vared ordered.

"As you command," said Devik.

"For now, I will not tell Talia about the incident. I agree with Lady Emmy that Talia does not need more stress right now."

Karid and Devik nodded.

"How are you feeling?" Karid asked.

"Better now that I'm in my own quarters," Vared said. "I should be back to full strength soon."

Devik smiled. "We are happy you are recovering so well, Vared. You had us worried."

Vared's fangs were bright against his lips as he grinned. "I have much to live for these days."

Devik and Karid chuckled.

"I've programmed several bots to travel the paths multiple times a day to keep searching for similar traps in the future," Devik said.

"He probably won't do the same thing twice," said Karid, his normally cheerful countenance was serious.

"We can't take the chance, though," said Vared. "We need to ensure the safety of the females."

Over the next several days, Devik and Emmy compiled the list, noting dates and times of each warrior entering and exiting the aquiponics area and by which door. While there were security cameras within the area, they primarily covered the center, not the outlying paths. Devik grumbled as he calculated how many cameras he needed to synthesize to correct the issue.

If they didn't have to deal with finding the traitor, Devik would have no complaints at all. Vared was healing quickly. Emmy was beginning to open herself up more to him and the other females. Her confidence was blossoming. He loved seeing her happiness. He only wished she was ready to true mate. His fangs had been elongating regularly.

"Wurvez, Tolvex, meet me in the on-call room," Vared's voice sounded from Devik's comm.

"Crek. Wonder what's going on?" Devik said as he rose from his desk.

"Well, get going and find out," Emmy said from her seat on his couch, waving a hand in the air.

"Vixen." He kissed her forehead. "I'll punish you later for your insolence."

She grinned. "Promise?"

He laughed as he left his office.

Devik met Karid in the hall.

"Do you know what this is about?" Karid said.

Devik's braids brushed his shoulders as he shook his head. "No idea."

Vared and Lady Talia were waiting for them in the on-call room.

"Watch this," growled Vared.

A recording of an Earth press conference accusing the Svesti of kidnapping the human females played. Growls emanated from Karid's chest as well as Devik's when he heard the call for military funding.

Devik looked at Lady Talia. Her face was set in hard lines. *She's not happy either.*

"What are we going to do about these lies?" asked Karid.

"Talia has an idea that has been approved by the king," Vared said as he nodded at her.

Lady Talia outlined her plan. Karid asked a few questions, then nodded with a smile.

"Emmy and I will help. Just tell us what you need from us," Devik said.

"I need to sit and make a list of everything, but I'll definitely need help," Lady Talia said. "Vared has arranged for the *Defiant* to send us regular updates on Earth's media so we can be sure to have the most current information."

Devik's tablet sounded an alert and he looked down to read it. He handed it to Vared, whose face hardened as he took in the information. Vared passed the tablet to Karid. Karid grinned widely when he saw what it said.

"*Kirani*, if we are done here, I have to speak to the males alone. Did you have anything else you needed at this time?" Vared said.

Lady Talia's face scrunched in confusion. "That's all I have for now until I compile my list." She kissed Vared's cheek. "I'll head out and you can do your super-secret ship business."

"Thank you." Vared smiled at her.

After the door closed behind her. Vared said, "Where is it?"

Devik took back the tablet and pointed. "It shows the Frezzian freighter passed by here less than a day ago."

"Are you sure it's the same one that was slowing down regularly at XB9428B where the Zuvgran lab was?" Vared asked.

"Yes."

Karid said, "I volunteer to find it and get some answers."

"You can't go alone and I need one of you here with this nonsense from Earth going on," said Vared.

Devik said, "You can take one of my security males or Jevax."

"Why Jevax?" asked Vared.

"He is aware that someone is trying to harm the females. He helped when Emmy was hurt in the aquiponics bay."

"Are we certain he isn't the traitor?"

Karid nodded. "Yes. He was eliminated early on. He was elsewhere on the security tapes during the poisoning of Ladies Talia and Emmy and also during the time frame when the upload that hurt Lady Talia was switched."

"Take Jevax. Bring him up to date on everything on the way. No heroics, Karid. Get information if you can, then meet back with us. You know our route." Vared stared at Karid.

"As you command. We'll leave within the hour."

After Karid left, Vared said, "Prep suitable transportation and supplies. Also, I want them to have emergency trackers."

"You know Karid won't like that," Devik said with a grimace.

"Too bad. If they don't need to use them, I'll be happy. However, if they need them and aren't equipped, I would be remiss as their commander."

"You couldn't have told him yourself?"

Vared laughed. "I'm still recuperating. I don't need the argument."

Devik sent a message to Jevax's section leader informing him Jevax was on special assignment for the foreseeable future. He then arranged for Hangar Bay Alpha to be empty for the next several hours and let the males know where to meet him. While Karid and Jevax were packing, Devik outfitted one of the smaller security shuttles with emergency ration packs, water pouches, nanosuits, and a variety of weapons. The *Tenacity* had a small brig, defensive weapons, and cloaking capabilities. He double checked the shuttle's maintenance logs to ensure all was as it should be. An extra medkit and some covert spying equipment rounded out his preparations. *Hopefully, that is everything they may need.*

Karid and Jevax arrived at the same time, bags in hand.

"Here's a list of what I put onboard the *Tenacity* in addition to what is normally stocked," Devik said as he forwarded the info to their comms. "The commander has also ordered emergency trackers for each of you." He held up two syringes.

Karid frowned. "We can inject them when we're on our way."

Devik's braids swooshed as he shook his head. "No, not taking the chance you'll disobey orders."

Karid grunted. He opened his mouth wide and Devik injected the tracker underneath his tongue. Karid made a face and moved his jaw in exaggerated circular motions.

"I hate these things. They make me feel like I've got a pebble in my mouth."

Devik and Jevax laughed. Jevax opened his mouth for his.

Devik said, "These are the upgraded trackers. We received a lot of complaints about the heat from the old ones as well as the fact that it was too easy to inadvertently activate them with the shorter codes. The activation code for these is clicking your teeth in a three-two-two pattern or tapping it directly with a claw in the same pattern. You should feel a minute of cold under your tongue to let you know the activation was successful. Inactivated, they should pass any frequency scan for trackers."

"With the Goddess' favor, we won't need them," said Jevax.

Devik nodded and stepped back. "Let me know when you finish your preflight checks and I'll open the bay doors. The engine signature you're following is already loaded in the *Tenacity's* computer. Stay safe and good hunting."

Devik watched them board the *Tenacity* and waited for the ramp to close before taking a position at the workstation closest to the corridor entrance. When Jevax requested clearance to depart, Devik entered his security code to open the bay doors. A force field appeared midway between him and the bay doors to protect him from the vacuum of space as the doors slid open. As he closed the doors after their departure, he said a silent prayer to the Goddess that their mission was successful and they returned unharmed.

Devik and the human females took over the War Room as they worked to enact Lady Talia's plan. Each female compiled a list of reputable journalists in each of their countries with contact information. They then expanded to other countries, researching Earth's internet to find more names.

Emmy and Devik compiled the videos for Lady Talia. Devik wasn't sure exactly what else Emmy was doing, but she and Lady Talia were constantly on Emmy's laptop.

Several days later, Lady Talia said she was ready. Devik coordinated Lady Talia's wishes to the *Defiant* so that she could contact her sister for help and introduced Emmy to their communications officer. She walked the male through various technical issues to transfer all the information to the appropriate Earth internet accounts. *I hope this works as Lady Talia believes.*

Chapter 26

Emmy sighed with relief once the *Defiant* successfully uploaded all the information to the places she wanted them. Long ago, she had set up numerous blind email and video accounts. She gave Talia access to one of each to use to keep her family one more step removed from the shitstorm that was going to hit Earth once the correct information was released publicly. *They deserve it, lying to the public so heinously.*

Talia ended the comm with the *Defiant.* She smiled, her brown eyes twinkling.

"Thank you all for all your help. We'll probably need to do more once everything hits the internet tomorrow, but the truth will be out there. I appreciate everyone making videos telling their stories. That, combined with the Svesti videos with Earth's leaders, will go a long way to establishing our veracity. We make a good team."

"If you need anything else, just let us know," Rachel said with a grin.

"They shouldn't have lied to us or to the public," said Ava. She spread her arms wide. "Huge mistake."

Everyone laughed.

Talia grinned. "I've got to go and hope my sister got the coded message to talk. This won't work without her and my son, Joshua, doing their parts."

"Do you foresee them refusing?" asked Natasha.

Talia shook her head. "No, we're close. They'll do what is needed." She frowned. "I'm just concerned whether or not the American government is monitoring them."

Lin said, "They're not in danger, are they?"

"I don't believe so," Talia said. "Thanks, again, ladies." She left the War Room.

Emmy listened to the chatter around her as she reached for two of Ava's cookies. Absently, she handed one to Devik before biting into the other. *Mmm, I don't know how Ava does it, but her cookies are addictive. Snickerdoodles today. Yum.*

Looking around, she was surprised at how proud she was of their efforts, how much she had enjoyed the past several days, and how hard everyone had worked to pull the plan together. *I guess trusting them makes all the difference.*

She sucked in a breath. *Is it that simple? Trusting him and trusting myself?* She tilted her head and tapped her fingers on her knee. Devik's tail wrapped around her ankle.

He leaned toward her and said quietly, "Is everything well, *milara*? You appear to be thinking deep thoughts."

She turned to gaze into his concerned teal eyes. Her own widened. *I do. I trust him with my secrets. I trust him to care, stay with me, and try to make things right. And now I trust myself to do the same.* She grinned widely.

"We need to go, Devik." She giggled at his brows connecting. "Everything is more than alright." Waving at the women, she said, "We're off. Got something we need to take care of."

Knowing grins flashed her way as she grabbed Devik's hand and pulled him behind her. She rushed them to his quarters.

"What's going on, Emmy?" Devik said once they were alone.

She tugged at his shirt to untuck it. He'd taken to wearing one more often to hide the scratches she sometimes left on his body during sex. Her hands slowed when she reached his warm skin. Sliding her palms with her fingers spread along his torso and onto his back, she mewled.

"I want to true mate with you, Devik." She smiled when she saw his eyes darken.

"Are you sure? I do not want you to have doubts." His nostrils flared and his large hands encircled her waist.

"I'm positive. I want to spend my life with you." An expression of pure joy expanded across his face.

Devik tapped his comm. "Tesix. I am forwarding all security calls to you. I have an important meeting and cannot be interrupted." After receiving an acknowledgement, he tapped his comm again.

"Now I am all yours, Emmy." He kissed her before carrying her into the bedroom. He undressed her, caressing her exposed skin reverently. He hastily stripped off his clothes.

Voice low, he said, "On the bed, *milara*."

She turned and crawled up on the mattress. Looking over her shoulder when she heard his growls, she shivered when she saw him licking his full lips at the sight of her backside. *No one has ever made me feel as sexy as he does.*

"On your back and let me give you pleasure."

Following his instructions, she sighed as he kissed a trail up one leg while his tail brushed a path on her other leg. He raised her knees over his shoulders. Slowly tonguing her clit, he increased the pressure on her swollen bud until she was panting and wriggling trying to get closer. He stopped and breathed on her.

"You are my partner, my love, and my reason for being, Emmy." Licking his way to her engorged breasts, he continued, "I love your heart, your mind, and your soul." He suckled on the stiff peaks and dragged his fangs across them. "You bring joy, laughter, and color to my life." He trailed warm wet kisses to her neck and ear. Breath hot, he said, "I will protect you always. I will never leave you behind."

She gasped as his cock entered her with his last words. Her hips rose to meet his in a steady rhythm. Her restless hands grasped at his flesh as their combined scent surrounded her. *This. This is making love. How beautiful.*

"I am yours." He grunted as his pace quickened. "You. Are. Mine. Forever."

"Yes. I am yours and you are mine, Devik." She tweaked his hard nipples causing him to hiss. "I love you. I will call no other male *mate.* Only you."

His chuckle was strained. "Come for me, *milara.*"

Tingles chased down her spine. His pace increased and his base node struck her clit repeatedly. Panting, she arched her back as her climax overtook her. She bit his shoulder hard enough to draw blood. His fangs dug into her shoulder and her pleasure expanded. Her body shuddered and her pussy spasmed uncontrollably squeezing his cock.

Surprised, she released his shoulder and stared at him. *Oh my god. His cock is vibrating better than BB ever has.* Wonder shone in Devik's eyes as he roared her name as he came.

Drawing in harsh breaths as they recovered, she savored his weight pressing on her. *I feel so safe with him.*

"Why didn't you tell me your cock could vibrate?" she said when she could speak again. He rolled them to their sides.

"I didn't know. It's never done that before." He looked pensive. "Maybe it's because of the true mating."

She traced lazy patterns on his chest. "Well, if you biting me means you'll vibrate, I suggest you get those fangs out more often."

Laughing, he brushed her hair from her face. "I'll take that under advisement." At the change in her expression, he asked, "What?"

Awestruck, she said, "Look." Her fingers were on his clan marking. "It's gold."

He drew back and glanced down at himself, then his eyes widened. "You have one now."

They both sat up and examined the changes in their bodies. Emmy said, "What does this mean?"

He grinned widely. "Oh, *milara*. It means we are fated mates. The Goddess has blessed us."

Fated mates? "Didn't you say there haven't been fated mates in a century?"

"Yes. We never even considered humans could be our fated mates." Softly, his claw outlined her new clan marking. "This is incredible." He hugged her close and dropped small kisses along her neck.

Sighing against his chest, she tried wrapping her mind around the fact that she'd found the one person in the universe who was meant for her. *It's unbelievable. But how else to explain it all?*

She raised her head and smiled. "Maybe that's the reason for your cock vibrating."

"We'll have to see if it'll do it again." He fell back and pulled her on top of him. Tugging on her nipples, he said with a wide grin, "So, how did I compare to BB?"

Laughing, she slapped his chest. "If your cock is going to vibrate on a regular basis, I think BB will be going into retirement."

After Emmy and Devik discovered his cock vibrating was not a one-time event, they discussed when to tell everyone about being fated mates. They decided to wait a little while since there was so much going on with Talia's plan to inform Earth of the truth.

They spent a lot of time in the War Room once Talia's videos went viral. The women sorted the press and social media by usefulness, so that Durek and King Sovex would have the most relevant information.

A couple days into the media frenzy, Devik became distracted. When they were alone in their quarters, Emmy rubbed his shoulders where he sat on a couch.

"What's wrong, mate?"

"We lost contact with Karid and Jevax. They haven't checked in today."

"Was their mission dangerous?" She dug her thumbs into a particularly tense knot to loosen it.

"It shouldn't have been. There is a Frezzian freighter we suspect has been supplying Zuvgran labs. They were following their energy signature to see if we can find other labs. If they were able to hack into the freighter's computers, then maybe we could find out where they've been. Worst case scenario would be to take a Frezzian prisoner and interrogate them." Devik groaned as the knot in his shoulder gave way. "Your hands are magic, *milara*."

She smiled as she massaged him. "Maybe they just haven't had a chance to check in. You know—following a lead or something."

He tilted his head to give her better access. "Perhaps. It's just so soon after Vared was critically injured. I hate to think something may have happened to Karid also."

She kissed him below his ear. "My big, strong warrior has a marshmallow heart. It's an intoxicating combination."

He grunted. "Come sit with me. It's my turn to rub your parts."

She shuddered. "Anything you say. Mate."

"It's been four days since we've heard from Karid and Jevax," said Devik with a worried look on his face. His tail flicked behind him in short bursts. He picked at the morning meal in front of him.

Emmy reached for his hand. "What can we do to find them?"

"They had emergency trackers, but as far as we can tell, neither has been activated. We sent out a message to all Svesti ships to scan for them." Devik shook his head. "I don't understand what could have happened."

"Can you track their ship?" Emmy's appetite waned as her concern for Devik and his friends grew.

"Possibly. But that means sending another team after them."

"Have you suggested it to Durek?"

"No, not yet." Sadness filled his teal eyes.

"Well, let's go do that now. You'll feel better doing something." She smiled gently as she squeezed his hand. "We can also tell him about us being fated mates. Maybe give some good news to offset the bad?"

He sighed. "You're right. Let's go talk to Vared." They cleaned up the remains of their meal and picked up their tablets. Before they left their quarters, he pulled her into his arms and rested his forehead on hers.

"Thank you, Emmy."

"For what?"

"For being you. Knowing you care and want to help eases the burden some." He kissed her.

"That's what mates are for, right?" Her fingers traced the lines on his forehead with her free hand. "To share the good, the bad, and the ugly?"

He smiled. "Never stop being you, *milara*."

"I don't know who else to be."

Chapter 27

"What can I do for you?" said Vared as Devik and Emmy entered the on-call room.

"I'd like to send Security Team Alpha to see if they can find out why we haven't heard from Karid and Jevax," said Devik. "I'm concerned."

"Have they all been cleared from the suspect list?"

"Yes."

"Who's on the team?"

"Kalix, Tesix, Xoriv, and Westov."

Vared thought for a moment. "Has Brauvix been cleared?"

Devik tapped his tablet. "Yes. He was on duty on the bridge for the first two incidents."

"Add him to the team. It's time he had more field experience and his abilities will complement the others on Security Team Alpha."

"I'd like to put Tesix in charge. His specialty is tactical."

"I agree," said Vared. "Is that all?" His lavender eyes glanced at Emmy.

"There is one more thing you should know," said Emmy. She reached for Devik's hand.

Devik smiled. "Emmy and I are mated."

"Congratulations, my friend." Vared grinned widely.

"It's a fated mate pairing." Devik's tail wrapped around Emmy's waist.

"Fated mates?" Vared said. "Are you sure?"

Devik and Emmy both pulled the collars of their shirts down to expose their gold clan markings. Emmy's true mating scar showed as well. Vared's grin grew wider as he tugged on his own collar showing his changed clan marking. *Two fated mate pairings? What are the odds? But I'm glad for my friend.*

"You and Talia, too?" Emmy asked with a happy smile.

"Yes. Two fated mate pairings. This is wonderful news for both our species," said Vared. He frowned. "Now we just need the humans to agree to the treaty."

"It may take awhile, but we'll get there," said Emmy. "You and Talia did a great job drafting a fair treaty. It truly will benefit both our races."

"From your lips to the Goddess' ears," Vared said. "We'll have to celebrate your mating when we arrive at Costonia."

"And yours," Devik added with a grin before his face fell. "I only hope Karid will be back in time to celebrate with us."

"We'll find him," said Vared with a determined look, his facial scar whitening. "I will accept no other alternative." *If will alone could make it happen, Vared could do it.*

Emmy left and Devik remained with Vared. Vared comm'd Brauvix and Security Team Alpha to join them. Vared briefed the warriors on the traitor, as well as Karid's mission. He nodded at Devik to continue.

"Finish your shifts, pack, and then meet me at the *Rectitude* in Hangar Bay Bravo. I'll have everything loaded except your personal belongings. Specifics for the Frezzian freighter's engine signature, the *Tenacity*, emergency trackers for Wurvez and Jevax, and last known position will be loaded for you. Tesix will be in command of this mission. Tell no one of your mission or the traitor." Devik looked at Tesix. "Check in daily. If you require more assistance, it will be forthcoming. Any questions?"

The males looked at each other, then Tesix said, "If we find them and everything is okay, what do you want us to do?"

"Make a field decision on whether to remain with Wurvez and Jevax as support or return," said Vared. "Depending on why we've lost communications with them, they may find the additional warriors helpful."

Tesix nodded. "As you command."

Vared's pinned each of the males with a hard look. "I already have two missing warriors. Do not make it seven. Am I clear?"

The five males thumped their chests with fists. "Yes, sir." The males filed out of the on-call room.

Vared looked at Devik. "They'll find them."

"From your lips to the Goddess' ears, Vared. I hope so."

Devik left the on-call room and repeated all the preparations he'd done for Karid and Jevax in Hangar Bay Bravo while adding additional supplies for the extra warriors. The *Rectitude* was larger than the *Tenacity* but had the same cloaking ability. It also had more defensive weapons, a larger brig, additional quarters and a small training area.

There were a couple hours left before the males would leave, so Devik joined Emmy and the other human females in the War Room to sort Earth's reactions to Talia's videos while he waited. They all paused when Vared's voice sounded over the speakers.

"Attention all hands. We are currently enroute to Talonka Six to answer a distress call. There has been a collapse in an arbixium mine and 281 miners are trapped. It is unclear at this time whether all trapped beings are Ermipas. Prepare for search and rescue and massive casualties.

"We should arrive in approximately eleven hours. Medical personnel, gather your supplies and coordinate the loading. Section Leaders, prepare your shuttles. Adjust rest periods as needed to be prepared. When we have more information on what may need to be synthesized and loaded, I will send it to you. Commander Durek out."

Devik checked his tablet for more information. *Crek. What else can go wrong?*

Rachel looked at Devik. "How can we help?"

He looked at the females, all waiting for how to assist a race they'd never heard of until today. *These are good females. We are lucky the Goddess made us compatible with them.*

"Lady Natasha, you will obviously be needed in the med bay. Medical personnel will be in charge of triage and treatment procedures on the planet. Perhaps Lady Lin could assist in gathering supplies."

"Of course. I'll have to ask the healers for information on Ermipa physiology, but I'm sure that won't be a problem," Lady Natasha said. "Come on, Lin. Let's see if there are any natural remedies for Ermipas that you might be able to prepare in advance as well." She and Lady Lin left the room.

Ava said, "I'll check with Talen and see if there are any special dietary requirements for Ermipas. I'll start making food for them, as well as for the warriors. I'll probably have to prepare some liquid and bland nutrition for some of the injured. I'll make sure the food for the Svesti is easily portable."

Devik smiled and nodded. "That would be helpful." Ava rushed out.

"We'll need a way to track the injured," said Emmy. "Do you already have a program I can modify for situations like these or should I come up with a new one?"

"We have a very basic one. I'll send it to you," said Devik. "If you can make it better, please do so."

"I'm on it, mate," Emmy bumped shoulders with him.

"What about me?" said Rachel.

"I think for now, it would be best if you worked with our supply master, Volax, ensuring we have the basics—blankets, cots, tents, etc.—to distribute to the shuttles. It looks like Talonka Six is transmitting what they think they'll need. Perhaps keep track of what goes where. I'll let Volax know you're coming."

"On my way," said Rachel as she left.

Emmy sighed. "Let's get to it. Maybe we'll get some time to rest before we arrive. It sounds like we'll be busy for several days."

He leaned over and kissed her. "There's no one else I'd rather be busy with."

Giggling, she said, "Remind me to explain the human expression 'getting busy' to you sometime."

He said in confusion. "Okay."

"Uncle, we are responding to a distress call. Our arrival on Costonia will be delayed."

"That works out well. I have a meeting with our co-conspirators in two days. The delay will give us time to put everything in place." His uncle's voice sounded eager.

"What are your orders?" Muscles tense, the male held his breath. *I didn't like using Nerid. While he is weak, the male did not deserve to have his brain muddled. I feel as if I'm too exposed.*

"Take no action, but keep alert for information that may prove useful. You must avoid suspicion. Do not contact me again until you reach the home world. Always Svesti."

The younger male released his breath slowly, and his shoulders relaxed.

"As you command. Always Svesti." Relief filled him as he disconnected the comm.

Several hours later, Devik met Emmy back in their quarters. He told her the search team had left. While they ate, Emmy told him she modified the program by adding triage columns for the healers. She also added multiple generic location columns that could be labeled based on where an incident occurred. When he questioned her, she said the columns could be beds, tents, floors, buildings, even towns. *I love her mind.*

"That's a good idea, *milara*. Before we leave the *Invictus*, we'll ensure everyone has it and understands it. The program should make it much easier to keep track of victims."

"I've coded it to automatically populate to a main computer, then that computer will update all the lists periodically."

He beamed at her. "Excellent. Anyone with the program would be able to tell a family where to find a loved one."

She ducked her head at his praise, heat rising on her cheeks. "Thanks."

"Come here, Emmy. It's been too long since I've held you."

She laughed and straddled him. Her fingers played with the hair at his nape sending tendrils of sensation down his spine. His hands stroked her back under her shirt. She wiggled on his lap, rubbing her cunt on his hardening cock. Her arousal scent rose.

"Are we getting busy?" she asked coyly.

He narrowed his eyes at her. "Does getting busy mean making love to my mate?"

Grinning, she said, "It means having sex. Love and mates may or may not be involved."

"When we get busy, love and mates will always be involved, *milara.*" He nuzzled her neck, dragging his fangs over her mating mark.

She gasped and bucked against him. "That's so sensitive."

He pulled his head back. "Good or bad?"

She tugged his hair to bring him closer. "Good, oh so good, Devik."

He smiled against her skin before licking the scar of his bite. She hissed and threw her head back. His tail slid under her shirt to rub her hard nipples. *She's so responsive. I'm a lucky male.*

Tightening his stomach and thigh muscles, he stood and carried her to their bed. His tail played with her clit as they stripped. She spread her lush thighs and his tail dipped into her hot, wet cunt. She moaned as the long, slow thrusts built her arousal. He grabbed her ankles and pulled her to the edge of the bed. He clasped her legs to his chest. Moving his hips in the same rhythm as his tail, his cock dragged over her clit.

"Are you ready for my cock, Emmy? Or should I make you come with my tail?"

Sweat glistened on her flushed skin. "Give me your cock, Devik. I need it."

"As you wish." He withdrew his tail, soaked with her wetness, and pressed it against her rear entrance. Her eyes widened.

Unable to wait any longer, he pushed his cock into her swollen cunt with one quick motion, pushing his tail into her rosebud simultaneously.

"Oh, yes!" Her hands grasped the sheets in tight fists and she tossed her head from side to side. "So fucking full."

Devik gazed at the erotic picture she made—brown curls awry, dewy skin, and her sheath gripping his cock. She clenched her inner muscles and he jerked.

"Move, dammit. I want more."

He chuckled darkly. "I'll always give you more, Emmy."

His claws pricked her skin as he held her in place. He slowly withdrew his cock while pushing his tail in deeper. She uttered one continuous moan as he reversed the motion. Point, counterpoint. Over and over. Faster and faster. Some part of him filled her at all times. Her moans became whooshes of air as the tension in both their bodies built. He moved a hand to finger her slippery clit.

Her body stiffened and she screamed his name as her climax overtook her, triggering his orgasm when her cunt seized on his cock and her ass squeezed his tail. Spasms of pleasure shook them both. Gasping for breath, he reluctantly pulled his tail and cock from her and collapsed face-first on the bed next to her. She rolled over to throw an arm over his back.

"Wow, Devik. Just wow." She laughed tiredly. "I'm impressed with your coordination."

He laughed as he rolled over. "You inspire me."

She smiled and kissed his pec. "I love you. I'm glad you didn't give up on me."

"I will never give up on you, *milara*. I love you more than I can say."

"Just keep showing me and I think we'll be good." She raised her head to give him a mischievous grin.

"Rest. We'll be busy once we reach Talonka Six." His claws threaded through her curls in a soothing, brushing motion.

"Mmm," she mumbled as her head rested on his chest. "Feels good."

He smiled to himself as her breathing evened out. *There is right and there is wrong and nothing is more right than this.*

Recap

Races thus far

Human - Enough said.

Svesti - Warrior Race. About seven feet tall, skin in various shades of bronze, semi-retractable fangs, tails, and retractable claws. Ruled by a King. Honorable race protecting many regions of space from the Zuvgran, including near Earth. Most Svesti females died or were rendered infertile thirty Earth years prior due to a virus released by the Zuvgran. Plural is Svesti.

Durelian - Mercenary Race. About seven feet tall, orange skin, three bulbous black eyes.

Ermipa - Mining Race. About four feet tall, furry, round head, oval eyes.

Estalan - Sybaritic Race. Known for its quality liquors and drugs.

Frezzian - Mercenary Race. Adverse to personal risk. Considered dishonorable.

Jalaxian - Warrior Race. About seven feet tall, blue skin, fangs, retractable claws and tail. Considered honorable. Many work as mercenaries after the Zuvgran decimated their world fifty Earth years ago.

Pellotian - Avian Race. Green skin and colorful wings.

Zuvgran - Warrior Race. About seven feet tall, gray skin, fangs, claws and horns. Ruled by an Emperor. Dishonorable race that invades planets to strip them of their resources and take the inhabitants as slaves. Considered violent. Plural is Zuvgran.

Planets and Space Stations thus far

Earth - Really not the center of the universe as humans might believe.

Costonia - Svesti Home World.

Talonka Six - Mining world closer to Costonia than Earth. Fourth planet in the Lestanus system.

Theron - Space Station approximately one quarter of the distance from Earth to Costonia.

XB9428B - Uninhabited planet, home to a Zuvgran lab.

Svesti Houses

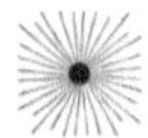 **Davelk** - Ruling House of Costonia.

 **Binova** - Primarily merchants.

 **Fresida** - Primarily educators and scientists.

 **Glixon** - Primarily merchants.

 **Kreliz** - Primarily scientists.

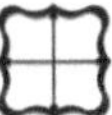 **Midnar** - Primarily agriculture.

 **Nuxar** - One of the two Houses that strictly adhere to the old ways of worship.

 **Ruxila** - Primarily agriculture.

 **Srotix** - One of the two Houses that strictly adhere to the old ways of worship.

 **Troliv** - Primarily merchants.

 **Vramel** - Primarily warriors and educators.

 **Yula** - Many Svesti healers come from House Yula.

 **Terran** - New human clan marking.

Characters

Humans

Emmy Norton - Australian, hacker.

Lin Chang - Chinese, botanist.

Rachel Llewellyn - British, MI-6.

Natasha Petrov - Russian, medical doctor.

Talia Sullivan - American, U.S. Ambassador of Interplanetary Relations, author.

Ava Taylor - Canadian, chef.

Svesti

King Traxen Sovex of House Davelk - King of the Svesti.

Lieutenant Devik Tolvex of House Vramel - Head security officer on the *Invictus*.

Lieutenant Triv'n Brauvix of House Kreliz - Communications officer on the *Invictus*.

Lieutenant Hozan Crulex of House Yula - Science office on the *Invictus*.

Canaan Durek of House Ruxila - Council member, Head Agricultural Advisor, and Vared's father.

Commander Vared Durek of House Ruxila - Commander of the space cruiser, *Invictus*, the flagship of the Svesti military. First cousin to the king.

Pluvi Frulix of House Srotix - Council member.

Bavin Hossix of House Binova - Royal Guard.

Merix Hunnek of House Nuxar - Warrior on the Invictus.

Grulen Jevax of House Midnar - Warrior.

Gal'n Kalix of House Binova - Security officer.

Rexus Markham of House Yula - Healer on the *Invictus*. Rank - Captain.

Nerid Mantoor of House Glixon - Warrior.

Madix Previv of House Fresida - Royal Guard.

Talen Previv of House Fresida - Warrior. Head Cook on the *Invictus*.

Ash'n Rivezt of House Yula - Head healer on the *Invictus*. Rank - Captain.

Narilla Rivezt of House Yula - Council member, Main Medical Advisor, Master Healer.

Klero Rovex of House Glixon - Warrior.

Nerob Sinoaz of House Troliv - Healer on the *Invictus*. Rank - Captain.

Raxus Sovex of House Davelk - Traxen's father and Costonia's previous king. Deceased.

Lerix Sproid of House Kreliz - Warrior.

Marek Tolvex of House Vramel - Council member. Devik's father.

Pex Tolvex of House Vramel - One of Devik's older brothers.

Rassix Tolvex of House Vramel - One of Devik's older brothers.

Solen Tolvex of House Vramel - One of Devik's older brothers.

Lieutenant Leriv Volax of House Kreliz - Supply Master on the *Invictus*.

Lieutenant Gat'n Wrox of House Fresida - Head engineer on *Invictus*.

Lieutenant Karid Wurvez of House Binova - Head tactical officer on the *Invictus,* second in command of the space cruiser.

Ril'n Xeliv of House Fresida - Admin to King Sovex.

Brestov Xoriv of House Fresida - Security officer.

Wing Raiders

Captain Makai - Leader of the Jalaxian mercenary group, Wing Raiders.

Crax - Jalaxian Wing Raider, specialty is weapons.

Kara - Human female in the Wing Raiders, specialty is technology.

Lezon - Jalaxian Wing Raider, specialty is medical.

Rain - Human female in the Wing Raiders, pilot.

Tren - Jalaxian Wing Raider, engineer.

Yaz - Jalaxian Wing Raider, pilot.

Other

Overseer Roho - Ermipa on Talonka Six, head of the Veba Mine.

Svesti Words thus far

Brellia - Small, rumik-filled pastry.

Cold season - Comparable to Earth's winter in the northern hemisphere.

Crek - Fuck.

Harvest season - Comparable to Earth's autumn/fall in the northern hemisphere.

Hot season - Comparable to Earth's summer in the northern hemisphere.

Kirani - Female feline found in the wild. Similar to Earth's lioness.

Leringa - Fruit that has a hint of spice when ingested.

Lunar - Month.

Maxiem - A large animal that resembles a hybrid between Earth's ox and cow. Used as a source of meat, milk and beasts of burden.

Mentok - Similar to Earth's myna bird, but larger and with plumage reminiscent of an Earth's peacock. Chatters incessantly.

Milara - Small brown bird with periwinkle/white chest and underside of wings. Known for its cunning.

Naroon - Large furry animal, similar to Earth's ape, with blue fur. Gregarious and known to be silly in their family groups.

Pertiza - Creamy yellow sweet yogurt made from maxiem milk.

Renewal season - Comparable to Earth's spring in the northern hemisphere.

Rulah - Small, furry animal similar to Earth's cat.

Rumik - Meat similar to Earth's ground beef. Comes from maxiem.

Shurlix - Similar to Earth's tomato, but yellow.

Solar - Year.

Tempika - Green berries that taste tart, but also sweet.

Trezoura - Capital city of Costonia.

Valadium - Steel-like ore when tempered is one of the hardest substances known in the universe.

Woolah - Red flower that blooms on Costonia during Harvest season.

Young – Baby/infant.

Youngling – Child.

Thank you for reading Devik and Emmy's story. If you enjoyed this book, please leave an online review where you purchased it. This lets other readers know whether they might enjoy it, too!

If you'd like to hear about Wavy's other books, you can sign up for her newsletter or find her social media links at wavymartin.com.